D1106049

A House of Secrets

A House
of Secrets

A NOVEL

Patti Davis

A Birch Lane Press Book
Published by Carol Publishing Group

A Birch Lane Press Book
Published by Carol Publishing Group
Birch Lane Press is a registered trademark of Carol Communications, Inc.

Editorial Offices: 600 Madison Avenue, New York, N.Y. 10022
Sales & Distribution Offices: 120 Enterprise Avenue, Secaucus, N.J. 07094
In Canada: Musson Book Company, a division of General Publishing Company, Ltd.,
    Don Mills, Ontario M3B 2T6

Queries regarding rights and permissions should be addressed to Carol Publishing Group, 600 Madison Avenue, New York, N.Y. 10022

The quotation in chapter 20 is from ROSENCRANTZ AND GUILDENSTERN ARE DEAD by Tom Stoppard, copyright © 1967 by Tom Stoppard. Used by permission of Grove Press, Inc.

Carol Publishing Group books are available at special discounts for bulk purchases, for sales promotions, fund raising, or educational purposes. Special editions can be created to specifications. For details contact: Special Sales Department, Carol Publishing Group, 120 Enterprise Avenue, Secaucus, N.J. 07094

Manufactured in the United States of America

10   9   8   7   6   5   4   3   2   1

Library of Congress Cataloging-in-Publication Data

Davis, Patti.
    A house of secrets / by Patti Davis.
        p.   cm.
    "A Birch Lane Press book."
    ISBN 1-55972-082-4
    I. Title.
PS3554.A93762H66   1991
813'.54—dc20   91-19328

To D.W.
in memory

ACKNOWLEDGMENTS

I would like to express my thanks to my editor, Gail Kinn, for her sensitivity and guidance, and for knowing when to push me and when to let me figure it out on my own. To my agent, Jack Artenstein, for believing in me and for fighting the battles I didn't have the patience for. To Larry Thompson, for still returning my phone calls. To Peter Fiebleman, for the Vineyard, the turquoise, and the gift of his writer's eye. To Tim O'Brien, for the letters and the encouragement. To Milton Wexler, for getting me this far. To Elizabeth Stone, for the picture. To Dian Roberts, for the beach, the walks, and for listening to chapters in progress. To Ron Meyer, for providing inspiration even when he didn't know he was. Thanks also to Dr. Leonard Schwartzman and Bruce Newberg for their help. And to the friends who understood and put up with my moods, which probably hit new levels during the writing of this novel: Paul Sand, Donna Burton, Bob Franco, Savina Teubel, Paul Grilley, Lee Horwin, Sue and Dino Barbis, Alan Wertzel, Ani and Jerry Moss, Ron Kovic, Lanetta, Molly White, Jon Wolf, Karyn Benskin, and Jody Evans—thanks for being there.

A House of Secrets

1

I am the child of storytellers. I have lifted up the edges of my parents' stories, looking for truth or lies, and I have found both. Lifting the edges of my own, I've seen questions scurrying away, frightened by the light. Often, I've let the questions go and put the stories back in place, back where they seem to belong. They are my guideposts across the uneven continent of my past, and, at times, they are the only things that seem real. The history of my family is a geography that changes, depending on who is telling the story.

When I was in the presence of both my mother and father, it was like being caught between two climate zones. My mother's red hair and flashing dark eyes radiated heat. Rachel Lawton rarely, if ever, spoke softly; hers was a voice that insisted on an audience. It was never meant for the soothing task of telling bedtime stories. Even her love was fire-whipped and furious, pulling us in and demanding to be recognized.

My father's hair was arctic white and his eyes watched the world with a clear blue calm. A portrait of him hung in our living room; the brass plate on the frame read "Clifford Lawton," but the eyes could have been anyone's, or no one's. They were cool and vague, focused on nothing.

I would hover between them, clinging to some invisible line of latitude, and I could almost feel half of me being licked by flames while the other half was washed by cool water.

My father wove stories in the dark. When I was small and my world was no bigger than New York, he'd leave for work in the morning and return in time to tuck me in at night. As he leaned over my bed in his business suit, I could tell what season it was by the scents that clung to the fabric of his jacket. Lamplight caught in the silver of his hair, until he switched the room to darkness and talked into the shadows.

A winged horse would form from his words, sleek and white in the dark space of my room. The walls would dissolve the moment I swung onto the animal's back, and child and horse would fly into the night sky, up over the city, higher than the highest buildings. The horse's mane would blow back against my face as my arms clung to the powerful muscles of his neck. Reaching my arm up at just the right moment, I could graze the edge of the moon; velvety and pale, it would leave a fine dust on my fingertips.

I spent my days looking forward to the nights, to being transported to worlds that seemed real only because I believed they were. My father gave my imagination permission to reach as far as it wanted.

I think now that I should have listened more closely to his stories, carved them more deeply into my memory. Because he may have been more present, more real, in the quick embrace of darkness than he ever was in the light.

My mother had told me he worked on Wall Street and, thinking she'd said "walled street," I imagined him spending his days on a street surrounded by walls. One evening, when he sat down on the edge of my bed, I asked him if there were any pictures on the walls of the street where he worked.

"Oh yes," he said, reaching to turn out the night-light. His voice hung on the air, ready to stitch together the seams of another story.

"There's one painting of a lot of people having a picnic on a grassy hillside. It was painted a long time ago, so they're drinking out of big stone jugs and they're wearing togas, and—"

"What's a toga?"

"Well, a toga is . . . It's . . . It's sort of like a sheet and it's tied around with ropes."

"Who wore them—the men or the women?" I asked.

"Uh, the men. But the women had something similar—longer, though."

"Longer sheets? They all wore sheets?"

"Carla—" My father's voice was starting to show his annoyance with my questions. "This was a long time ago. They didn't have department stores to shop in. Anyway, above them, sitting on clouds, are cherubs."

"In togas?"

"No, cherubs don't wear anything."

"They're naked?"

"Carla, they're cherubs. They have wings on their backs. They're little naked angels who come down from heaven."

I heard my mother's footsteps approaching my room and the story started to unravel; cherubs fell off clouds and thumped against the earth.

"Clifford, aren't you finished saying good night yet?" With the sound of her voice, clouds rushed away and the entire painting started to crumble.

"I'm telling Carla a story. I'm almost done."

"Well, it's past her bedtime. I think sleep is a little more important than stories."

My father waited until my mother's shape no longer filled the doorway, until the sound of her footsteps had disappeared. "I think stories are more important, but don't tell your mother I said that," he whispered.

"Don't the cherubs have parents to make them wear clothes?" I asked, happily reassembling the painting, calling back the clouds. "God doesn't make them get dressed?"

"Well, I . . . no, I guess not. I suppose God doesn't care about things like that."

Weeks later, I asked my mother if cherubs got cold when they sat on snow clouds. She was checking the dinner table for a party they were having that night. Pink curlers decorated her head, and she was in her robe, moving around the table, straightening silverware, scrutinizing place cards.

"I don't know," she said, giving me a puzzled look. "Is this from one of your father's stories?"

"Yes, and the other people wore sheets."

"Well, you should ask him, then. I don't know much about cherubs or people in sheets. Now, Carla, you and your sister are going

to eat early in the kitchen, all right? And I want you to stay out of the
way tonight."

"Yes, ma'am."

My mother's stories were tethered to the earth. Her eyes never
strayed to far horizons; they stayed fixed on the world she had
constructed, hammering each nail so that it could withstand any
unforeseen catastrophes. She was always on the alert for loose boards
and unseen fissures. Hers was a world of order; she spoke of knowing
rather than imagining.

She told me once about falling in love with my father; the minute
she saw him, she knew they would marry. To her, love was like a
strong wind that relieved her of the responsibility of navigating—its
sense of direction was so infallible.

One of my favorite stories was of the night I was born. It was
October, and my parents pulled their car into Manhattan's Friday
evening traffic, trying to make it to the hospital before my mother's
labor pains were too close together. In her version, she was the calm
one while my father teetered on the brink of hysteria. He ran a red
light, narrowly missing several pedestrians who yelled obscenities at
him, and was pulled over by a policeman.

"My wife's having a baby!" he shouted to the cop who peered into
the car.

"Listen, Officer, we really don't have time for a ticket," my mother
said, perfectly in control, according to her. "If you really want to be
helpful, you can give us a police escort to the hospital. Otherwise, you
might have to help deliver a baby right here."

They got a police escort, which was my favorite part of the story—
my birth being heralded by a siren screaming through the streets of
Manhattan. Of course, my mother was the only one who knew they
had plenty of time to spare, but at least my father didn't get a traffic
ticket.

Sometime after my sister Lily was born, another chapter was added
to the story. According to this new, embellished version, I bellig-
erently "hung on" to my mother; my adamant refusal to enter the
world forced the doctor to reach for the scalpel and remove me
himself.

"It was very difficult," my mother said, staring at me in a way that
made me shift my weight uncomfortably. "The doctor has forbidden

me to have any more children. You probably don't remember, but I had to stay in bed the first three months I was carrying Lily because they were afraid I'd lose her."

It sounded horrible, and I felt responsible for the whole gruesome mess. I stopped asking to hear that story, although sometimes it was repeated anyway.

Only once did my mother speak of magic. I had been frightened awake by nightmares, and I heard her footsteps moving quickly down the hall toward my room. I was four years old, and in the next room Lily, barely two, slept the clear, sweet sleep of a childhood too new for nightmares. While in the darkness of my room, the chair had become a grizzly bear, crouched and ready to sink his claws into my throat, and ghosts huddled under the bed, laughing low and soft behind their long white hands.

"I have something for you," my mother said, removing a small plastic bottle from the pocket of her robe. It was filled with gold glitter, each tiny piece shaped like a star. She tapped some into her palm and scattered it over me; perfect gold stars caught in my hair, floated onto the pillow, and nestled in the wool blanket.

"Magic dust," she said. "It will make you have beautiful dreams."

Protected by my blanket of gold stars, I dreamed of flame-colored trees, the leaves ripe and crisp with the smells of autumn. They skittered across the ground, running away from the breath of winter that curled around a corner of the sky.

Years later, I asked my mother if she remembered that night and her eyes shone as she nodded, fingering the edges of a time-worn picture. But there was much that she refused to recollect, and a part of me could never forgive her for the half-light of her memory.

As time stripped childhood from me I became, to my mother, a symbol of her own doubts, her own pain. My sin was growing into a woman—an accident of birth I was helpless to change, although there were moments when I would ask God why He had cursed me with the one affliction that was destined to turn my mother against me.

That night, though, framed by a nimbus of yellow light from the hallway, my mother's face was like a soft cameo, appearing out of the darkness to chase away my nightmares.

I have become a storyteller, too, and, finally, I have decided to tell the story I've spent my life running away from. It is the story of a little girl in a house of secrets, of soft days on the sea, and nights when the moon glittered with magic that she tried to catch, but couldn't.

And it is a war story, ending as all war stories do—with no winners and losers, just wounded and dead.

2

A fog bank is rolling down the beach, and I am watching it from my deck. It is almost to my house; in minutes, it will engulf me. It's June and the fog stays until late morning, lifts for a few hours, then returns in the afternoon. At least, that's what it does in Malibu—I don't know about the rest of the world.

I'm waiting for more than the fog; I'm waiting for Beck's key in my lock, for my dog's race to the door—he assumes someone who has a key is worthy of being welcomed and not worth a bark.

I called Beck and asked if he would come over and stay the night—something that's usually restricted to the weekends. This midweek request is like raising a flag, signaling trouble, sending out an SOS.

The fog has almost reached me when I hear Tully's paws tear up more of the carpet on his way to the door. With his Doberman tracks marking the way, I'll never need to post an exit sign.

"Hi," Beck says—like a question—coming out to the deck and into thick white air that's timed its arrival with his. I told myself I wouldn't cry, but I do as soon as I see him.

"Carla, what's wrong? What happened?" His arms slide around me and the fog holds us in its palm.

"I had a miscarriage," I tell him, my face against his neck, my lips scraping across his skin as they form the words.

Beck pulls back and looks at me; his eyes mirror my sadness.

"I'm sorry."

"It's probably silly to be upset. I mean, it wasn't even really a baby yet, was it? Just a few cells. I wouldn't even have known if I hadn't rushed in for a blood test when I was only four days late. But it's the second one—the second in less than a year." My words are speeding up, trying to cover up the pain underneath—because it embarrasses me, because I think I should be stronger. But Beck sees it.

"You have every right to be upset," he tells me, his thumb wiping a tear off my cheek. "You don't have to apologize for that."

My arms tighten around him, asking for reasons, asking for assurance that he's really there, that he's not going to go away.

"I feel like I'm being punished, Beck."

"Oh, now wait a minute—we're not going to start with this Old Testament stuff again, are we? Like there's some vengeful God up there tossing lightning bolts down on you? Why are you sure you deserve punishment?"

I pry myself away from him and move to one of the deck chairs. As I sit down, I notice how fast the fog is moving—ghost streams float past my face.

"You know why. Because I went down to a county hospital at the ripe young age of twenty-four and had them sterilize me. The fact that they could reverse it years later and put me back together doesn't wipe my slate clean. It's still there on my record—you know, the record that determines how many lightning bolts you deserve."

Beck pulls a chair up close to mine and sits down. "This is not a criminal record, Carla. I think they should have hidden the Bible from you when you were a kid."

"But don't you get it? I let my mother win when I did that. I fought my whole life against her, and I put up a good fight. She hated me for growing up into a woman, she tried to punish me for it whenever she could, she tried to destroy that in me. I fought her with everything I had. But the moment I walked into that hospital and asked them to make sure I could never become a mother, I handed her her biggest victory."

"And then you turned it around," Beck says. "Why don't you congratulate yourself for that? You took it back as your own victory. They told you that you should be able to have a baby."

"I know, but doctors don't know everything. They only know that physically I'm put back together. They studied medicine, not karma."

I think back to the operating room, white and cold as a glacier, the sound of instruments clinking in the tray, and the doctor's face, lips pressed tight as he patiently worked on putting me back together. I had insisted on staying awake, opting to be made numb from the waist down rather than being excused from the whole experience. Humpty-Dumpty keeping watch over the repair job.

Repair—it makes me think of cars and stereos. But then I move beyond the mechanics; I consider the unknowns, the mysteries that medicine can't unravel. The karmic charts divided into columns—accomplishments and failures, victories and defeats. This is where the Old Testament comes in.

We go to bed early, before the moon has moved across the sky. I need the darkness, and Beck doesn't argue. As I slide in beside him, I'm grateful for the space he takes up in the bed, in my house—in my life.

My eyes adjust to the dark and I can see the outlines of his face in the moonlight.

"Does it scare you that I love you?" I whisper to him, my leg across his, my arm balanced on his chest.

"No."

"Sometimes I feel like it does."

His body shifts slightly and I imagine that the bed just got wider and he has moved to its farthest edge. We're still tangled together, but something has changed.

"Is this about living together?" he says. "We've gone over this before, Carla. It wouldn't work out—two writers under the same roof? Besides, Tully will only surrender his side of the bed to me a few nights a week, and I'm not about to argue with a Doberman."

Tully groans and stretches out on his cushion in the corner, adding punctuation to Beck's argument. The moon has floated to the center of the window, and molten silver falls into the room.

"So we just live together on the weekends and retreat to our own houses during the week?"

"It's been working okay for a year," Beck reminds me. "We get a lot of work done that way, don't we?"

"Maybe you just don't want that much company," I tell him, my finger circling his nipple, trying to make it hard. "But then, maybe I don't either."

I think about what I've just said, as my hand moves over to his other nipple, trying to make him symmetrical. Lately, my writing is an excursion into the backwaters of my life. There are ancient, murky areas I venture into—an explorer through my own history— trying to make sense out of it the only way I know how. With words. It's a solitary journey, one in which traveling companions aren't allowed. It seems to always come down to boundaries, to dark lines between the acres of the soul—I need to cross them alone.

"You were the first man I ever told," I say to Beck, the rise and fall of our breathing measuring the space between us.

"About your criminal record?" he jokes softly, one of his legs changing places with mine, moving on top, pinning it down.

"Yeah. I used to lie to men. If they asked me about birth control, I said I was on the pill. I was afraid of their judgment."

"How did you know I wouldn't judge you?" Beck asks, his voice trailing off, crawling toward sleep.

"I'm not sure. Maybe it was your reading glasses. Men with reading glasses have always inspired trust and confidence in me."

"Uh-huh."

I met Beck at a writers' seminar; my only reason for attending was that he was going to be there on one of the days, reading passages from his fourth novel—glimpses of a work in progress. His three other novels were conspicuously placed in my bookshelves, and I had read each more than once.

There was no sun that day—a sky like gray wool. I got up at dawn, walked Tully on the beach, and tried to ignore the nervousness shivering in my muscles. My hands felt unsteady and uncooperative, arguing with me every time I attempted to bring a mascara wand or a pencil close to my eyes.

I wanted to meet Beck. I knew I would. It was the certainty of this that was unnerving me, as though I were careening toward something preordained. I resisted the temptation to practice my introduction in the bathroom mirror—rehearsals like that have always ended up sabotaging me.

I'd intended to be demure and sit in the back of the room, but I watched myself heading down the aisle toward an empty seat in the second row, wondering how I could ever have considered sitting anywhere else.

He was thinner than I thought he would be—narrower and taller. Gray was sprinkled through his black hair and dotted his beard like ashes from an errant fire. He was wearing jeans and a blue sweater, a shade lighter than his eyes; somehow I had thought his eyes were brown even though I had looked at his photographs countless times. He unfolded reading glasses and balanced them on his nose.

"I used to laugh at people who wore these," he said, peering over them at his audience. "So, please, no one laugh."

No one did. No one made a sound as he read from the novel he was working on and shared some of the struggles he'd had with the characters. I was astounded at his generosity; maybe after several novels it's easier to reveal the dilemmas, the piles of crumpled paper, words crossed out with angry slashes of ink.

When he finished, I waited for others to crowd around him before getting up to wait my turn.

"Mr. Eller, I'm Carla Lawton," I said, knowing his eyes had brushed across mine several times while I was waiting. "I've admired your work for a long time."

"Please call me Beck. Mr. Eller sounds very professorial. Carla Lawton—I read your first novel. I was impressed."

"You did? I mean, you were?" I imagined him sitting down with my book in his hands and immediately recalled passages I wished I could change.

"That surprises you?" he asked, smiling.

"Sort of—I guess I never considered you would know my work too."

Something about his eyes wouldn't allow me to avert mine. I felt like he was seeing more than I wanted him to—lasers cutting through to vulnerabilities I preferred to protect. I suddenly knew why I had rushed around the house that morning, vacuuming, dusting, throwing sweatshirts and sandals in the closet, carrying out a week of newspapers. I had bought fresh flowers the day before, I made sure no dishes were left in the sink, no damp towels hung in the bathroom . . . it all made sense to me now.

"I've read each of your novels several times," I told him as we walked out to the parking lot together. "Sometimes I reread them when I'm in the middle of working on my own and I run dry. They always inspire me. It's either that, or wash my hair. That usually gets me unstuck too."

"What else? How else do you get unstuck?" His eyes bored into me again; the gray in his hair was the same color as the sky.

"I walk on the beach," I said. "Since it's right out my back door."

"Ah-hah. I knew if I stayed in L.A. long enough I'd meet someone with a magic key to the beaches inhabited only by the rich and famous—and by invited guests, of course."

"You're invited to walk on the beach anytime," I said, knowing where this was going and unwilling to change the collision course we were on.

On the Coast Highway, with Beck in my rearview mirror. I wished for the traffic to thin out, wished for a speedier journey to my front door—all of this a foregone conclusion that had nudged me a day earlier.

Tully was wary of him at first, possessive of his role as the only male in the house. I watched Beck coax him into accepting his presence there. Tully is the determining factor in every relationship I consider; I trust in his dog-wisdom, wait for him to make up his mind.

"It's nice to live alone, isn't it?" Beck said, studying the books along my shelves. "After ten years of marriage, the past year on my own has made me think it's probably better for a writer to live alone." His voice was even and controlled; I liked the timbre of it—deep and resonant, a sound I could feel as well as hear. I could feel it between my legs.

"When did you start writing?" he asked, still looking at book titles.

"When I was about ten. I had to hide it for a long time, though. My mother didn't want me to write—she burned some of it when I was younger."

He didn't say anything, but he didn't need to.

"Do you have any children?" he asked quietly.

"No—I'd like to, but no. Not yet." I wanted suddenly to tell him all of it and I knew that, before nightfall, I would.

It had been four months since I lay exposed and open under the glare of surgery-room lights, watching the doctor's face for signs of progress. "I've put you back together," I wanted his face to say. "Tell me I'm whole again," I prayed, "undamaged, the past reduced to a line of scar tissue."

But it was hours before he leaned over me and answered the question my eyes had been burning into him.

I pushed open the sliding glass doors and looked at the gray clouds lapping over each other; a light rain had started to fall.

"Do you still want to walk on the beach?" I asked Beck. "It's raining."

His arms around my waist answered me and I found myself kissing him as rain drifted across the deck and into the house.

"I knew this was going to happen," I said.

"When did you know?"

"I'm not exactly sure. But for some reason I ran around the house this morning cleaning up with the diligence of a hotel maid—this is not typical behavior for me. I guess at the time I didn't realize I was expecting company."

He kissed me again and I returned it, liking his mouth, wanting more of it.

"I don't know about this, Beck. We only met a few hours ago—I don't even know you."

"Yes, you do."

I lit a single candle in my bedroom and left the door to the deck ajar so the smells of rain and sea mist could drift in and wind could choreograph the candle flame's dance of light along the walls. I unbuttoned his shirt, studied the paleness of his skin—a winter body, no lines of suntan to mark the boundaries between seasons. I imagined him in a snowy landscape, sitting by a fire, surrounded by books.

He lifted my sweater over my head, his mouth finding my breasts. But when his hands moved down to my skirt, I stopped them. "I have to tell you something," I said. "I had some surgery a few months ago— I did something pretty stupid in my twenties—I got sterilized." My words were soaked in fear and running for the finish line. "I had it reversed four months ago."

He didn't say anything for a moment and I could hear the seconds counting down my fear.

"Please say something."

"You weren't stupid—it was just something you did. It'll be okay," he whispered, sliding my skirt off my hips.

Something inside me relaxed then, surrendered and laid down its weapons. I told him about the hours ticking by in white silence, a world somewhere outside—sunlight and voices and the bloom of spring flowers. Nothing bloomed in that room; it was sterile, frozen as a glacier, silence rattled only by the sound of steel instruments dropping in trays.

I didn't feel afraid to lie down with Beck, to let him touch the ridge of swelling below my belly.

"I still feel kind of fragile, though," I told him. "I haven't been with anyone since..."

He ran his tongue over the scar and his hands pulled my thighs apart, reaching inside to my fear, to where I thought I might be parched as dried bones, breakable as mended china.

"I'm scared."

Don't be, his hands answered as they drew into their grip the pulse of blood and the heat of wanting him. When I felt him inside me, there was no more fear, only the rush of pulling him in deeper and wanting to be nowhere else in the world.

I looked around for my mother—she had always been there, with every man I had been with—arms crossed, horrified and angry. I had wanted her there, needed her fury, delighted in her horror. But this time she was absent, and I didn't care.

My lip was bruised for a week from biting down on it when I came. I was sorry to see it fade—the tiny blue reminder that I wasn't dead. I could still sweat and cry out and beg for him to stay inside me just a little longer.

I don't ask Beck to stay with me past his usual two cups of coffee. The morning is still gray and early, but he wants to go home and write, and I don't want to feel guilty about keeping him from it.

"You okay?" he asks, as he looks around for his keys.

I find them under the paper and hand them to him. "Yeah—I'm glad you stayed with me last night, though."

"Are you going to be able to write today?"

"I don't know. Probably not. I'm supposed to go visit my mother." I don't have to explain this to him; one activity often precludes the other.

"Doesn't that seem sort of masochistic under the circumstances?" he asks me.

"It's masochistic under any circumstances. I might as well just go through with it."

We kiss good-bye at the door and I go back into a house which now wears reminders of him—extra dishes in the sink, blankets thrown back from both sides of the bed, the sports section open on the coffee table. And his parting words that keep tapping me on the shoulder. It is masochistic to visit my mother; it always has been. But I keep doing it, out of habit, or tradition, or needs I can't let go of.

3

I was six when my parents decided to move from New York to California. It was a white December day when Lily and I were told that our lives were about to change and, for a while after that, our two-year age gap seemed to close, and we were united in the singular task of adjusting to a new reality.

But there was one thing Lily and I didn't share; my mother started turning a different face toward me. I tried to blame her anger on our relocation; I told myself that some strange shift must have taken place on our passage across the continent. But I soon learned that it had nothing to do with exchanging one coast for the other; it had to do with me. It would always have to do with me.

I still force myself to remember her the way she was when I was small—holding my hand and walking me through the New York seasons. But it's like remembering a different person. I see my mother's face as it was then, shiny and laughing along with me. Her dark red hair was tied back in a scarf and she wore no makeup except lipstick. I draw that picture in my mind frequently, so that I won't forget how she once was.

During our last winter in New York, the windows wore wreaths of frost. I would look down from our living-room window at children playing in Central Park, hurling snowballs at each other—balls of white ammunition exploding against the backs of whoever didn't run fast enough. I could see their faces transformed by screams and laughter, but I was too high up for any sound to reach me.

On an afternoon of watching these soundless games from the vantage point of our penthouse, the maid carried in a tray with four mugs of hot chocolate on it. Lily trailed behind her, four years old and tiny—lost in a plaid dress that was too big for her.

"Meeting," Lily said, sitting down next to me on the window seat. She preferred an economy of language which usually brought an admonition from our mother to speak in complete sentences. But I enjoyed her ability to communicate in phrases of one or two words.

"What about?" I said. Even then, my sister seemed to know things before I did.

"Don't know."

Our parents appeared in the living room and sat down on the couch after handing us each a mug of hot chocolate, Lily's being only half full in deference to her age and habit of dropping things.

"We have some very exciting news," my mother began, smoothing a wrinkle from her wool skirt and slipping her high heels off under the coffee table. I was always nervous about news that our parents considered exciting; I buried half my face in the steam curling up from my mug and waited.

"We wanted to be absolutely sure about this before we told you children," my father added.

I sank deeper into the steam.

My mother smiled at my father. "Your father, girls, is going to start his own business, out in California," she said brightly. "He's going to have his own company, with a friend of his."

"You won't be here anymore?" I asked my father, wanting to hear his contribution to this "exciting news."

"We're all going to go," my mother said. "we're going to move to California. Isn't that thrilling?"

"What's California?" Lily said.

"It's another state," my father answered. "The sun always shines there. It's always warm."

"When does it snow?" I asked. I couldn't conceive of a state without winter.

"It doesn't," my mother said. "You can go swimming in winter."

I glanced at Lily; she was blowing into her mug, trying to make bubbles, and I knew that I was the only one in the room who had reservations about this move. I also knew that it was not negotiable; the decision had been made, and we were being informed after the fact.

Within days, the apartment was filled with boxes of all sizes, and Lily became on of the busiest people there; an endless array of hiding places had been provided and she was determined to take advantage of the situation.

"Carla, have you seen your sister?" I heard at least a dozen times a day. Everyone else was too busy to look for her, so the job fell to me. Usually, I found her sitting in a box having tea with an imaginary friend.

One afternoon, when my sister had vanished and my services were once again in demand, I looked in every box and couldn't find her. I started to wonder if she had been sealed into one of the boxes that had already been carried out. Maybe she was on her way to California without the rest of us. But when I heard whimpering from inside the wine closet, I knew she had at least escaped that trauma.

"Lily, what are you doing in here?" I said, coming into the cool, dark closet and closing the door halfway, dividing the small space into shadow and light.

"Everything's leaving," she said, looking at me with wide, wet eyes.

"But so are we, remember? We're moving to California."

"I don't know what that is, though."

"I don't either—but I guess we'll get used to it."

Lily stared off into the shadowy space that hid us from our parents. She was tiny and frail, like a figure from inside a music box. Her hair would eventually be as red as our mother's, but then it was still pale. Everything about Lily seemed pale, as though she could be easily erased.

I held out my arms and she came into them, her small hands clinging to me, with her fingernails that she was biting even then. It is a habit she has never lost.

Lily and I were led onto the plane in our matching winter coats and black patent-leather shoes. It was our first time traveling by plane.

"What if we fall out of the sky?" Lily asked.

"We won't," our father said. "It's a plane, Lily—it's supposed to fly."

"Yawn so your ears will pop when we take off," our mother told us.

"Why do I want my ears to poop?" Lily said.

"Not poop, Lily, pop. so they'll feel better."

"It sounds like it'll hurt," my sister the skeptic said.

Eventually, Lily got tired of asking questions; we both fell asleep and, when we woke up, we were landing in Los Angeles, New York somewhere far behind, lost in the air currents and vapor trails.

When I remember the limousine ride from the airport, I can feel again the strangeness of the new world we'd landed in—the palm trees and the warm breeze in my hair, even though it was January and the world should have been cold and white. My ice skates were carefully packed in a box, but I think I knew then that I would never use them again. There was more, though, than just the unfamiliarity of a winter without snow.

My mother's voice filled the car that day; she was cheerful and animated and full of plans. But I heard something else beneath her words—something that made me turn and squint through the sunlight to see if it was really my mother talking. It was the first time I didn't believe my mother's laughter, the first time I heard danger beneath it—a quiet hum of anger that would grow louder over the years. I felt fear settling in my bones, winding around my ankles. Fear was my introduction to California, and it became the one thing I would steel myself against—on a thousand different occasions when I would stare back at my mother's fury with eyes that refused to cry. I would walk away from her proudly, not letting her see the trembling in my muscles or the wounds that her words had opened in me. I would never let my mother know how much she frightened me.

In my memory, that fear might have first surfaced in me at twenty thousand feet, somewhere between New York and Los Angeles—a huge mysterious serpent that stirred and lifted its head. But it was probably born long before that—if only I could remember.

Our new home was a rambling, five-bedroom house perched on a hill; it had a swimming pool, a fenced-in backyard, and an oak tree that invited climbing. From the deck, we could look down on the sea

and the city at the same time, like monarchs surveying our kingdom. Our family grew; we got a black and white collie named Daisy who patrolled the pool protectively while Lily and I learned to swim.

We grew in strange ways as well. Another child came to inhabit our house—my older sister, who had died at birth. But some people are never allowed to die. They are continually resurrected by those who need them to be alive. It's a testament to the strength of my mother's illusions that she could turn the spirit of her dead child into a solid, immutable presence in our house. I felt the existence of this child; I collided with her in hallways, moved over to accommodate her, ached with the threat that she would have been everything I couldn't seem to be. Any mention of her perfection could make me flare with embarrassment and shrink away, ashamed that I couldn't equal her. She could have been my enemy, but I decided to make her my friend, because I needed an older sister I could turn to, tell my secrets to. And I needed to become like her, so my mother would like me.

"She was so tiny," my mother told me. "And this angelic little face..."

"Was I tiny?" I asked her.

"Oh, no, Carla, you were a big baby. I've told you this story—I couldn't even deliver you. They had to do a caesarian. It was a very difficult birth."

So that was my first crime, I thought. I was large, I took up space, my size demanded to be noticed. I practiced feeling small, tried talking in a soft voice, but then I would forget and my real voice would return. I would pass a mirror and notice how much of it I occupied.

I wanted my mother to talk about me the way she talked about my dead sister, the ethereal child who had come to live with us. I had to make her my friend so that I could learn from her.

I envisioned her as pale and soft, able to cool the red heat of my mother's anger with her sweetness. And, over time, I came to imagine her with me everywhere; I felt her floating behind me like a shadow. At night, she would lie beside me, listening to the dreams I could tell no one else. I imagined her comforting me, teaching me, her voice like silvery whispers, coming to me alone.

But I learned that my imaginary guardian could not protect me from everyone. One night, when the rain was relentless and Lily had gone to bed asking if we would float away, this ghost-child deserted me.

Daisy was allowed to sleep in the house on rainy nights. We would make a bed for her on the service porch, just off the kitchen. It was almost ten o'clock; I was supposed to be in bed, but I crept past the ribbon of light under my parents' door and went out to the service porch.

"Hi, Daisy—we have to be quiet," I warned her, as her tail started wagging against the washing machine. "Come on, let's go get a snack."

With Daisy at my heels, I went into the kitchen and found, in the refrigerator, the rest of the lemon meringue pie we'd had for dinner. I put a slice of pie on a plate, got two spoons, and crawled under the kitchen table, coaxing Daisy to follow me. With the tabletop as the roof of our cave and the chairs forming the walls, I fed our dog pie until her whiskers were covered with sugary white meringue.

Daisy heard it before I did—the sound of footsteps coming toward the kitchen. I hid the plate behind her back and wiped my mouth with my sleeve. My mother appeared at the mouth of our cave, her face stern and unamused.

"What are you doing, Carla?"

"Nothing...talking to Daisy. We were playing, sort of...we couldn't sleep, so we were pretending this was a cave and we were out in—"

"What have you been eating?"

"Nothing," I lied, noticing the meringue still coating Daisy's whiskers.

Daisy gave me away; she got up and slinked past my mother, leaving the plate with the remains of our pie exposed. My mother reached in and pulled the plate toward her.

"You call this nothing?" she said, showing it to me.

"No, but it was just a snack—Daisy and I were sharing it—I gave her her own spoon."

My mother moved away from the table. I could hear her opening the refrigerator and putting something on the table above me. Outside, rain was pelting the roof, and from somewhere far away, the sound of thunder echoed through the night.

"Come out, please, Carla."

I crawled out to find the rest of the lemon meringue pie on the table and a spoon beside it.

"Finish that," my mother said.

"I can't—it's too much." It was growing larger before my eyes—I had fallen down the rabbit hole and the pie looked like it could swallow me.

"Well, you should have thought of that before you went sneaking through the house in the middle of the night. Honestly, Carla, I think the worst thing that happened was that you were deprived of an older sister who could have taught you how to behave. I obviously am not getting through to you that rules are rules and you don't disobey them, and I can't watch you every second. At least with an older sister you would have an example to follow. Now start eating."

My tears dropped onto the pie as I forced bite after bite into my mouth. Finally, when I leaned over and threw up on the floor, my mother removed the platter and said, "Well, I hope you've learned your lesson."

I had learned a more valuable lesson than my mother could know. I had learned that even ghosts can desert you; my secret companion, the imaginary friend I hid in my shadow, could change her allegiance in a moment. I lay in my bed that night, sick and humiliated, and I looked for her, but the corners of my room were darker than ever before and I knew I was alone.

4

My mother's house sits above the fog that yawns somewhere behind me. She looks down on it from a throne of harsh, searing sunlight. This seems oddly appropriate to me. There are times when, approaching her house, the smell of scorched earth seems to catch in my nostrils.

What I visit these days is my mother's silence—no less imposing than her voice once was, but a little easier to handle. She has become a medical mystery—a woman turned into a pillar of silence for no particular reason, at least none that the doctors can decipher. A series of small strokes has been one explanation, but there is more to it than that, and they can't find it in any textbook.

For years now, she has stared vacantly, focusing on nothing. Numb and childlike, she waits for visitors whose names she no longer says, and may no longer remember. Only my sister Lily has kept her rightful place in our mother's memory. A soft obedience comes over her body as Lily tends to her. With everyone else, there is an impenetrable coat of armor, a silent warning to stay away.

I sit with my mother once or twice a week; I talk about nothing, or anything. It doesn't matter. She is far away, exactly where she wants to be. Her eyes follow shadows moving across the lawn, marking the passage of another day.

Sometimes, when I sit with her, I think it might all be an act, this blank page she has become. She has sealed herself off, pretending not to comprehend, waiting to catch us at some act of treachery. The nurse who takes care of her speaks to her in a slow, patient voice—loudly, as though she's speaking to a hearing-impaired child.

"Careful," I often want to say. "She could be making a fool of you."

One afternoon, I almost thought I was right. As she sat watching raindrops travel down the window, my mother turned to me with what looked like recognition. I waited for her to say, "Carla"—waited for her mouth to form around the syllables of my name. But her eyes glazed over again and she said nothing. I should have known, I thought later, as I walked to my car, rain trickling down my neck. She would never break her silence for me.

But I still could be right; my mother is a master of disguise. I think about her latest transformation and I wonder if it will be her last, if this will be her finale. It's not the first time she has transformed herself, and she might still have the ability to surprise me.

To reach my mother's house, I drive through streets that haven't changed since I was a child. Gardeners mow the lawns into wide, even blankets of green, and the flower beds are planted in perfectly aligned rows; no snail would dare nibble at the petals. In this neighborhood, maids walk the babies and the dogs. It's hard to know who lives in these houses; they drive Jaguars and Mercedes into garages and close the electric doors behind them.

I turn up the steep driveway lined with rosebushes that always seem to be blooming; if any have ever died, they've been replaced so quickly no one noticed. In my memory, I can still see my mother standing along the driveway, clipping roses and putting them in a basket that's looped over arm. Her sun hat is tilted down over her face, putting it in shadow.

There is a tightening in my stomach that always happens when I get this close to the house. There is too much history here, too many phantoms. My parents built the house of their dreams—a house of secrets—and even though my father is gone and my mother is lost to silence, the secrets still live here. They dart from corners, teasing, laughing...and then they retreat again.

Lily opens the door when I ring. She spends at least an hour a day with our mother, sometimes more. My suspicion is that, with each visit, she's flirting with the laws of osmosis, slowly siphoning off our mother's personality and absorbing it as her own.

Today Lily is wearing gray linen slacks, a white blouse buttoned to her neck, and a gray cashmere sweater with tiny pearl buttons, I glance at her shoes—gray pumps with bows—and notice the sheen of nylon at her ankles. I'd bet money she's wearing panty hose under her slacks. The only things that give Lily away, that show she's not yet become Rachel Lawton, are her hands. Her nails are still ragged and bitten down. Her fingers usually curl in, trying to conceal the damage.

"Been raiding Mother's closet again, Lily?" I ask, hoping that some shred of humor comes across, because I do find it amusing, this cloning process.

"Carla, you're the last person who should masquerade as a fashion critic. Look at you—your sweatshirt is falling off your shoulder, your jeans are torn—you look like you've just been raped. Why don't you at least sew those up so your knees don't poke through?"

"As a matter of fact, I was just raped. That's why I'm a little late. Where's Mother?"

"Where she usually is," Lily answers, clicking across the hardwood floor and disappearing into the den where I know my mother is sitting stiffly in her wheelchair, staring out across the flat blue surface of the swimming pool to the city beyond. The wheelchair is not a medical necessity; physically, she can walk and does sometimes. Most of the time, however, her mind refuses to acknowledge this ability.

Lily and I take our usual chairs, on either side of our mother. This is how we spend these hours, talking across her silence, each waiting for a glimmer of recognition to ignite the flat brown of her eyes.

"So, what's new?" Lily asks.

I'm tempted to tell her about my miscarriage, but Lily is childless, too—by circumstances she doesn't even know she designed. She married a man almost thirty years her senior who promptly had a heart attack four months after their wedding and has been in fragile health since. She bought a station wagon, talked incessantly of filling it with kids, and then complained that her husband's doctor warned him about the exertion of sex.

"Not much," I answer, opting for vagueness. "I'm just writing, as usual."

"Your book?" my sister asks me, in a voice that could be our mother's. Lily knows I am writing about my childhood—our childhood. Her eyes narrow and her voice changes whenever she mentions it.

"Uh-huh."

I look at her carefully rolled hair, almost as red as our mother's once was, at her gold clip-on earrings, and I wonder how a thirty-one-year-old woman can choose to look so old.

"Lily, what are you hoping for with all of the days you spend sitting here? What do you want from Mother? A word? Eye contact? What?"

"I'm not hoping for anything," Lily says, her shoulders pulling back so her spine is arrow straight. "I'm here to be supportive. She needs us now more than ever. She needs to know we're here. But I suppose supportiveness is not a concept you've ever embraced, is it, Carla?"

"She hasn't the slightest idea that we're here. When are you going to accept that? And where would I have learned about support for family members? It wasn't an idea that ran rampant in this household. Lily, don't you ever wonder about all the lies that were told? Don't you ever want to know why?"

"What lies? You're the only one who sees it that way." She adjusts the blanket on our mother's lap, tucking it in around the bones of her hips.

I reach for my sister's wrist, but she pulls it back quickly, before I can touch it, before I can remind her. "You saw it like that too, Lily—you saw it that day. And you became part of the biggest lie of all. Why don't you admit it?"

Her eyes burn with tears that threaten to spill over, but probably won't. I can see the rage behind them. At this moment, her eyes remind me of our mother's—dark flames that can singe your soul if you get too close.

"You know why this makes you uncomfortable?" I ask her. "Because I know what you heard, and what you saw. You know as well as I do what went on in this house. You just trained yourself to run away from the memories. Congratulations, Lily—I never could quite master that. Sometimes I don't know who's luckier—you or me."

Lily stands up and takes the handles of our mother's wheelchair. "I should put her down for her nap."

"Yeah—right—you do that. Sleep has always been a good excuse, hasn't it? Except that I know you weren't asleep. I heard you, too, Lily—I heard you crying on some of those nights."

She turns our mother's wheelchair and takes her out of the room. Watching my sister from behind, I could be looking at an old home movie of our mother in a younger time. Her hips are as narrow, her stride as determined and rigid as Rachel Lawton's once was.

"God, Lily, where did you go?" I whisper to no one.

I should put the words in a bottle and float it down a slow river of memory to my sister. But she would probably just let it drift by.

When I get home, I take a yellow pad and pen out to the deck where the sea mist is already thick. I try to be brave in my journey back to the places in childhood I would rather forget, but sometimes I don't feel brave. I have memories which, I have been told, are not memories at all, but the fantasies of an overactive imagination. And there are holes in my memory, like black holes in space. I'm afraid to approach them, afraid I will be sucked in, lost forever in a world of black confusion.

But there was a witness; Lily heard things sometimes. Voices leaked through walls and doors, but she will always pretend she heard nothing.

After Daisy and I were caught with our late-night snack, an intercom was installed in my room so that any sound or movement was piped into my parents' room. I was also no longer trusted to put myself to bed, or to get ready for bed alone. I was escorted, like a prisoner who must always be watched.

The first time it happened, I wasn't sure why my mother's footsteps were behind me. I was eight, my bedtime was later than Lily's, and, every night, I would walk softly past her door and into the bathroom which was between our two rooms.

The bedtime ritual had started out the way it always did. I went into my parents' room, kissed them good night, said "I love you," because this was expected and required. Going to bed without saying I love you was a crime in our house.

On this night, my mother stood up from her chair where she had been reading and moved toward the door. I glanced at my father, looking for a sign, looking for help, wanting him to snatch me back into his arms, to protect me, but he was watching television. He saw nothing unusual in my mother's movements.

I walked out of their room, down the hall, and heard her walking after me. Her footsteps pounded in my ears, resonating danger. When I got to the bathroom door, she was so close I could smell her perfume, and when I went in, she followed me, closing the door behind us. The room suddenly closed in on me; it felt smaller than it ever had, and my mother seemed larger. I turned and looked at her, waiting for her voice, waiting to hear the reason for her presence there.

"Go on," she said, crossing her arms in front of her chest. She had on a long pink dressing gown and matching slippers; her diamond wedding ring caught the light and bounced back shards of color. "Get ready for bed."

The shaking started deep inside me, but I was determined to keep it hidden. It was all I could do with the fear that my mother stirred up in me; I could only hide it and pray that it wouldn't give me away.

I took my toothbrush and leaned over the sink, letting my mouth fill with toothpaste foam before spitting it out, trying not to look at my mother's reflection towering behind me.

"I'm finished," I said, facing her again after rinsing out my mouth.

"No, you're not." She pointed to the toilet.

I felt my face flush and something deep inside me started to tremble.

"I don't have to go."

"You have to go to the bathroom before you go to bed, Carla. And we're going to stay in here until you do." Her voice was getting louder; it was filling the room, running down the walls, drilling pinholes into my bones.

"I don't have to," I said again.

"Carla, sit down!" my mother yelled, pointing again to the toilet.

I sat down on the lid, taking nothing off.

One hand grabbed my arm, pulling me to my feet, and the other stripped the clothes from the lower half of my body.

I obeyed only part of her command. I sat, but I clenched everything my body. It was a slender thread of victory that I clung to—the knowledge that there were actually some things that were resistant to her rule.

"You have to make everything difficult, don't you?" she said, her voice slapping against my eardrums. "We'll just stay in here all night if we have to."

I sat, half-naked, and cried; my eyes were the only part of my body I couldn't control—I held onto everything else.

Later, long after my mother had deposited me in the dark of my room, I tiptoed across the floor, holding my breath. I opened the door so slowly that the intercom couldn't pick up the sound, and crept into the bathroom. On my way back to my room, I stopped outside my sister's door and listened to the soft rhythm of her crying. I knew she had heard, as she would on many nights after that. It was a scene that was repeated until my mother tired of it.

But before she gave up, she recruited another soldier to her side.

My pediatrician's office was painted with lambs and chickens, designed as a distraction from needles and stethoscopes. But I preferred watching the needle pierce the flesh of my arm and the mysterious serums disappear into me, inoculating me against diseases that were only names to me.

After a Band-Aid was put on my arm, my mother stood up and said, "I'll wait for you outside, Carla."

The doctor sat down beside me on the table. "Your mother tells me you're having a problem, Carla."

"I am?"

"She tells me you refuse to go to the bathroom."

"I go—just not in front of her."

"That's not what she tells me," he said. "It's very unhealthy—you could weaken your bladder. How are you going to feel if you have to wear diapers when you grow up?"

"Diapers?"

"Oh yes. It's dangerous what you're doing."

"But I'm not doing anything. I mean, I am doing something, just not while she's watching. Why don't you tell tell her not to watch?" I said, suddenly angry at him for joining my mother, for enlisting in a war he didn't understand. "Why are you taking her side? Why don't you believe me?"

"Carla, your mother is concerned about you. So am I."

On the way home, my mother drove too fast through Beverly Hills. I leaned against the door, afraid to look at her, holding onto my anger like a lifeline.

"They say the middle child is the most difficult, and I guess they're right," she said, screeching to a stop at a red light.

"Who says that?"

"It's just said, that's all."

"How do you know my older sister would have been better than me? She's dead."

My mother pulled the car over to the curb and wheeled around to face me. My hand closed around the door handle, ready to turn it. I thought of running down the street, away from the car, away from her, but I didn't know where I would go.

"Don't ever say that again," she said in a voice so sharp it sliced the air between us.

I wedged myself against the door and didn't speak the rest of the way home.

My father came into my room that evening before dinner.

"Why do you treat your mother like this?" he said.

"Like what?"

"Carla, you turned away from her in the car and wouldn't speak to her. She doesn't deserve that kind of treatment from you and I won't allow you to hurt her like this."

I knew what I wanted to say to him; I could taste the words, feel them rolling around in my mouth, but they wouldn't come. I wanted to ask him why he allowed her to hurt me, lie about me, tell him stories that made him not like me.

"I'm sorry" was all that came out. And I hated myself for my cowardice.

I lay in my bed that night, sinking into the darkness, and I didn't imagine my sister's ghost beside me. I thought it would be better if she died completely, disappeared from our house and our wars. "I can never be like you," I thought.

It is almost dark when I finish writing. I take my pages into the house, start to turn on lamps, then change my mind and look for candles and matches instead. I don't think I can take too much light right now. I have taken a child out of the shadows, and I need to send her back, to where she feels safe.

I light a candle for the little girl standing frightened and embarrassed in the bright glare of the bathroom light, and for Lily, in her bedroom, turning her face to the wall and pretending not to hear. I light a candle for my father, who chose to believe what looked like truth. I don't light one for my mother. I don't have that much forgiveness yet.

5

The message on Beck's answering machine says he's not there, but I know he is, so I talk to the tape until he answers.

"Hi—it's me. I know you're writing, I'm really sorry to disturb your work, but I needed to talk to you for a minute. I won't interrupt you for very long, I just—"

"Yes, Carla."

"Hi—I have a writer question, or maybe it's a writer dilemma. I'm not exactly sure. I'm writing about these things that are memories to me, but are lies to the only other witness who still has a voice—Lily. What if I'm wrong? She thinks I'm wrong."

"Does it matter?" Beck says. "They're real to you. That's all you need to know."

"I feel like all my old fears and doubts have been resurrected and are marching across my desk, leaving little footprints on the pages. I think there are about seven of them—I should name them— Grumpy, Sleepy, Dopey—"

"Where's Snow White?"

"I think she fell in a ditch."

"Get her out and give her a pen," Beck says. "Look, Carla, your memories are your reality, and all you can do is write about them. Lily's not at your typewriter, you are. And no one is going to burn your pages anymore."

I look past my desk, out the window to where a flock of seagulls is flying over the water. I remember how I used to dream of having wings, how I used to pray for them, promising God that I wouldn't do anything stupid like fly too close to the sun.

"You're right. Thanks, Beck—I'll clean these footprints off my pages now."

I used to look for magic in people's eyes. I looked for it in my father's, but the magic he possessed was in his stories, in tales spun in dark rooms—never in his eyes. I could find the sky there, and wide miles of blue ocean, but never the glimmer of magic that would have let me escape a world that too often felt tilted against me.

The territories of escape are fragile, the boundaries changeable. I preferred to be a vagrant in the lands my imagination created, but I was constantly pulled back by those who had little patience for my wanderlust.

In my friend Timmy's house, though, my imagination could go wherever it wanted; no one reined it in. Timmy was my first friend in California, the first friend I made in school, and the only one who had magic in his eyes; it danced out of them and tapped me on the forehead like a shiny wand. We were nine years old, but in our imaginations we were ageless.

He lived alone with his mother, a retired actress who wore silk, feathered robes and high-heeled slippers until noon and smoked cigarettes in long holders.

My mother would take me to his house on the weekends, but reluctantly.

"Aren't there any other children in your class you want to play with?" my mother asked me on several occasions.

There weren't. Timmy understood magic; he understood the ethics of magic, and the lure of escaping into its realms.

"Peter Pan shared his magic with the other kids," Timmy said earnestly. "That's very important."

"Do you have magic?" I asked him.

"Uh-huh. In my sleep I do."

"What happens then?"

"I go to beautiful places," Timmy said. "The clouds are gold and fluffy and there are talking animals."

I would imagine him in that place later, after he had died from the cancer that was starting even then. Talking to animals, bouncing on gold clouds as though they were trampolines.

There were boxes and trunks full of magic in his house too—costumes that his mother had saved from her years as an actress. We would rummage through them, the dust-smell of time rising up in our faces. Make-believe was sewn into the seams and no fantasy was out of bounds.

I would transform myself with shawls and huge fake jewels that sparkled in the light and made me feel like a princess. I would paint my lips red, powder my face, and spray myself with perfume. And I would twirl and dance through Timmy's house. He would lead me down the stairs, my handsome escort taking me to a carriage pulled by six white horses.

We created kingdoms—safer, more peaceful kingdoms than the one I came from and would return to when the clocks chimed and the carriage turned to dust.

One afternoon, rain was washing down hard outside and warm air was blowing out of the heater. It had been raining for days. Timmy thought it would probably rain for forty days and nights, and we should start making a list of all the animals we would need to round up and herd onto the ark.

"Don't we need to build the ark first?" I asked him.

"We'll make the list first—then we'll know how big the ark needs to be."

Our list was two pages long and Timmy and I were the only humans on it.

"Let's carve our initials on the wall inside the closet," he said. "So when the flood stops and someone finds the house, they'll know we were here."

"Who will be left to find it?"

"I don't know—people who are born after the flood, I guess. And we'll be there to find it, because we'll have an ark."

But Timmy wouldn't be there; I knew it that day as I watched his tiny hand clutch the scissors and press the point into the closet wall. Already he was disappearing; his skin was becoming transparent, barely opaque enough to cover the green map of veins.

At Timmy's funeral, I sat wedged between my parents, small and bewildered in a sea of black. I stopped listening to the words and the weeping and concentrated instead on where Timmy might be right then. I wanted him to be floating somewhere high above, where the air was soft, where sadness and pain didn't exist.

"Do you think he's dancing tonight?" I heard his mother ask later, after the funeral when we gathered at her house to eat and talk in low voices. She was sitting in a corner, and my mother had taken me over "to pay your respects, Carla." I wasn't sure what respects were, so I just shook her hand.

"I'm sure he is—of course, he's dancing," my mother told her, patting her on the shoulder. She steered me away, whispering, "She's in shock. That's why she's not making any sense."

But she made perfect sense to me. I thought Timmy probably was dancing, skipping from cloud to cloud, tossing stars over the moon.

I went up to his bedroom, to the familiar Wild West wallpaper and the toy chest, painted with ducks and rabbits, and trees with tops like green balloons. It was a scene that would never change. It was happiness made immortal—never to be touched by death.

I opened the closet door and stood eye level with our initials— wobbly lines pressed into the paint. The crooked lines of our lives that we believed would last after the flood. Already the closet smelled musty, as though it had been closed for a long time. In that tight, small space, his spirit tugged at me, drew breath from my lungs. Finally, I was forced back into the wider space of his room, where I sat on the small bed, shuffling through memories.

Footsteps came down the hall, and I recognized them as my mother's. Fear shivered through me, but she came in, sat down beside me, and put her arms around me. Gratefully, I buried my crying in the perfume smell of her.

In that moment, she was both mother and stranger, returning me to the fold of arms that were at once familiar and foreign.

"I know you miss Timmy," she said. "I know it hurts a lot."

I let her voice wash over me like a warm tide, permitting myself to forget that tides change, fooling myself into forgetting that her voice could snap like icicles falling from eaves.

In my memory, Timmy was there, smiling as the light deepened in the room and the sky turned purple outside the window.

As my mother and I got up to leave, I was sure I heard the sound of tiny footsteps, dancing between the darkening air currents.

One night, at the dinner table, my father cleared his throat, looked around the table at us, and said, "I have a surprise."

I stared out the window at the city lights, glittering below as if they had been put there for our viewing alone.

"Lily, get your pigtails out of your food," my mother said. "What's your surprise, Cliff?"

"I bought a boat." My father lifted his water glass in a toast, but my mother waited a second before raising hers.

"A boat? You don't even know how to drive a boat—or sail a boat—or whatever you do with it," she said. "What in the world do we need with a boat?"

"Rachel, need has nothing to do with it. I want to learn about the ocean—get out there in the deep blue, just me and the whales. It's good for a man's soul."

"Whales?" Lily said, suddenly interested.

My mother arched one eyebrow. "This must have cost quite a bit."

"Dear, we have quite a bit. We're wealthy enough to afford this, believe me."

"I certainly hope so," my mother answered, her tone darkening. "We do have two children to educate, and Carla looks like she'll need braces."

I ran my tongue over my teeth, trying to determine if this was true. I didn't even have all my permanent teeth yet, so I couldn't imagine how my mother had made this diagnosis.

"When do you plan to use this boat?" she continued.

"I thought I'd take off Fridays, give myself a three-day weekend. I'm my own boss now—I can do things like that."

"Uh-huh. Well, we'll discuss this boat thing later," my mother said. That always made me nervous—discussing things later. It didn't even involve me this time, and it still made my stomach tighten. I glanced at my father to see his reaction, but he was calmly spooning tartar sauce onto his fish and seemed to be engrossed in the task. Lily was arranging her potatoes in the shape of a whale. My mother jingled the silver bell that was always beside her place setting and the maid appeared with a refilled serving tray.

To this day, I hate the sound of bells; they remind me of summoning servants and it never seemed like a very cordial way to summon them. I'd have preferred it if my mother had just yelled for them by name—at least it would have had a more personal touch. I don't even like to pass those people from the Salvation Army at Christmas time, ringing bells and asking for money. I usually give them something, because I want to help, but also because I want them to stop ringing the damn bell.

On a hot, sun-drenched day my mother dressed Lily and me in white cotton shorts and navy blue shirts. She wore white slacks, a yellow blouse, and a wide-brimmed white hat. We were going to see the boat for the first time, and my mother believed in dressing appropriately for all occasions. She hurried around all morning, making sure we had a fully packed picnic basket, a first aid kit, and sun lotion.

When we parked our car at the marina, the smells of fish and saltwater filled my head; I heard water slapping against the sides of boats.

My father walked ahead of us and came back with a stocky, suntanned man who had elaborate tattoos on each arm. They twisted and rippled with his muscles whenever he moved. I couldn't take my eyes off them.

"This is Roy," my father said, smiling broadly. "He's going to teach me to be a sailor."

Roy shook hands with each of us and, when he got to me, I pumped his arm up and down so his tattoos would move some more.

"Carla, that's enough," my mother said, leading me away.

I stood beside my father and Roy for the rest of the day, trying to memorize the new words I was hearing. I was determined to learn everything that was being taught so that I could understand my father's fascination with taking to the sea.

The sun was orange and falling into the water when we docked the boat and set our feet on solid land. I could still feel the movement of the sea in my legs. Lily's nose was sunburned and my lips tasted salty.

"I'm not sure this is such a good thing for the children to be exposed to—the people down here, I mean," I heard my mother say as we walked back to the car. "Carla wants to get a tattoo now."

My father laughed. "Oh that—she'll get over it."

But I would never get over my love of the sea, and I would never stop wondering if I heard the same call my father did when he stared out across the whitecaps.

6

The first stop my school friend
Jackie and I made after the bus dropped us off in the mornings was
the restroom. We had each stolen bras from our mother's lingerie
drawers and we began our school days by stuffing them with Kleenex
so that, despite our grade-school uniforms—navy blue pinafores with
prim white blouses—we could look like teenagers. At least that was
our intention.

We were eleven, impatient with youth, and anxious for time to
speed up. We were best friends, although Jackie's friendship was
more conditional than mine; she reminded me, in various ways, that
she could withdraw it at any time.

Jackie wore cashmere sweaters over her uniform and a gold
identification bracelet which she never removed. Her blond hair was
always set in a perfect pageboy. She was allowed to attend her parents'
dinner parties and was well versed in the language of the upper crust
of society. She knew about crystal and china and which fork to use.

Jackie chose me as a friend because the balance of power between
us was too tempting for her to discard. I looked like I needed a friend
and she was the girl who everyone wanted as a friend.

I was too tall, my hair was chopped off above my ears, a decision my
mother made despite my protests. I raised my hand too often in class
and gave too many right answers. The girls in my class smirked at me
and said "Brainchild" in low, derisive voices as they passed me in the
corridors.

"Let's steal some nylons and wear those too," Jackie said one morning through the partition as we were stuffing our mothers' bras.

"But we already have to hide in the stalls when we change for gym," I argued. "It'll take even more time to get undressed and we'll get caught."

"Carla, you are so boring," Jackie sighed in her most adult voice. "It'll be fun. God, you're always such a chicken about everything."

"I don't know..." I said, as the bell for classes rang through the speaker system.

But I did know. I knew I would do whatever Jackie suggested, because defying her would mean walking from class to class alone, conspicuous in my solitary passage. Companionship defined our importance; being alone was the scarlet letter no one wanted. We were tethered to the concept of partnership. In the classroom and on the playing field we were instructed to choose partners or teams. It was a training ground for the exercise of power, and the lesson was not lost on us.

I would wait, when sides were being chosen or my classmates were organizing themselves into pairs. I knew Jackie would either choose someone else or wait until the last moment to align herself with me. I hated her power over me, yet I watched myself surrender to it every time.

But at night, I would lie in bed and sink into the dark comfort of my solitude. I would listen to the desert winds that howled down from the hills and hear in them voices meant only for me. I would open the blinds and stare at the moon's stark white eye. I felt safe like that, alone, with dark winds rattling the windows and the moon watching me.

I thought, if I could only remain alone like that, I wouldn't be afraid anymore; I wouldn't hurt anymore. It was when footsteps approached, and the boundaries of my solitude were crossed, that I became weaker.

It was Halloween. We had gone trick-or-treating in Jackie's Beverly Hills neighborhood the year before; that year she was coming to my house.

"I asked Leslie and Cheryl to come along too," she said at the end of the school day as we were climbing onto the bus.

"To my house?"

"Of course, dummy—that's where we're going trick-or-treating, isn't it? So I asked them to go with us—it'll be fun."

I heard the echo of Leslie and Cheryl's voices—the sound had trailed me too many times at school, their laughter crawling up my back and into my ears. I wasn't at all sure that Halloween was going to be fun.

"Their mothers said it was okay," Jackie added, as if to further emphasize that these plans had evolved without my knowledge. I wondered how long ago they had been confirmed.

I was dressing as an Indian. The year before I had gone as a cowgirl—just for the sake of fairness—but my heart was with the Indians. I had a black wig—braids that reached the middle of my back—a white leather dress with beadwork on it, and moccasins.

"You don't have a mask!" Lily said through the green head of her turtle costume. "Everyone will know who you are."

"We could put war paint on you," my mother offered.

"The women didn't wear war paint," I said. "Only the braves wore it when they went into battle." I knew that from my father's bedtime stories.

My mother put on her camel's hair jacket and tied a scarf around her head; she was taking Lily trick-or-treating.

"Carla, your friends should be here soon. Please watch out for cars and don't eat so much candy that you get sick," she said as she guided Lily—a tiny, round turtle—out the door. I suddenly wished I was Lily, young enough to be escorted through the trip-wire night.

I went back into my mother's dressing room and stood, framed by my reflection on three sides. I saw, looking back at me, a braided Indian maiden with dark, timid eyes and a wide nose, dressed in fringe and beads. I would have preferred a loincloth and war paint; I would have felt more confident confronting the tricks and treacheries of Halloween.

I heard the doorbell ring and I knew, even before my father called out, that Jackie had arrived with Leslie and Cheryl.

Jackie was dressed as a princess—pastel pink layers that rustled and scratched when she moved, and a rhinestone tiara on her head. Leslie and Cheryl were both witches—green-faced beneath their pointed black hats, capes swirling around them and long black plastic nails glued onto their hands.

I joined them, caught between royalty and evil, a remnant from another culture, another people—conquered and shuffled off to reservations with their silent pride and their beadwork souvenirs where they wouldn't be conspicuous reminders of how America was really founded. I wanted the war paint then; I wanted a bow and arrow and a sharp tomahawk—weapons against the echoes of history. But I was too late.

"Be careful," my father said as we trudged down the driveway. "Don't be gone too long."

He was framed in the lighted doorway, smiling and waving his hand. Halloween meant something different to him.

We passed other trick-or-treaters on the streets—monsters and wounded soldiers and furry animals with long tails; they all seemed happier than I felt. I lagged behind the other three; distance was my only weapon.

"Come on, Carla! What a slowpoke!" Jackie yelled over her pink tulle shoulder, and the three of them giggled.

There was a half-moon and a thin wash of fog drifting through the streets. In my neighborhood there were not many streetlamps and those that were there cast only a faint amber glow on the asphalt. We had flashlights, like the other trick-or-treaters we passed. My objective was to keep my three companions at the farthest tip of my flashlight beam. But I closed the distance whenever Jackie reproached me for falling behind. I didn't want to give myself away—an imitation Indian with nothing to assist her in the battle that might be looming.

Our bags were getting full and I was starting to feel more comfortable; maybe I'd been needlessly suspicious. There was still giggling and whispering that seemed aimed at me, but perhaps that was as bad as it was going to get.

We came to a vacant lot where Jackie and I had picked wildflowers one afternoon.

"Carla, remember that path you showed me at the end of this lot?" Jackie said.

"Oh, great—a secret path!" Cheryl said. "Where does it go?"

I welcomed the chance to take the lead, guide them into terrain that I knew and they didn't. "It leads to the canyon down below," I told them, my moccasins swishing through the low weeds. "There are some horse corrals. I go down there sometimes and pet the horses." I heard my voice growing more authoritative; I thought of leading them down the narrow path, under hanging branches and over crevices with which I was intimately familiar and they were not.

I was almost to the beginning of the path when I heard the crash of footsteps behind me. Before I could turn, I was on the ground and my arms and legs were pinned down by two witches. My flashlight had flown from my hands and I could see its light beam rolling over the lip of the hill. Jackie stood over me, her eyes shining in the half-light of the moon.

"Now you can be a real Indian—don't you want to know what that's like?" she said, and kneeled down beside me. She unsnapped my dress and Cheryl sat on my legs while Leslie moved down and took off my moccasins. My arms were unguarded; I could have hit them, tried to defend myself, but I lay still. My defense was going to be my silence, my lack of tears, and the dull ache in my stomach that I would swallow and never reveal. I listened to the branches move above me and tried to count the stars as my tormentors stripped me naked to the cold night air, giggling and calling me Pocahontas.

They were still laughing when they ran off carrying my clothes, leaving me on the ground, still and bare as a reed. I waited for the night around me to grow quiet before I stood up and stretched my arms to the sky, placing stars at the tips of my fingers. I needed to prove to myself that I was tall and straight and nothing could defeat me; I could prowl through the night like an animal, wordless and quick. My eyesight would grow keener and my feet would become thick and calloused to help me travel faster.

I stood at the edge of the path, wondering which way I should go. I heard the whisper of ghosts on the wind, felt spirits, long dead, stirring in the ground under my feet. The moon watched me with its half face, but my eyes could trace the outline of its dark side. I thought of making a bed from branches and waiting out the night, reading the patterns of stars until the sun rose and I would stare into its core without going blind. That was how powerful I felt. But maybe my power was only an illusion—the night had cast a spell on me that would be devoured by the red heat of the sun. I started walking in the direction of my house, finding trails behind yards and in between shrubs. Jagged pebbles stuck to the bottoms of my feet and the sky moved above me; the cold air stung my skin, but I had no tears. I was

tall as the stars and thin and dry as a wind current. When I heard
voices or footsteps coming in my direction, I would stop and crouch,
breathless and still. I was transparent—clear as ice—the darkness
would not betray me.

I knew I would have to cross some streets to get to my driveway; as I
got closer, I listened for danger, watched for the thin beams of
flashlights to bend around corners and find me. Anyone holding a
light was the enemy; only the creatures scurrying through the
darkness could be trusted. I stopped often, crouching on all fours; I
was forming pads on my palms, on the soles of my feet; my skin was
growing thicker, sealing in the heat of my blood.

A dog barked at me, but I said, "Shh..." and he fell quiet. He
knew I was not the enemy.

When I got to the foot of my driveway, I felt my head start to bend
and a shiver travel through me. I was transforming, turning back into
a naked little white girl, not even an imitation Indian. I stared at the
sky and clenched my fists; I was not going to lose my power. It had
been given to me—it was mine to keep, at least until morning.

I knocked on the front door and heard footsteps approaching—I
could tell they were my father's.

"My God, Carla! What happened?" He reached for me and wrapped
his arms around me; his gesture was rough, desperate, a frantic effort
to conceal my nakedness.

"I'm okay, really." Words felt foreign on my tongue, as though I had
been silent for a long time.

He pulled me inside and shut the door. I smelled my mother's
perfume and knew she and Lily had already returned.

"Rachel! Come here!" my father yelled, his voice scraping against
my ears.

"No," I said, too softly for him to hear.

I tried to read my mother's expression when she came down the
hallway and saw me; it was somewhere between anger and disgust,
but it didn't really matter. Either way, I knew I was in for a long
night of questioning.

"What in the world—" she began, and then as she got closer she
squinted at me, her eyes moving up and down over my body. "Are you
hurt?" Her voice accused me, blamed me.

"No."

"Well, I think an explanation is in order."

"Rachel, don't you think she should put on a robe first...or something?" My father was clearly uncomfortable.

My mother hooked her hand over my elbow and led me into my bedroom. Lily's door was closed, no light shone underneath, but I wondered if she was really asleep or sitting by the door listening.

"Go get your robe on," my mother said.

I was colder then than I had been earlier, prowling through the dark on damp, rocky soil; my teeth were chattering and I clenched my jaw to make the sound stop.

Wrapped inside my blue terry-cloth robe, I followed my mother into the living room, where a fire was burning and my father was sitting in his usual chair reading. I tried to imagine myself still out in the night, crouched by a fire I had built from twigs and fallen branches; the image made me feel stronger. I sat on the warm hearth and felt the heat travel up my spine.

"Well?" my father said.

"Some kids knocked me down and stole my clothes. I don't know who it was." I wanted to add, "Can I go to bed now?" But I restrained myself. I knew they wouldn't let me go that easily.

"What did they look like?" my mother asked, arching her eyebrow in a way that suggested she didn't believe me.

"I don't know. It was dark...and I closed my eyes."

The doorbell rang and it suddenly occurred to me that my tormentors had to return to my house. Jackie's mother would be picking them up. My father opened the door and I heard Jackie's voice.

"Did Carla come back? We got separated and we looked all over for her. She was lagging so far behind, I'm not surprised..." It was her most adult, conciliatory voice, the one she'd learned from her mother.

My father led them into the living room and I turned my face toward the fire; I couldn't meet Jackie's eyes. In some black corner of my heart I imagined the flames engulfing the three of them—two witches and an evil princess going up in smoke. But it wasn't an image I could hold onto—it felt too evil. My victory would be silence, complete withdrawal from the power they had once wielded over me.

"Carla tells us that some children attacked her," my mother began.

"That's terrible!" Jackie said, with just the right note of horror in her voice. "I kept telling her to keep up but she got so far behind. Who would do such a thing?"

I could feel Jackie's eyes boring into me, but I kept my face turned toward the flames.

"What did they look like?" Leslie said, confident that the three of them had won an important victory

"I don't know," I said to the smoldering logs.

A car came up the driveway—Jackie's mother—at least they would be gone soon.

"I'm going to bed," I announced, and walked past them, meeting no one's eyes.

I heard the sounds behind me—voices, doors opening and closing—but I pretended they were miles away. Once in my room, I turned out the lights and opened all the shades. I felt safe again in the darkness, my power was still there.

The wind had come up; it billowed the curtains and filled my room with the smell of woodsmoke. I sat on the bed and looked out at the sky, wishing I had enough power to create miracles. I would change myself into a boy, remove myself from the betrayals of girls. But I knew it was impossible. My body was already changing—breasts were forming on my chest and I had hair where I used to have none. I had to find other ways to make myself invulnerable to the treacheries that threatened to entangle me. I would trust no one, tell no one my secrets. The black wind shivering across my skin told me that was all I could do.

I didn't abandon my resolve not to speak to Jackie after her betrayal on Halloween night. I made friends with boys instead. I learned their jokes, became a co-conspirator in their plots against girls. I would tell them who was wearing a bra so they could sneak up behind and pull the strap, releasing it with a hard snap designed to inflict pain on pale girlish skin. One boy presented me with crayfish claws he'd found in a frog's stomach while he was dissecting it in science class. The plan was to put them in some squeamish girl's gym locker, although he had no particular person in mind. I, of course, had the perfect victim and I acted legitimately shocked when Jackie screamed and threw them on the floor. I no longer minded that my hair was short; it made me look more like a boy. I didn't care that I gave the right answers in class or that I set records in track and could outrun all of the girls and most of the boys. The girls who had wielded power over me sensed my determination, and shied away from it; the boys had an ally who could infiltrate the territories forbidden to them.

At first, Jackie taunted me, trying to lure me back, but I knew the game now. Leslie and Cheryl were her chorus, echoing her challenges, mimicking the cadence of her voice. But I was immune; I would squeeze my eyes shut and see myself walking naked under the half-lit eye of the moon, the stars trailing my journey. Their voices would fade and break into tiny splinters of sound. Eventually, they got bored with the effort.

The rains came that November and my father complained that the weather was keeping him from going out on his boat.

"Damn rain. It always rains on my days off," he'd grumble.

"It's been raining all week, Cliff. I don't think God singled you out specifically," my mother said in a soothing voice. She seemed to have a particular insight into God's motives and patterns.

One Saturday, the sky was a clear, brilliant blue, but to the north a line of storm clouds hovered menacingly. I walked into the living room . . . and into an argument already in progress.

"Cliff, how can you even think of going out sailing on a day like this? The forecast is for rain, and look outside—you can see the storm that's coming," my mother was saying.

"Oh, you know the weathermen—they're always wrong. Besides, those clouds are going the other way."

Neither of them was looking out the window, so I had no idea how they each had so much confidence in their predictions.

"Are you going sailing? I want to go," I said.

"Now look. You've got Carla started. Oh, Lord, just do what you want. I can't talk sense to you, Clifford Lawton. I swear, this boat has become an obsession with you." My mother turned abruptly and left the room, probably assuming that my father would follow her to smooth things over. But he didn't.

"Go change your clothes, Carla. Roy's already on his way to the marina to meet us."

By the time we got there, it was obvious that my mother was much better at forecasting the weather.

"I don't know," Roy said, narrowing his eyes at the sky. "Pretty big storm, looks like."

"Well, we'll just go for a short one," my father answered.

We pulled out of the harbor and into open water; the sea was gray and choppy and the smell of rain laced the wind.

I had believed my father's weather prediction and hadn't brought my rain slicker, and the storm was bearing down on us, a black conquest of the remaining blue sky.

"Let's turn back!" Roy yelled.

"Okay." I could tell my father loved this; it was an adventure that my mother had almost taken from him with her protests, but here he was, the boat slapping against the whitecaps while he yelled into the wind and tried to outrun the rain. I stood beside him as the clouds broke and rain slanted into us. If he didn't care about getting wet, neither did I. I lifted my face and opened my mouth, feeling the sharp pellets of rain and the softer, subtler taste of salt spray.

"You're getting awfully wet, Carla!" he yelled, his voice rising above the sound of the wind. "Want to go below?"

"No!"

By the time we got home, I was shivering and my lips were blue.

"Good Lord in heaven," my mother said when she saw us walk in the front door.

She put me in a hot bath and bundled me in flannel pajamas and a thick robe. I got to eat dinner by the fire, and my mother kept feeling my forehead.

The next morning, I woke up with a sore throat and a fever which got worse as the day progressed. I ended up missing nearly a full week of school, and much of that week was lost to the delirium of a raging fever.

Graddy, our cook, would come into my bedroom and play cards with me and I would try to imitate her accent. She was from Alabama and was the only black person I knew. Her skin was the color of dark maple syrup and the palms of her hands were pink.

"I wish my hands had two colors," I told her once. "Look—mine are boring. Both sides are the same."

She laughed and pulled me against her. Her body was thick and reassuring; I would try to make her laugh so that she would hug me and cushion me inside her arms. There was a scar angling across her cheek that I asked her about, but she just shook her head and said, "It's nothin' for you to concern yourself with, child."

I think she sat with me most of the day when my fever reached its peak, but everything seemed to be floating. I saw things through a haze and heard voices as if they were coming to me from some distant, cavernous place. I remember Graddy sitting on my bed, but she moved in and out of focus. I remember touching her scar—the long, raised ridge of it felt smooth and shiny.

"I'll tell you about it, child," I think she said, but I wondered later if I had dreamed it in the heat of my fever. "I was tryin' to save my son—they were takin' him and I knew what they were gonna do. This one man, he pulled back with a whip and got me in the face. The blood went in my eyes and I couldn't see. I was nearly thrown back off my feet. Now this scar's all I have left of my son."

When my fever broke that night, I woke up drenched in sweat, my hair stuck to my head and my lips dry and cracked. Graddy and my mother changed my sheets and brought me a clean nightgown. When my mother left the room, I touched Graddy's scar and asked, "Were you here today?" It seemed like a memory, but it was misty and just out of reach, so I wasn't sure.

"Hush now—you go to sleep. You were burnin' up with fever today. Likely as not you don't know who was here."

But weeks later, when I was playing cards with Graddy in her room and she went out to the kitchen for a cup of coffee, I opened the drawer of her nightstand. I knew I shouldn't be snooping, and even as I slid the drawer out, I didn't know why I was doing it. My hand seemed to have a will of its own. In the drawer was a yellowed newspaper clipping with a picture of a young black man, hands bound behind his back, hanging from a tree. I knew then that her visit hadn't been a dream.

When I went back to school, I was still light-headed and weak. My mother wrote notes for the teachers, asking them to excuse me from gym class and to please make sure I didn't tire myself out. I was starting to like how I felt—as if I were watching everything through a fogged-up glass. It made me feel removed, invulnerable, especially to the girls who still occasionally snickered and pointed at me. The boys were nicer; I had joined their ranks. I didn't squeal or run away from bugs or shudder at the dead things floating in jars of formaldehyde in the science room. I would put my nose right up against the jars and examine the tapeworms and the rat fetuses. The boys wanted to know about my illness, and if I'd thrown up—I said yes even though I hadn't.

I was still in my post-fever haze when our afternoon classes were cut short and we were told to line up ouside. One of the teachers was lowering the flag to half-mast and the principal announced that President Kennedy had been shot and killed. From the row behind me, I heard Jackie gasp and say, "My God"—which was her latest expression. Then she fainted—not a real faint, but one she had learned from watching old movies. She even had her hand across her forehead. The rest of us were too stunned to help her. She lay on the ground for several minutes while we stood in numb silence, trying to understand how this could have happened. We knew about Lincoln—

certainly it was possible for a president to be killed—but that was a long time ago, a page in our history books, not someone who had come into our living rooms and talked to us from the other side of the television screen.

Slowly, those around me recovered their voices; some started crying, some mumbled that they couldn't believe it. Jackie decided to get up from the ground. I was caught in silence—I couldn't contribute to the sound swelling around me. I had learned, in a matter of days, that there was no limit to betrayal; it wasn't restricted to girls or to schoolrooms and Halloween nights. It reached farther than that; black boys hung from trees like sad fruit, and bullets whistled along their deadly paths, shattering flesh and lives and changing the course of countries.

My mother was crying when she put me to bed that night; her eyes were swollen and bloodshot. She looked smaller to me, as though the sadness had made her shrink.

"Nobody's safe," she said, but not really to me. Her voice floated on the lamplight, directed at no one. "I get so worried when your father's picture is in the newspaper and in magazines. They keep saying he's one of the richest men in the country. It's bound to make some people angry and jealous."

I had seen some of the pictures of my father, and I had overheard enough of my parents' conversations to know that my father's investment firm was very successful. It didn't occur to me until that night that someone might hate him for his wealth.

My mother hugged me good night, but it felt different—not as insistent as it usually did. In our family, there was a protocol involved in saying good night; kisses and hugs and I-love-yous were mandatory. I liked Graddy's hugs better; hers felt like a thick, warm blanket you could curl up in. My mother's arms demanded, held on. But on this night they wrapped around me with a willingness to let go.

School was canceled for four days. The only thing on television was news of the assassination. Graddy took two days off, leaving in a black dress and hat.

"Where are you going, Graddy?"

"To church," she said. "We need mountains of prayers right now. It's a sad time, child. A sad time for the world. It ain't never gonna be the same. You'll see."

All the sadness in the house made me feel like I was still floating, still riding on waves of fever. Lily kept asking questions and my parents answered her with soft, faraway voices.

"She doesn't really understand," my father whispered to me.

I took Daisy for long walks to the top of the hill behind our house. Sometimes I took my kite and I'd watch it dance on the wind currents. I wished myself up to its height—miles above the crying and the funerals. Layers of thick blue air between me and men dangling from trees, and fallen leaders lying in pools of blood.

8

My breasts were growing. I would touch them late at night, under the covers, trying to measure any new growth with my hands. Other girls in the locker room after gym class were measuring me, too. Their eyes crawled over my chest— spider trails of curiosity and judgment—trying to see whether I was going to be the next one to graduate into a bra. Not one stolen from my mother's drawer and stuffed with Kleenex, but one bought for me and stuffed with me.

There were only two other girls in my class who were wearing bras—"trainer bras"—as though breasts needed guidance on their way to maturity. It made me think of instruction booklets—*How to Train Your Breasts*. Although I had no idea what they would be trained to do. I'd looked at my mother's, and they didn't seem to do anything except be there.

I'd looked at my mother a lot, although it always left me feeling confused and frightened, with a vague sense of awareness that this was exactly her intention. She had a habit of marching into my room naked; it wasn't the nakedness that frightened me, it was the way it charged into my room like a battle cry.

It was usually associated with something I needed to be lectured on, and I would end up standing clothed before her nakedness, hearing her voice rise, wondering where to put my eyes. I would try, sometimes, to turn and run into my imagination. I'd think of a scrapbook picture I'd seen of me as a baby, nursing at her breast. I'd think of the gentleness of the human body, the gift of milk into a baby's mouth, into my mouth. It was a way of reminding myself that once upon a time her breasts had nourished me, her arms had carried me at safe heights.

I wasn't sure what had changed, or why... but some part of me knew.

It was all connected to the changes in my body, to the swelling of my breasts and the way my hips were becoming wider than my waist. I could chart my mother's anger, its steep ascent—when she had to explain things to me, like how a man puts his penis into a woman to make a baby, and how I would soon start bleeding every month.

"Do I have to?" I said.

"Don't be ridiculous, Carla. It's part of becoming a woman."

But that process already seemed fraught with dangers and unpleasant requirements. Women had to do things to themselves—my mother had already told me that, years before, when I'd made the mistake of asking what the rubber bag and hose were that hung in her bathroom.

The answer didn't follow immediately; it came two days later when my mother came into my room naked and told me to come into her bathroom with her.

"You asked what this was," she said. "I'm going to show you. It's a douche."

The word meant nothing to me, but what followed did. She sat down and I watched from the doorway, as I'd been told to do, as part of the hose disappeared inside of her. I knew if I tried to run I would only make things worse. So I watched, nine years old and frightened, and later that night I cried and prayed in the safe darkness of my bedroom that God would change His mind and let me wake up as a boy—or a crow or a dog or a tree stump. Just not as a girl.

On the practical side, my breasts seemed to be the biggest problem. I was growing out of my clothes; buttons were pulling loose and fabric was stretching where it hadn't before. My school uniform was fine; apparently whoever designed those had biological changes in mind and had left plenty of room. But my other clothes were becoming uncomfortable and potentially embarrassing; I could look down and see gaps between the buttons—windows into flesh that was growing in new ways.

When we had school dances, our uniforms were not required. It was a chance for girls to express themselves with frills and bows and for boys to complain about the suits and ties that made them look like they should be standing in church pews holding hymnals.

It was also a chance for my mother to dress me—in clothes I'd outgrown. Dresses that flattened my breasts, that were ruffled and young, that ridiculed the years that were shaping me. I understood then, more clearly than ever, that there would be no absolution for my sin of growing up—growing into the woman I would eventually become. My body was starting to look like sex; it was starting to smell like sex; I knew it from my hands' nightly travels over its changing territories. To my mother, this made me the enemy. It was a war I would never win, but I was determined to walk away with a few battles to my credit.

I adopted a new strategy. I acceded to my mother's choice of clothes, smiling sweetly, agreeing that the ruffled, pastel, puffed-sleeve dress she pulled out of my closet was perfect. And when she left me alone, I would get a pair of manicure scissors and sabotage the zipper by carefully cutting out one of the teeth. Then, armed with an impenetrable act of innocence, I would go in to my mother and ask her to zip me up, knowing the zipper would break in a matter of seconds.

Since I usually waited until the last minute for this finale, I would be sent back to my room to "just put on something." Which meant I could choose. Which meant I had won.

But there was always defeat looming on the road ahead. My prayers weren't answered; my body kept changing, inviting my mother's anger. It was only a matter of time before it would betray me completely, cutting me off from my childhood and hurling me into the world of women, the world of the enemy—the world that I feared the most.

It was a passage marked by blood. It happened at night, seeping from some inner hollow of my body onto the sheets. But first it came into my dreams—before the moment of waking up and rolling over, wet warmth sticking to my flesh, prying me awake.

Before all of that, my dreams saw it coming. A red moon floated through them, fevered and hot, leaking into the sky that bent over my sleep. Something heavy and new rumbled in my body, pushed my legs apart, and sent my hands out to catch what was abandoning me.

I turned on the bedside lamp, peeled back the covers, and my childhood fluttered away on fast wings. It left behind a message of blood.

It was three-thirty in the morning. I stripped the bedclothes off, dragged the sheet into the bathroom, and put the red stain under a running faucet.

I was afraid to let my mother know—afraid of exposure, reprisals, interrogations. I had to erase the evidence, send it down the drain in a watery red stream. But it wouldn't all come out of the sheet; there was still a pale red spot on the white that I attacked furiously, scrubbing it with soap. Lady Macbeth cursing the heavens, cursing the spot, driven mad by the evidence.

I slit open the box of Kotex that had been put under the sink for the inevitability of this moment—I slit it in the corner so it would look unopened. And I removed the emblem of my initiation into womanhood. Wearing this new emblem, I took the wet sheet back to my room and lay on the mattress to spend the rest of the night with the red moon leaking between my dreams, between my legs, between sleep and fear.

I thought it would work—changing my own bedclothes at dawn, piling the soiled sheets on the service porch—just another innocent bundle of laundry.

"Carla, may I see you for a minute?" my mother said, coming into the kitchen where I was sitting at the breakfast table in my school clothes, hoping for a fast getaway. A spoonful of cereal froze in midair, on its way to my mouth. I followed her back into the service porch. Damn spot, I thought, it gave me away. It exposed my crime to my mother and now I'd have to pay for it.

The sheet was spread out on the washing machine, the now-pink spot an advertisement of the transformation that had visited me during the night.

"Why didn't you tell me about this?" my mother asked.

"I don't know," I said to the floor, my voice whispery and thin.

"What?"

"I don't know," I repeated a little more forcefully.

"Are you wearing something?"

"Yes," I answered, squeezing my legs together, wishing for time to speed up, wishing to be anywhere else but right there at that moment.

"Come with me," my mother told me.

I followed again, back to my bathroom where she first checked the box under the sink, locating the scissor-slit on the corner.

"You were trying to hide this?"

"I don't know," I repeated again.

Just as my mother was reaching for the edge of my dress, I heard the school bus honk outside.

"I have to go," I said quickly, stepping back from her hand—from its exposure, its humiliation.

"You have to take one of these with you—you'll need to change," she said, ripping open the box and handing me my new identification. She looked like she'd rather throw it at me.

I ran for my bag, shoved the Kotex in it, and sped out the door, onto the bus like it was a coach sent down from heaven.

But I knew it wasn't. It would take me to school, where there were girls I had to guard myself against. And it would bring me home, to battles I had already lost.

Lily is spooning soup into our
mother's mouth.

"Bet you twenty bucks if I were holding the spoon, she'd spit it
out," I tell her, as our mother obediently opens her mouth, accepts
the spoonful of soup, and swallows.

"That's not funny, Carla."

"I don't think it was meant to be. Everything was always more
acceptable if it came from you. Do you suppose, if you had been the
writer instead of me, that Mother would have destroyed your writing?
I mean, would it have been okay if it had come from your pen rather
than mine?"

Lily puts the spoon down and turns to me. She is wearing an orange
silk blouse, a lighter orange than her hair, and her face, caught
between these two shades of the same color, looks paler than it
usually does.

"Mother had good reason to be upset with your writing," she says.
"It was depressing. It probably still is."

"Upset is one thing, destroy is another. You do remember the
destroy part, don't you, Lily?"

"Yes, Carla, I remember."

"That's a relief—so you only have partial amnesia, huh?"

Our mother coughs, and Lily picks up the napkin and wipes a string
of saliva from her mouth.

"Is this why you came here today?" she asks me. "For a confrontation?"

"No—it wasn't preplanned. It just seemed like a good idea once I got here."

I get up and head for my old room; it's suddenly important for me to see it, to revisit it, to listen for the call of ghosts and the echo of words I was afraid to write down.

It still looks the same—cream-colored wallpaper with vertical rows of red roses, matching curtains and beige shag carpet. I always wondered why my mother never redecorated the room after it was no longer mine. She put overnight guests there, as though showing off the shrine she had preserved for her wayward daughter. I sit on one of the twin beds and remember some of the nights I couldn't sleep, when it seemed I could hear the roses opening and closing around me, their blood-red petals moving in rhythm to my breathing.

I go to the drawer that I once regarded as my infallible hiding place. I lost words and pages, watched them vanish forever before I realized that, in order to write, I had to learn to hide.

I was ten and I had written my first story. It was about a child who lived in a house of shadows. There was one room she was not allowed to enter; she was told that something evil was locked inside, and she was forbidden to even linger outside the door. One day, she emptied the key drawer in her mother's desk and tried each key until she found the one that fit.

She opened the door and found, inside the room, the most beautiful little girl she had ever seen, with long blond hair and bright blue eyes. A cloud of gold dust hovered around her.

"I knew you'd come," this angelic girl said, in a voice that sounded like tiny bells from a faraway hilltop. "I knew you wouldn't believe them that I was evil."

One afternoon, as I was playing with Daisy in the backyard, my mother appeared. White pages fluttered in her hand, but I couldn't look at them; all I could see was the bright red on her fingernails.

"I'm sure you know what this is," she said. "I didn't know you had taken up writing, and I certainly don't understand this."

"You weren't supposed to understand it. You weren't supposed to read it," I said. But I had been careless; I had left it on a bookshelf in my room under some schoolbooks.

"Is this supposed to represent this household—shadows, locked-up children, warnings about evil? There are so many cheerful things in life. Why don't you write about them? Lily would never do this, nor would your older sister, if she had lived. I'm sure of it. God had to curse me with a middle child."

"Can I have my story back, please?"

"No, you cannot. I will not have this depressing drivel in my house."

I never found out what she did with it; I searched through the garbage for a week and never found it. But I knew I had to find a hiding place for my future compositions.

I peeled away the lining in my sock drawer, and for months I slid in page after page, gently pressing the lining back like a blanket over my words. I still don't know what gave me away; maybe the stack of pages got too high and looked too obvious.

I came home from school on a rainy afternoon and found them in my mother's possession.

"I think you have some explaining to do," she said, meeting me at the door. The rain washed down behind me as I stood in the open doorway, my mother filling the space in front of me. I considered making a run for the rain, but my body felt frozen in place.

She led me into her bedroom and sat down in a chair by the fireplace. I stood like a soldier facing a commanding officer; I stared stoically into the flames and the sputtering logs.

"I thought I told you about this depressing writing."

"Why did you go through my drawers?" I asked, weakly—a feeble attempt at gaining victory in a battle that was already lost.

"I was putting your clean socks away. Don't change the subject on me, young lady. This is very disturbing, reading this distorted account of your life. My God, one would think you've been chained in a basement and forced to survive on bread and water."

"Can I go, please?" I knew what the the finale was going to be, and I didn't want to watch the words I'd labored over in the late, sleepy hours of night destroyed.

"Yes. Go to your room and stay there until dinner," my mother said.

I realized that I could remember much of what I'd written. For weeks, I devoted myself to ravaging my memory and re-creating what I could. As I filled up page after page, I peeled away corners of wallpaper, slid papers under my mattress, hid others in suitcases that were stored in cabinets I could only reach by standing on a chair. I calculated that the likelihood of my mother finding everything was not great; at most, I would only lose part of what I'd written.

None of my pages were found again, although I know my mother looked. I found traces of her presence in my room, smelled her perfume on the air and in my drawers, as though it couldn't resist betraying her. There were words, though, that I would never be able to remember. They had healed me somehow, but their magic had been stolen.

I go back to the den where Lily is putting a blanket around our mother.

"Lily, I'm going to go," I tell her. "I'm sorry I'm in such a rotten mood today."

But I'm not really sorry. I drive too fast down the driveway and through the tree-lined streets, trying to escape the floodlight of sun. I don't slow down until the road meets the coast and the air seems softer. Only then do I feel safe, far away from my mother's determination to allow no secrets but her own.

Beck's car is parked outside my house when I get there, but neither he nor Tully greets me when I walk in the door. I find them on the beach, sitting side by side, facing the sea in some mysterious communion that I'm reluctant to intrude upon.

I sit down beside Beck on the sand, my silence leaving room for him.

"I needed to escape my typewriter," he tells me, as though he has to explain his presence here.

"I know the feeling."

"Let's take a walk," Beck says, standing up.

It's late afternoon, but the fog hasn't been blowing in these days; all that's left of it is a thin layer of clouds over the sun, making the light silvery and smooth. Birds occupy the shore, lingering on the sand, their reflections small and perfect on the mirror-gray of the low-tide beach. They scatter as Beck and I approach them; they lift off and circle over us, waiting for us to get out of the way so their landing strip will be clear again.

"This book I'm working on is taking me into some strange territories," he says; our footsteps have left long trails behind us.

"I haven't asked..."

"I know—your restraint has been admirable. But I should tell you something about it—where it's coming from, at least. It has a lot to do with corners of the mind we don't like to look at because they look like madness and probably are. I guess in some way I'm doing what you're doing—traveling back to places that aren't so pleasant."

"Beck, you're not going to tell me you had your high school yearbook picture taken in a straitjacket, are you?"

"No," he laughs, "not quite. But I escaped going to Vietnam in a rather unique way—I had a friend drive me to a mental institution and commit me. He told them I'd taken too much acid, and I acted convincingly frayed around the edges. I voluntarily locked myself in a world where insanity is the common denominator. The password is anything that makes no sense."

I stop and face him, circling my arms around his waist. "Why haven't you ever told me about this?"

"It's the kind of thing you want to wait on, Carla. It makes lousy cocktail chatter and could probably throw a small wrench into a relationship if it's brought up too soon."

"So how long did you stay?" I ask, trying to imagine Beck wandering through dank halls with people whose minds had spun out of control.

"About six weeks. Sometimes I hid the drugs I was supposed to take, but there were times I couldn't. You know what gets you after a while? The sounds. The moaning, the incoherent monologues, the sounds of keys and doors slamming. I thought while I was in there that I'd figured out why van Gogh cut off his ear—to escape the sounds of madness. The sounds came first, not his own madness. The biggest struggle was hanging onto the thread of my own sanity while I was keeping up my act . . . and blocking out the noises that kept trying to suck me in."

"This is what you're writing about?" I ask after we've turned back toward the house.

"Not specifically, but it's where the story finds its roots. There are things I don't quite remember—just like you—in my case, it's probably due to the drugs they were giving me."

"In my case, they *should* have been giving me drugs," I tell him. "I wouldn't have minded dulling my senses a little."

His hand moves to the back of my neck, his fingers thread through my hair. "I just thought I should tell you."

"I'm glad you did."

I think of the nights when I have awakened to find Beck staring into the blackness, as though he is listening to an ancient drummer only he can hear, and it makes sense to me now.

10

The July air is dry as cinders, even at night; wind scrapes against the house. I hear it in my sleep, through my dreams...until Beck's body curves around my back, pressing into me, and his hands slide around my ribs and find my breasts. I open my eyes to the soft blue of early morning and the feel of him hard against me. Turning to him, tangling myself around him, I open my body to his.

I taste sleep on him, smell sex drifting out from under the covers, and I close my eyes again, painting the morning gray in my mind. I want clouds to move into the sky as Beck moves deeper into me, and rain to pour down and wash away the dust we've let gather on us.

Beck falls asleep afterward, and Tully comes over to paw at me. He doesn't understand why I'm not up yet. I put on a robe, walk quietly out of the room, through the house, and let Tully down on the beach. He looks at me, waiting for me to come with him.

"You're on your own this morning," I tell him.

When the sun pushes its way into the sky, I am sitting on the deck drinking coffee, watching Tully trot through the waves. I don't want to shower Beck off of me; I can still feel him between my thighs. I think about the pages I want to write today and decide that this is an appropriate state to be in. Inspirational, in fact.

"Are you daydreaming?" Beck asks, coming onto the deck with a cup of coffee, his shirt unbuttoned over faded jeans and bare feet.

"Not really. I was thinking about what I'm going to write today. I'm using you for inspiration."

"Oh—well, that could mean any one of a number of things."

"I'm writing about first sex—actually, first almost-sex. You remember—the keeping your clothes on kind? Remember when anything was okay as long as it was done without unzipping your pants?"

"Rings a bell," Beck says, and laughs softly.

"How old were you?" I ask him.

"I'm not exactly sure. But I think I'd progressed to solid food and two-syllable words. How old were you?"

"Thirteen. It was my exit from grade school. I figured it was important to enter high school with as much education as I could get. So did you love her?"

"Who?"

"Whoever you first had clothes-on sex with." I look at the tiny lines around his eyes and try to imagine him younger.

"Jesus, I don't think so. Whatever emotions I had were well below the level of my heart," he says.

"Yeah, me too."

Two hours later, I am still in my robe, still smelling like sex, still getting inspiration from it. The wind is angrier now, but I try to ignore it as I fill up pages, organizing memories into stories.

His name was Redge Brillstein. He had bad skin and long, slender fingers—musician's fingers. In eighth grade he was the only boy taller than I was, which might be why he became my boyfriend, although he used that term more than I did. With his thick, black hair, and long nose, he reminded me of an exotic bird. I liked him because of that, and because he was smart and read almost as many books as I did, and because he had a penis.

We'd sneak off during lunch hour, looking for hiding places where we could explore each other wordlessly—hesitant, wet kisses and sweaty hands groping under sweaters. His breath always smelled like wintergreen Lifesavers; I'd still find the smell in my hair hours later. It was part curiosity, part hunger, and part the lure of the forbidden. But more than all of this, it was a way to defy my mother and prove to myself that she hadn't frightened me away from growing up.

Eventually, we found the perfect hiding place. In the backstage area of the auditorium, there was a panel cut out of the floorboards; the space underneath was used for storage, but there was nothing down there when we discovered it. We'd lower ourselves down and slide the panel back, the darkness clamping down on us. The space was deep enough for us to sit up, although our stolen hours were spent lying down. Sometimes, people would walk across the floor above us, and we would laugh into each other's mouths, exchanging breath and muffled sounds.

We got less awkward the more we practiced. Our tongues learned to tease and our hands grew more certain in their exploration.

At first, I was frightened by the changes I felt in Redge's body as he lay on top of me, but I learned to move underneath him in ways that sent tiny shudders of heat through me. Sometimes, with his face buried in my neck, and his wintergreen breath soaking into my hair, I'd open my eyes and imagine the floorboards parting and my mother's face staring down at us. Her mouth would gasp, her eyes would call me names...and I would press my crotch into Redge and feel heat bloom inside me.

It went on for more than a month; we were bold and confident that our disappearances would go unnoticed. But I forgot that old enemies remain enemies, and their eyes are keen.

I underestimated the ingenuity of revenge.

Our heads emerged from the floor one afternoon—like gophers sneaking out of their tunnel—to find the principal, the school nurse, and Jackie waiting for us at the backstage entrance. The principal led Redge away, the school nurse took me, and Jackie walked away victorious. I had removed myself as a player in her game, and she hadn't found anyone else who would bend to her will the way I once had. She had waited, and watched, and had finally been rewarded with the perfect opportunity to get back at me for going AWOL on her.

"Did you and Redge have intercourse?" the nurse asked me. Her eyes looked fishlike through her glasses.

"No, we were doing our homework," I said. I hated Jackie, and if I couldn't make her pay, I was willing to aim my anger at anyone who happened to be in the way.

"Carla, don't get smart with me. This is very, very serious."

"We did not have intercourse, all right? We kissed, and unless they've been keeping something from us in science class, you can't get pregnant from that."

"You have no regrets about this? No apologies?"

"No."

"Fine. Maybe you'll feel like apologizing to your parents."

"I doubt it."

I sat in the nurse's office until my mother came to get me, and I stared out the car window on the ride home.

"You are not to associate with this boy anymore," my father said later that evening. "We've already told his parents that he is to stay away from you."

"Why are you blaming him? He didn't force me to do anything. We both went down there. How do you know I didn't force him?"

"He's Jewish, isn't he?" my mother asked in a vague, noncommittal tone that failed to disguise feelings no longer vague to me.

"What does that have to do with it?" I asked defiantly.

"Nothing," she shrugged.

"We don't care who is to blame," my father went on. "You two are not to associate with each other anymore."

"Kind of hard when we're in the same classes," I mumbled as I left the room.

"What?"

"Nothing," I answered, mimicking my mother's tone.

I was determined to defy their orders, and I fully expected Redge to go along with my rebellion. But when I approached him the next day at school, he said, "Carla, I can't talk to you," furtively looking around and refusing to meet my eyes.

"You're going to go along with this?" I said. "This is a free country. We can talk to whoever we want!"

He shook his head and started to move away from me.

"You chickenshit!" I yelled.

Redge Brillstein was much more courageous underground than he ever could be standing up, in full view of everyone. I had no patience with his fears; I was too intolerant of my own. I understood anger—it was my survival kit—and anyone who retreated from it was swallowed up in the distance I put between us.

11

Beck and I are driving down Melrose to an art gallery, the streetlights and Hollywood neon humming around us. In the year that we've been together, Beck has never suggested going to a gallery; I chalk it up to research for his book, which is how I explain any unusual behavior these days.

"You know how Jung talked about the dark parts of the personality being in shadow?" he says.

"I think that's the point at which I stopped reading Jung. It started sounding too much like my childhood. Does this have to do with your book, or are you about to tell me you're going into therapy?"

"At the moment, I'm talking about my book." A siren wails somewhere in the distance, the sound growing thinner as it speeds in a direction that doesn't involve us. "I was thinking that it was applicable to what I'm doing—the idea that there are parts of ourselves that haven't been integrated. It's frightening when you think about it."

"It's starting to frighten me," I say softly, aiming my voice out the window.

"What?"

"Nothing. Who is this artist we're going to see? I didn't know you kept up with the art scene."

"I read something about him, he sounded interesting," Beck says, turning onto a side street, away from the neon hum into the dim wash of streetlamps. He parks along the street and we walk back to Melrose.

The gallery is crowded and rock music is turned up too loud. It's the hard edge of the art world—the black leather contingent with hair that's either been mowed into short, angular shapes or dyed with paintlike colors. The eyes are tough, show-me eyes. I know the look; I used to practice it, back when we drew thick black lines along our lids and wore pale, chalky lipstick. The lips in here are red, or a purplish wine color, like old injuries.

I glance at Beck; in his faded denim jacket and white T-shirt he looks like a painter—some eccentric recluse who has ventured out of his canyon studio to check out the new wave of artists. It doesn't matter that he's almost twenty years older than most of the people in the gallery; he blends in. I don't. At thirty-three, I feel like a relic in my jeans and turquoise jewelry. My sapphire-blue sweater might be the only spot of color in the room—a misplaced peacock. Only after I have a plastic cup of cheap white wine in my hand do I turn my attention to the artwork.

I realize why Beck wanted to come here. On one canvas, gray-black vines crawl over a woman's rigid body; her eyes are open in a wide death-stare. Naked men sit on either side, holding the ends of the vines as though they are tightening them. I move on and stand in front of a pale sky with black, faintly human shapes floating in it. After a few minutes, I see that they are not floating—they are hanging from chains. Underneath, where the earth should be, a huge pair of hands is cupped as though waiting to catch the dark figures when they fall from the sky. Cigarette smoke drifts between me and the canvas, and I look at the girl who has moved up beside me—short, white-blond hair stiffened into spikes and the requisite black leather jacket.

"Heavy shit, huh?" she says. "And he's only twenty-four. Makes you wonder what he'll be painting when he's sixty."

"Landscapes, probably."

She looks at me from beneath heavy lids and too much mascara. She's not sure if I'm joking, and I offer no clarification.

"I mean, he really captures it, you know?" she continues, turning back to the painting. "The meaninglessness of life—a real existentialist message."

A man with black hair and pale skin comes up behind her and slides his arm around her waist.

"This is my boyfriend, Scorpion. I'm sorry, I don't know your name."

"Carla. Hi, Scorpion. Excuse me, I'm going to get some more wine." I'm glad to be moving away from them; I'm suspicious of people named after arachnids.

I zigzag my way through the crush of people, refill my wineglass, and look around for Beck. He's standing in front of a painting that takes up most of one wall; it's in two panels. In one, a group of people are buried up to their necks in a sandpit; their faces register terror, their mouths are agape. Their hands would probably be covering their mouths or reaching out to plead for mercy—if they had hands. But only their heads are uncovered, as though planted there like some strange crop. In the other panel, another cluster of people is standing, facing the sandpit. Their lips are curled back with hatred, their arms are hurling stones and broken bottles at the planted heads.

"Take a good look at the faces in each panel," Beck says. He's been studying this painting for a while, I decide. I compare the faces in both panels and realize they are the same. I count, I go one by one, comparing hair, noses, eyes. They are identical; the people taking aim are the same as those planted neck-deep in sand. The cheap wine is turning to vinegar in my stomach, and a headache is blooming in my temples.

"Can we go now, Beck? I'm starting to feel like a sardine."

We squeeze ourselves out of the gallery and into the quieter rush of night wind. As we walk back to the car I glance at the sky and imagine all the stars that have been made invisible by the city lights.

"So what did you think?" Beck asks.

"Well . . . I hope this is just part of your research and not something you're planning to hang in the bedroom."

"Jokes aside, Carla, can't you see how unique his work is? Especially being so young, to be grappling with the concept of death like that . . ."

"His youth is what makes it more disturbing—almost as disturbing as your preoccupation with death ever since you've started this book. I don't even really know what it's about. You give me little pieces here and there. Are you ever going to let me in on the basic story, or do I have to wait until it's published?"

I wait for his face to change, for him to shut me out, but he doesn't.

"Okay, I'll give you the outline of it. It has to do with a man who starts to have trouble sleeping. More and more, just as he drifts off, something jolts him awake—some horrible wave of panic overtakes him. If he gets past that and gets deeper into sleep, he has gruesome dreams and they wake him up. Gradually, he realizes that he's dreaming of a murder, and the panic comes because he doesn't want to wander into that dream again. So his nights become terrifying."

"His own murder or someone else's?"

"He's not sure. That's what starts the journey. Is it a memory of another life, of his own death, or of a murder he committed? Or some horrible, hidden fantasy he's been submerging that he's now falling prey to? To figure it out, he has to go in both directions—retreating into a past that may or may not exist, and trying to sort through wishes and fantasies that he's not even consciously aware of."

"And the outcome?"

"I don't really know yet. But somehow, he has to be able to sleep again. That has to be the end result if he is to hold on to any thread of sanity. And to do that, he has to put an end to the dreams. Have you ever had dreams about death?"

"No... I don't think so."

But something, on the dark ride home, starts to stir and untangle itself from my memory. It feels dusty and brittle—something locked away too long that has to be handled with the tenderness of an archaeologist lifting fossils out of the earth. At first, it's just scattered pictures—a child standing over an open grave, fingers that point accusingly. I hang on to the pictures, tuck them away until I crawl into bed. When Beck is asleep, I take them out and lay them side by side, like yellowed photographs. Only then do I go back for more.

When I was seven, we'd been in California for almost a year. In December, the house was decorated for Christmas; colored lights were strung along the eaves and pine boughs sent their aroma through the rooms. It started with my mother complaining that she needed more help—one live-in maid wasn't enough. My mother couldn't be everywhere at once, there were not enough hours in the day. All these complaints were angled at me, as though I expected her to multiply and fill every room, and had whittled the days down, scraped time away hour by hour. It continued with her leaving the dinner table in tears, losing her appetite, losing weight.

And then she was going to die. Or so I was told.

"Mommy is going to break, and it'll be your fault," Lily said, a tiny messenger bearing a grim forecast.

"What are you talking about?" I said. I was older, I knew better. People did not break, only parts of them sometimes, but those parts were always mended with casts you could write your name on.

"A nervous breakdown," my father said to me later that night. He came to tuck me in, and in a hushed, serious voice he told me my mother might die of a nervous breakdown, and it would be because of me.

"You have to stop being so difficult," he said. "She can't take all these problems. You're stubborn. You argue about the littlest things. You don't want to have this on your conscience, Carla."

Throughout the holidays, I watched for signs. I imagined my mother cracking down the middle and splitting into two halves, or crumbling into a million tiny fragments that would be lifted up and scattered by the first strong wind. I imagined them floating up the chimney, drifting toward the clouds.

On Christmas day, I was pulled aside by one of my parents' friends—a woman I called "Aunt" even though she wasn't.

"Your poor mother is doing her best to hold herself together," she whispered. "And you have to help. How are you going to feel when they're lowering her into the ground and you're standing by her graveside, knowing it was your fault?"

I think that's when the dreams started, although this is vague. I rummage through the memories, trying to put them all in order. Pieces are missing and can't be retrieved; I remember the dreams, though. They emerge from the dust perfectly intact, blazing with color.

In one, I was standing at the edge of a huge grave as a casket was being lowered into it. I was tiny and everyone else was large. Even Lily towered over me. Their eyes were boring into me, burning me, singeing my flesh. I was not crying in this dream; my eyes were dry, frightened. Somehow, I had caused my mother's death, but I didn't know how, or what I had done.

In another dream, I was being chased by a group of people. I was running as fast as I could, but it was getting harder because tears were flooding from my eyes and washing to the ground. I was almost up to my knees in the saltwater tears, and my feet would barely move. I always woke up moments before the people got to me.

Beck is sleeping so soundly, his breathing is deep and loud. I slide out of bed and put on my robe. As soon as I move toward the door, Tully gets up, following me through the house, out the sliding glass doors, and onto the deck. The tide is out and the waves are small and lazy; a thin sliver of moon hangs in the sky. Tully stands next to me, leaning against my leg as if to assure me of his presence. I stroke the velvet side of his ears.

A star falls through the black sky as though it's been tossed from its silver heights into the deepest part of the ocean. A meteor, but I like the thought that I can see a star fall.

I realize how courageous Beck is in turning to face his demons, allowing them to lead him into caves where the sounds of madness wait for him. Where death purrs in his ear. There's something wild and uncharted about what he's doing. I'm not as brave; I escape to the predictability of tides and the safe dome of stars. I bury my dreams of death, and wait for morning.

12

By thirteen, my childhood had long since disappeared, but Lily's looked as though it might never end. It seemed eternal, drifting on as though outside the boundaries of time. While my parents discussed which high school to send me to, Lily collected rainwater in plastic buckets and stood in the shower while my mother poured it over her head.

"My hair has God's tears on it," she would announce, swaddled in towels, her face shiny and damp. I think that was something I made up when I was very young, before I outgrew the right to be baptized with rain from God's eyes. But it didn't matter; I had passed out of an enchanted zone into one fraught with seriousness and subterfuge. My sister was the new recipient of soft laughter unfolding like petals around her, of nightlights in dark rooms to shine away fears.

Lily was eleven, but childhood games still seemed to fit her. It was as if she had found a way to stall the march of time, had learned to alter herself to fit my mother's preference for things small and delicate. Her body was still that of a little girl—flat and angular, and in need of protection. My parents had designed Lily in some secret, careful language that only they could hear, and she had molded herself perfectly to their design. She had our mother's coloring—red hair framing a pale, chiseled face, and sharp, brown eyes. Her movements were small and precise; she could have navigated her way through a room full of fine crystal without breaking a thing.

I was dark and sturdy, and not good around fragile things. I was uncomfortable with the changes that had visited me despite my hostility toward them. My body had organized itself into monthly cycles, the passage of my childhood a matter of history. I had grown into stern-voiced lectures about high school and the hazards of going to a public school, which was the school I had requested. These schools were considered havens for children of undesirable families, children who dressed poorly and didn't know any better... and boys. There were, of course, boys in public school and they were now regarded as dangerous by my parents ever since I was caught under the floorboards with Redge doing "God knows what." It was decided that I would go to a private girls' school.

"Come in to the den for a minute, Carla," my mother called out one evening after dinner as I was racing back to my room.

"Your father and I have decided to send you to Tipton Girls' School in La Jolla," she said after I sat down. Her voice was not asking; she was presenting me with a bought-and-paid-for gift which was mine whether I wanted it or not.

"Well, what do you say?" my father asked. "It's a nice school. Your mother is going to take you down there this week to see it. I would think you'd be pleased."

"Uh-huh."

"That's it?" my mother asked, looking at my father with a wide, startled expression. "This is an extremely expensive school, and with that last escapade on your record... well, it wasn't easy to get you in. The least you could do is show some gratitude."

"Okay," I said, showing none.

My father flicked on the television. "That's it, then, I guess. We told you our news. We had hoped for a better response." His attention turned to the screen, dismissing me.

"When you're ready to stop being so sullen and uncommunicative, you let us know," my mother said, her eyes holding me for another second.

I went back to my room and closed the door, wishing it had a lock on it.

Silence had become my armor. I hid inside it, knowing it stirred anger in my parents. It was my citadel, my refuge against winds that were always blowing the wrong way. I'd been found guilty of the crime of growing up, and the onslaught of my mother's anger was my sentence. I retreated, frightened, but holding on to my own anger. I commanded my face to show nothing, instructed my voice to become mute. I became hard as glass; words bounced off me and judgments were only smudges on a surface nothing could penetrate.

Only in the blackest hours of night, when sleep whispered through the house, did I peel off my slick armor and tend to the child inside. I would lie in the dark, shivering, wondering what other transformations time had in store for me. So far, no one seemed pleased with my evolution. I allowed myself tears only in those thin, solitary hours; by morning their traces would be gone.

I felt the most comfortable out on my father's boat, standing between him and Roy. They treated me like a son, and I let myself pretend I was. But I knew it was the magic of the sea—a spell that was inevitably broken when we returned to land.

The image of my dead sister's ghost was again betraying me. She looked frail now, like Lily—an eternal child. I was outgrowing her, becoming someone she never would have allowed herself to be.

The idea of going to an all-girls school should have bothered me more than it did. I was going to be dropped into the den of the enemy. But I told myself I didn't care. I had walked naked through the treason of a Halloween night, refusing to cry, refusing to be defeated. I had learned silence; I had learned to hide.

That night, with my parents' announcement replaying in my mind, I couldn't sleep. The house felt still and quiet, and I tiptoed through the dark, down the hall, past my parents' bedroom, to the kitchen. I had heard that warm milk helped to bring on sleep. I doubted the truth of that, but it was something to do.

Once in the kitchen, I managed the whole process with a minimum of noise. I washed out the saucepan and cup and replaced them in their proper cabinets without rattling any of the other dishes.

On the way back to my room, as I passed my parents' door, I heard their voices floating out into the silence of the hallway where I stood in the shadows of the late-night house, listening to a conversation I was never meant to hear.

"She's always been difficult," my mother was saying. "She couldn't even be born easily. But it's just getting worse. She won't even speak half the time—she's always shutting us out."

"Maybe it's just a phase," my father said.

"She's thirteen—it's an awfully long phase, don't you think? Sometimes I think the wrong child died."

My mother's words sliced through the stillness, jolted me from my frozen spot, and propelled my bare feet across the floor, back to the safety of my own room, where I lay staring at the ceiling, wondering if I had been born under a dark star.

It was cloudy on the Friday morning my mother and I were to drive to La Jolla to visit the high school that had already been decided upon. It was only a small consolation that I was missing a day of school. I was going to be introduced to a school only for girls; there would be no boys to be my allies.

I stood in the driveway that morning beside my mother's Cadillac, waiting for her to come out of the house. I stared at the sky and prayed for more clouds to rumble in—black clouds that would crack open with torrents of rain so our trip would be canceled. But the sky looked back at me, pale and unthreatening. It was April; the season for angry storms had passed.

We were pulling onto the freeway when my mother broke the silence that had hung over us for half an hour. I had been staring out the window with my forehead pressed against the glass, trying to entertain myself with license plates and buildings.

"You can sit there sulking if you like, Carla," she said, "or you can try to make the best of it. It would be nice if you made a good impression today—you are being introduced to what will be your new school. I realize you don't want to be with me today. You've made your point."

"I didn't do anything."

"No, of course not. You just squeeze yourself into the corner there and stare out the window as though I don't even exist." Her voice was changing pitch and I felt the car accelerate.

"You exist—you're driving," I said, aiming my mouth at her and firing, realizing as soon as I did that I had made a terrible mistake. My body snapped against the seat belt as we lurched forward, dangerously close to the car ahead of us. My mother was not looking at the road; she was turned toward me, screaming.

"You are the rudest child I have ever known! I just can't do anything right in your book, is that it? If you think I'm going to let you talk to me like that..."

I was no longer listening to her words; I was listening to the sound of my own death roaring toward me at a speed I couldn't even calculate. I heard it in the wind rushing through the windows, in the tires speeding along the asphalt, in a car horn that blared out when we started veering into the next lane. I saw my body, broken and limp, lying on the freeway like a pile of rags. I wondered if cars would stop, or if they would just drive over me, leaving me flat and thin as cardboard.

Only when I heard the police siren did I realize I might not die after all.

My mother pulled over to the shoulder and I watched her face change as the policeman approached the car. She no longer looked angry; she was almost crying. She was deflating before my eyes, appearing thinner and more fragile than she had moments earlier. She handed the officer her license, but before he could look at it, she said, "Officer, I know I was speeding, but my daughter was being so impossible I completely lost my temper. I don't know what gets into her—she just makes life as difficult as she possibly can. She pushes and pushes—"

He handed the license back to her. "Okay, ma'am, I'll let it go this time. I have kids, too—I know how they can be. Just be careful. You could have had a bad accident." He leaned down and looked across my mother to me. "You be nice to your mom, now."

My mother thanked him and watched in the rearview mirror as he walked back to his car. She turned to me, pulled back her hand, and slapped my face. I felt the numbness start; I memorized its passage across my face, its progression into pain. It was the first time my mother had ever slapped me. It would not be the last.

"I hope you're satisfied," she said. "Look what your smart-aleck attitude has caused."

She pulled the car back onto the freeway and we drove the rest of the way in silence. I kept my face turned toward the window, pressing back the tears that wanted to pool in my eyes, forcing them down my throat. But beneath the stone surface of my will was a mother lode of fear. I had received another lesson in the dangers of my mother's anger—a slippery embankment I would spend years trying to avoid. But whichever way I turned, I ended up there, staring down at the rapids, praying I wouldn't fall in.

Since that day, I have stood at the threshold of other people's anger, and, each time, I am met by a frightened young girl, clinging to the only dignity available to her—her refusal to cry. I have left Beck holding the tattered remnants of arguments that unraveled long before they were completed—because I bolted, startled by visions of a speeding car filled with screams and my own body lying broken on the road.

Silently, we drove up a steep, winding road to the gates of Tipton Girls' School.

My mother pulled up to a two-story Spanish building, the tires crunching across gravel. Nestled in the gloom of overhanging trees, it had been discolored by age and ocean air. Ivy crawled up one of the walls, and thick clusters of ferns bordered the front steps.

"Mrs. Tipton is going to show us around and then she wants to talk to you alone," my mother said, checking her face in the mirror and rummaging through her purse for lipstick.

"She named a school after herself?" I asked, as my mother turned her lips redder and blotted them with Kleenex.

"It's her school. What else would you have her call it?"

Still shaky from our argument on the freeway, I decided it would be wise not to answer.

Mrs. Tipton was large. So was the room where she greeted us, but she seemed to fill every inch of it. The floors were dark oak—the color of chocolate—and watery light came through tall, leaded-glass windows. There were bookcases along the walls and a desk in the corner, but the center of the room had been left empty, as though they were preparing for a square dance. But only Mrs. Tipton occupied this arena, tall and thick, looking like she had been raised on farm equipment. Her white hair was pulled back severely from her face and done up in a braid that wrapped around her head, just behind her ears. Reading glasses hung from a gold chain around her neck. The rest of her was navy blue. I would realize, years later, that I never saw Mrs. Tipton in anything but two-piece suits. She had the same suit in a variety of colors, and that was her wardrobe.

"Mrs. Lawton, how nice to finally meet you," she said. Her voice was low and resonant; it bounced through the empty room and seemed to linger after she had stopped speaking. "And this must be Carla." My hand felt lost in hers; I felt her strength as she gripped my fingers.

She led us through the dormitories and past some of the class-rooms—curious eyes turned from blackboards to windows as we passed. The uniform was plaid skirts, white blouses, and saddle shoes. But the eyes were the same—taunting, demanding, eager to control. Girls' eyes.

When she showed us around the grounds, I decided that Tipton wouldn't be a bad place to spend my high school years. The bluffs overlooked the sea, and a narrow path led to a huge boulder where I could sit with my back toward the lair of girls and their treasonous ways, and watch the tides change far below me.

When we finished our tour and returned to the same wide, sparsely furnished room, my mother left me alone with Mrs. Tipton. She led me over to the desk and motioned for me to sit down across from her.

"You have an excellent academic record," she said, peering at me over her reading glasses as she thumbed through my school records.

"Yes, ma'am."

"But I see you've had some discipline problems."

"Well, I . . . yes."

"You know, Carla, sometimes young people get into trouble because something is bothering them that they don't feel they can talk about. Do you understand what I mean?"

"I think so." I liked the lines at the corners of her eyes; they made her look like she was smiling even when she wasn't.

"I like to think that my girls feel they can come to me with anything, Carla—with any problem, no matter how small or large—rather than lashing out in an inappropriate way. Maybe I can help them come to a solution about whatever is bothering them. Do you think you could give that a try?"

"Yes, ma'am, I think I could," I said. I had a sudden urge to tell her about the thin stacks of pages I'd hidden in my room at home—the words that had become one of my biggest secrets. But I stopped myself; I wasn't sure how much of our meeting would be related to my mother.

She walked me to the door with a firm arm around my shoulders and, when she said good-bye, her hand reached up and touched my cheek—the same cheek my mother had slapped earlier. I learned that this large, imposing woman with a voice that could fill an auditorium was sparing with her judgments and generous with her love for the girls she regarded as her own while they were under her protective wings. My mother, smaller and more delicate, knew the subtle art of tyranny, the cold precision of its rule.

I slept on the way home, stretched out on the back seat and let the speed of the car drive my dreams. I saw myself carried by swift air currents, winged and flying over marshes and wetlands, high above the gentle rise of hills and the dark green of canyons. I knew I would not fall. I passed blue herons, gliding with their legs trailing loosely behind them, and sea birds flying in perfect formation. I didn't need the earth; I had the wind to hold me up, wings to guide me, and clouds to cover me. My only reminder of another life was a crumpled piece of white paper clenched in my hand, penned with words I could no longer decipher.

I woke up as the sky was turning pink; it seeped into the gray, and I watched the gentle exchange of color.

I had gotten used to California's pastel seasons. I'd stopped looking over my shoulder for rust-colored autumns and white winters. My father had driven me up steep roads high above Los Angeles where a soft patchwork of wildflowers blanketed the hills. I remember a soft edge to even the hottest summer days, the smells of warm, baked earth and eucalyptus that filled my head.

That was before the earth stopped forgiving us and started returning to us the poisons we've unleashed on her. I remember with perfect clarity the deep blue that the sky used to be, the fragrance of blossoms that hung on spring breezes, the untouched hillsides blooming with alyssum and blue lupine.

Because the sky may never be that blue again, and because my dreams no longer allow me wings, I have to remember.

13

The summer before I went away to Tipton was a long procession of slow, sweltering days that rolled by, broken only by the night flow of sea breezes.

My mother and Lily never went out on the boat anymore; Graddy would pack a picnic basket and put me in charge of it.

"Make sure Carla eats her lunch, Cliff," my mother would invariably say as she followed us out the door, chasing us down with things we had tried to forget, like zinc oxide for our noses and lips.

Sometimes my father brought other people along; these men were introduced as his clients and they would receive most of his attention. I overheard conversations about huge sums of money and buyouts and other terms I didn't understand. But I noticed the seriousness, the edge of secrecy.

On these days, Roy would take me aside, give me sips of his beer, and tell me stories of how he had rescued people at sea and nearly died himself. I doubted these stories, but his knowledge of the ocean and its mysterious inhabitants I believed. He told me how whales and dolphins nurse their young, are fiercely loyal to their herd-mates, and communicate in indecipherable sounds. He taught me about sea lions and stingrays and jellyfish whose deadly tentacles trail far below the surface of the water. The sea became, for me, an exotic blue kingdom, descending to unimaginable depths, far below the reach of sunlight. Roy would transport me to this watery world of soundless beauty, as if he knew I needed an escape.

I think of his lessons now, as the death toll rises and the bodies of whales and dolphins are heaped into blood-soaked piles by men who don't share his reverence for the sea, as the waters of the oceans become uninhabitable. I think what the world might be if there were more people like Roy, who saw the earth as a fragile, mysterious gift to be worshiped and protected.

The days we didn't go out on the boat, we spent by the pool. It was the summer that the fog didn't come, that the sun beat down unforgivingly. There was a tenuous, lazy truce in our household. Carefully, I reached out for my sister, ignoring the misgivings that tugged at me, arguing with them, trying to believe that they didn't belong. But I was to learn that Lily had become a master of stratagem and deceit, a cunning player in a game that still ensnared me.

I was sharing my Beatles albums with her; we would sit in my room in the afternoons, sun-browned and wrinkled from hours in the swimming pool, while outside a white-hot sun crawled slowly across the sky. We sang along with the songs we had memorized and occasionally our voices caught the harmonies and blended together in a single, sweet sound. It was one of the few times I felt I had a sister.

We traded small pieces of trivia, things that have relevance only to children.

"Did you know if you dropped a penny from the top of the Empire State Building and it hit someone on the head, it would kill them?" Lily said.

"Everyone knows that. I bet you didn't know that if you get a tapeworm from eating pork that's not cooked enough, it'll grow to about ten feet and start eating your stomach away."

"Yeah," Lily said, excitedly, "and then you'd die and your finger-nails and hair would keep growing while you're inside the coffin."

She was catching on; ten-foot worms and dead people with growing fingernails were infinitely more interesting than pennies dropped from tall buildings.

It was a while before our mother discovered where we were disappearing to in the afternoons. She walked in one day while we were sitting on the floor singing along with "I Want to Hold Your Hand."

"What are you doing?" she asked, as though it wasn't obvious.

"Singing," I answered, reaching over to turn down the volume.

"Lily, why don't you come with me?" my mother said. "I'm going to cut some roses to put on the dining-room table. You can hold the basket for me."

"I can help, too," I offered, wanting to stay with my sister.

"No, we can do it ourselves. You girls have spent enough time together today. Why don't you clean up your room, Carla?"

"It's clean."

"Then find something else to do." Her voice was a door slamming, a curtain coming down, a hand throwing the switch.

My eyes snagged Lily's as she was being pulled from the room, but only for an instant. She grew smaller as the distance swallowed her, and I knew she would never really come back.

"Want to listen to records?" I asked her the next day.

"No. Mother says you're a bad influence on me."

I took the arrow and went back for more. "Why does she like you better than me, Lily?"

"Because I know how to be good. You don't."

My sister, the expert, the keeper of secrets even darker than those harbored by the rest of us, and ours was a family impeccable in the art of keeping secrets.

I tried to find my sister's eyes again, tried to recapture the one instant when I looked at her and thought I was seeing through. I tried in the only way I knew—with secrets. But I used someone else's secrets and became the cause of someone else's wounds.

"Mother thinks Graddy is getting too old to do her job properly," Lily said one day. "She thinks she might have to hire someone else."

Graddy was the only live-in maid we had; her domain was the kitchen. Two other maids alternated days, sweeping through the rest of the house with vacuum cleaners and dust rags, and loading the washing machine with whatever was lying around.

"She can't do that," I said, annoyed at Lily's tone of false maturity. "Graddy's part of the family."

"No she's not—that's silly. She can't be part of our family. How could she possibly be? She works for us."

Lily was standing in the doorway to my room where I was playing records by myself.

"You don't know what she's been through, Lily. I found something in her room." Using a technique I'd seen on television, I turned up the volume on the record player and spoke in a low voice. "Her son was murdered. I saw a newspaper picture. They hung him. That's how Graddy got that scar on her face—she tried to save his life."

I was confident that if Lily knew Graddy's life as I did, she would come to her defense and persuade our mother to let her stay no matter how old she was.

"That's awful, but it doesn't have anything to do with what kind of work she's doing," my sister answered, sounding so much like our mother it made me shiver.

Something cold lodged at the base of my spine and started inching its way up. Lily's expression had changed; her eyes were harder, refusing to let me in. And when our mother's footsteps sounded in the hall, Lily got up and left, not waiting for whatever excuse had been manufactured that day.

It wasn't until the following day that I learned the enormity of my mistake, that I realized how reckless I had been. I went into the kitchen shortly before noon to see what was for lunch and found Graddy sitting at the kitchen table, crying silently. I saw her wounds; her face looked damaged, but somehow beautiful in its naked portrayal of pain.

"Graddy, why are you crying?" I put my arm across her broad shoulders, feeling my spine shiver again, wishing I could ignore its message.

"I'm gonna be leavin'," she said in a hoarse voice. "You shoulda told me you foun' that picture, honey. What possessed you to open my drawers?"

She wasn't angry; her eyes were asking me to give reason to her pain, and my only answer was my own pain and the flood of tears behind it.

"Why did she have to tell? I thought I could trust her. I never told anyone before, Graddy, I promise." My voice was tangled in my throat, fighting through sobs. "I don't know why I opened your drawer—I know I shouldn't have. I'm so sorry—it was terrible of me. I just don't understand why she had to tell. It shouldn't get you in trouble—you didn't do anything."

"Your mama doesn't want you to know about such things—said I shoulda been more careful. Don't matter, honey. She woulda found another excuse. This one jus' happen to fall in her lap."

"Graddy, you can't leave—you're my only friend in this house."

Graddy's crying had stopped; she was trying to quiet mine, holding me against her chest so my sobs were muffled and my tears soaked the white cotton of her uniform. "You might be right about that, honey," she said. "You're special, Carla, don' you ever forget that. You don' have to be like anyone else. You're different—don' matter if no one understands that. You just keep bein' special."

"I love you, Graddy," I said, holding on to her so tightly my arms were trembling.

"I love you too, sugar. I always will."

I stayed crumpled against her until my crying subsided and was replaced by anger. Only then was I willing to leave the safe space of her arms. With my tears shining on her skin, Graddy looked at me with the soft ease of uncomplicated love. It was her final gift to me. "Don' you blame yourself, honey. Woulda happened jus' the same." But it wasn't her words that stayed with me; it was her eyes, showing me what love is supposed to look like.

I went out to the yard and sat between some trees with Daisy, preparing myself to face my mother. My anger had congealed into a slender reed of hatred, razor-sharp and unyielding. She had hurt someone I loved and she had used me to do it. I knew I would never forgive her, and I stroked Daisy's head and asked her how people could be so cruel, finding only a distant answer in the brown eyes that stared back at me, that looked only for kindness.

I found my mother in her bedroom, sitting at her desk going through some papers. I had passed Lily in the hallway and had averted my eyes; at that moment, I didn't care if I never spoke to her again.

"What is it, Carla?" my mother asked, glancing up from the letter in her hand.

"Why did you fire Graddy?"

"Now, Carla, I think you know the answer to that. I'm not going to have the help exposing my children to horribly violent things."

"I'm not exactly a child—I'm going to high school in the fall. Do you think I don't know about prejudice? And she didn't expose me to anything. I opened her drawer and found the picture. It was my fault. Why don't you take it out on me instead of Graddy? I'm the one who deserves the blame."

"Be that as it may, I will not have this going on in my house."

My mother's voice was calm and studied. I heard my own voice lash back at her with the force of a whip. "It's because she's my friend, isn't it? You don't want me to have a Negro friend. You're as prejudiced as the people who killed her son, except you don't go around hanging Negroes, you just fire them instead!"

"Carla! How dare you? You apologize this instant."

"I will not. It's true, goddamn it!"

My mother stood up so quickly the chair tipped over. She lunged toward me and slapped my face, but I'd been expecting it. I clenched my teeth and stared, dry-eyed and defiant.

"Where did you learn language like that, young lady?"

"Which? Goddamn or Negro?" I hissed at her.

She pushed me toward the door. "You go to your room and stay there until you're ready to tell me where you learned swear words like that. I will not permit that kind of language. You were not raised in a gutter."

"You'd love it if I told you Graddy taught it to me, wouldn't you? Well, she didn't. And I'd rather live in a gutter than in this *goddamn* house!"

I slammed my bedroom door between us. I looked at my face in the mirror and saw the handprint emblazoned on my face, and I wished it had been a whip, slashing my cheek; then I would have a scar like Graddy's—an identical brand that would unite us forever.

My father got home a little before five. I listened to the familiar sound of tires on the driveway, turning into the garage. And I knew that, shortly, I would hear him approaching my door. I waited for footsteps, the ominous prelude to another confrontation, the final act to arguments he was never there to witness.

I thought of my mother demanding to know where I had learned to swear. It was absurd for her to think I could possibly remember, and I wondered how long she would leave me in my room to ponder this impossible question. I pictured weeks going by, midnight forays into the kitchen to get food and water so I wouldn't shrivel from starvation.

"Whatever happened to Carla?" I imagined my father asking at about the third week. "I haven't seen much of her lately."

"Oh, she's still in her room trying to remember who taught her to take the Lord's name in vain. Now that you mention it, I suppose I should see if she's still alive," my mother would sigh.

And she would crack open my door, certain that the stench of death would engulf her. But there I would be, a thermos full of water and three weeks worth of cupcake wrappers and Frito bags littering the floor.

I shook myself out of this imaginary drama when I heard my parents' voices; they were both headed for my room.

My father came in first, looking at me with a stern, disappointed expression. He sat down on the twin bed opposite me, and my mother moved in beside him, marshaling forces.

"Carla, your mother tells me you screamed and swore at her."

"I've never been spoken to like that in my life, Cliff."

"She screamed at me, too," I said. "She didn't swear, but she screamed."

My father's expression hardened, his eyes turning to blue glass.

"Carla, your mother runs this household, and if she decides to let someone go, it's for good reason, and it's up to her. You have no business—"

"She has no right to fire Graddy," I interrupted. "It's not fair!"

"We will decide what's fair and what is not," he said. "Now I want to know where you learned language like that—like what you said to your mother earlier."

"At school."

"Who at school spoke like that?"

"I don't remember."

"Well, you'll be sitting in here a long time, then, until you do," my mother said.

I considered my options—a criminal weighing a plea bargain. Name names or face prison. I folded.

"I learned it from Jackie," I said, seeing her face in my mind, bending over me in the dark Halloween night. "She talks like that all the time."

My parents glanced at each other.

"I'll have to give her mother a call," my mother said.

"I can tell you some of the other words she taught me," I offered.

"That won't be necessary, Carla. We'll discuss what your punishment should be and let you know later. For now, you can stay in your room until dinner," my father told me, the same stern expression molding his features.

I didn't care how they decided to punish me: Jackie would be sharing my punishment. It would be my final message to her—a reminder that the Halloween moon had been on my side, bending its light to guide me, and that her treachery was something I could match.

14

I know the novel Beck is working on is changing him. I've felt it in his sleep, restless beside me, as though his dreams are full of shrapnel. And I see it in his body; he's let his hair and beard grow longer, like an animal growing extra fur to protect him from a world that's suddenly grown colder.

I've felt it, too, in his lovemaking.

As I drive to my mother's house, I squeeze my legs together, feeling the places that are still raw inside me. A light rain is falling and as the wipers push the mist across my windshield, I think of how he pulled my legs tight around him, as if the force of my muscles could save him from drowning. I can still feel the weight of his mouth, hard against my shoulder, and the way he pushed into me, trying to get deeper.

These are the imprints on my flesh, the sensations my thoughts should not be crawling through while I'm getting closer to my mother's driveway. But the incongruity of it is too tempting. It feels forbidden, this re-creation of last night while I'm crossing the boundaries into my childhood neighborhood...which is why I'm doing it.

I think of how he grabbed my hair and rolled me on top of him. "Wait," he said, a second before it would have been impossible to wait. And we lay there, shuddering, balanced on the edge, his fingers pressed into my spine. But I didn't want to wait anymore; the seconds were collecting in my body, gathering force. I started to move against him, against his will—fighting him, wanting him, and we finished together. But then it was as if the room got darker and I couldn't find him; he had moved away from me into his own world, closing the passageways behind him.

In the darkness, with sweat cooling on my skin and my breath still ragged and short, I wished I could see more of him; I wanted him to be like flat, open land where you can turn in any direction and see forever. But the fact that he isn't like that is probably part of the attraction.

I arrive at my mother's and find Lily in the bedroom, sitting at the foot of the bed, guarding our mother's sleep. Her stocking feet are tucked underneath her and her green jersey dress floats around her.

"I put Mother down for her nap a little early," she says when I walk in, as though she's required to explain any change in the usual schedule.

My mother's eyes are closed, but it's hard to tell if she's sleeping. I look for a flutter of eyelashes, a parting of the lids, trying to determine if she's really asleep before turning my attention back to Lily.

"I'm a little late," I say finally, satisfied that my mother's eyes haven't moved. "I had to talk to Beck for a while."

"How is Beck?" Lily asks, as I sit down in one of the armchairs by the fireplace. This room makes me nervous; I remember pages of my writing being tossed into the flames. Smoke drifts back across the years and stings my eyes.

"He's okay."

"Just okay?"

"Well, I'm being generous," I concede. "He's at his lawyer's office right now. He got in sort of a fight—a one-sided fight, unfortunately. He punched a guy who cut him off in traffic, and now the guy's talking about suing him."

Lily gets up, picks up our mother's pill bottles from the nightstand, and goes back to the foot of the bed.

"Well, you can hardly blame the man," she says. "Why did Beck do that?"

"I don't know—lost his temper, I guess."

I look at my mother, who is lying motionless on the pillows. It's like looking at a blank television screen. Lily has opened one of the bottles, dumped out the contents on the bed, and is counting the pills.

"Lily, what are you doing?"

"Counting the pills."

"Okay—let me rephrase this question since I can see that you're counting pills. *Why* are you doing that?"

"To make sure that the nurse isn't forgetting any of Mother's medication. I know how many pills should be in here if she's getting them when she's supposed to be getting them."

She puts the pills back in the bottle, opens the next one, and repeats the process.

"You do this all the time?" I ask her.

"Yes." Her tone tells me she thinks this is an absurd question. Doesn't everyone count pills because they mistrust the nurse they've hired?

I watch her calculations, the concentration that creases her forehead.

"You should have been an accountant, Lily—or a pharmacist."

She doesn't answer, and I decide it's just as well. Lily is doing exactly what she was born to do—guard our mother.

"What does she need medication for?" I ask her.

"Don't be ridiculous—look at her."

"I have looked at her. So have half the doctors in Los Angeles, and no one can figure out what's wrong, so how do they know what medicine to give her?"

My sister looks at me with studied patience. "Carla, it's important that she sleeps."

"So they're sleeping pills? There are four bottles there—they're all sleeping pills?"

"No. Others are for her digestion, for regularity, blood pressure, I think—I can't remember all of them. But she's supposed to be taking them."

I sit silently and watch my sister finish her task. I wonder how many other things in the house she counts and catalogs.

"Do you know everything that's in the refrigerator and the pantry, too?" I ask her after several minutes.

"Mostly. Someone has to run this house, Carla. I don't notice you volunteering."

"No, and I don't think you will, either. I wouldn't want to intrude on your territory."

I feel an argument waiting in the wings and I want to make my exit before it takes the stage.

"I want to get home and see how Beck made out at the lawyer's office," I tell Lily, moving toward the door, brushing past my mother's silence. "What will you do if you find too many pills in there?"

Lily's fingers stop counting. "I'll talk to the nurse about it."

"Talk to her or fire her?"

"Talk to her."

"Oh—well, it's encouraging to know that some traditions are being broken in this household."

I drive away from my mother's house with the storm moving above me, vacating the sky, which is now half covered by black clouds and rain and half stripped down to blue.

When I get to my house, there is a perfect arch of a rainbow and a fainter one above it. A double rainbow—it's supposed to mean something, but I can't remember what. Neighbors are standing out on their decks, on the beach, heads tilted back, staring at the bands of color bending across the sky. The evening sun is gilding the edges of the escaping clouds. As I watch, the rainbow fades upward from one end, leaving half an arch—brilliant and incomplete.

By the time Beck comes back, the rainbow is gone and the clouds have abandoned us for another piece of sky. The evening is cool and purple.

"So what happened?" I ask him.

"We'll probably be able to settle it for his medical expenses and whatever he thinks his pain is worth," Beck says. I stand beside him, first star of the evening pinpointed between us—a beacon in the sky he rarely looks at these days. Lately, his eyes don't pull me in; they hold me at arm's length.

"How badly was this guy hurt, Beck? How hard did you hit him?"

"I broke his nose. He probably needed a nose job anyway."

"Well, I bet he'll drive with his window rolled up in the future. Beck, couldn't you just buy a punching bag or something? Join a gym? Wrestle alligators? I mean, you can't just go around slugging people who piss you off on the road."

"Carla, get off my back, okay? I've already been lectured by my lawyer. That's enough for one day."

"Yeah—sure."

I call Tully and take him down to the beach, a hurt child trailing in my shadow. She runs from voices that turn harsh; she catches up to me, clings to me, her tears pooling in my eyes. She wants me to run through the night with her, away from voices that claw at her, away from the land mines buried in terrain that once looked like safe meadows, back when her eyes were young and saw only green.

She holds tightly to me. She knows me too well; she is my history. She gropes for my breast, wanting to be nurtured, but I push her away. "I'm not you anymore," I whisper into the wind. "I can't feed you anymore."

15

There is probably a Jackie at every school. After a few weeks at Tipton I learned that, this time around, her name was Rochelle. But the names become irrelevant. These are girls who share a common agenda—the quest for power and popularity. They are the girls who get their college yearbooks signed by the entire football team and most of the Drama Club, who grow up to date only millionaires, who fire servants on Christmas Eve, who flirt with your husband and then offer lunch and consolation when he files for divorce. Their eyes can hunt you down, and even their softest words hide thorns. I watched them as cautiously as I watched my mother.

Rochelle had golden blond hair and wore tiny pieces of gold jewelry that announced, "My parents have money and they spend some of it on me." She was a year ahead of me, but I saw her at meals, gym classes, and school assemblies. Rochelle was never alone. There were always girls following her, attending her, agreeing with her, and laughing with her.

The morning assemblies were required. We gathered in the auditorium to pledge allegiance to a flag that was mounted at the corner of the stage. Schoolgirls with other things on our minds, we dutifully put our hands over our hearts and recited words we'd learned by rote. I'd been told that the only time the morning assembly was canceled was the day Mrs. Tipton's husband died the year before. It was regarded as crucial that we begin the day by asserting our patriotism, unless death or some natural disaster interfered.

Across from the flag, on the opposite wall, was a portrait of Mrs. Tipton's son—blond and blue-eyed—stiff in his crisp military uniform. He wore the bland smile of a boy dreaming of medals and flags unfurling.

"Her son disappeared in World War II," Rochelle said one morning when we were leaving the auditorium and heading for the dining room and a breakfast of thick oatmeal that never seemed to soften no matter how much milk was poured on it.

"His plane was shot down," someone else added, eager to embellish Rochelle's story.

Rochelle stopped and faced us, stalling us on one of the narrow, wood-chipped paths that connected the buildings at Tipton. White azaleas bloomed beside her.

"He might not have died," she said. "They never found his body. I think he just didn't want to come home. I think he's living somewhere in Europe, probably sitting in some little café right now. I bet he lives in Greece."

But I didn't believe her. There were mornings when Mrs. Tipton would read a poem that her son had written or some prose, and her eyes would simmer with pride in his words. He never would have been forced to hide pages under mattresses and drawer linings, and I couldn't imagine him running away from that freedom.

One day, near the end of my first year, I knocked on the door of Mrs. Tipton's office. It was a warm afternoon and the sun rested heavily on my neck and shoulders as I waited there. Her low voice told me to come in.

"Yes, Carla—what can I do for you?" she said as I walked across the wide room and sat down beside her desk.

"I wanted to ask you about your son's writing," I said.

"Oh, how sweet. He was a beautiful writer, don't you think? I like sharing some of it with you girls."

"Well... I wanted to ask if I could read some of his poems—if that would be okay, I mean. I write, too."

Mrs. Tipton hesitated for a second; her hands straightened some papers on the desk, moved a pencil holder. "Yes, your mother mentioned that you wrote."

I should have known that my mother had been there before me, I should have seen her footsteps, picked up her trail.

"She said she was a bit disturbed by your writing," she added.

"Did she tell you she burned some of it?"

"Now, Carla—"

"She did—she searched my room and found it and threw it in the fireplace."

Mrs. Tipton's face was set and serious; her eyes studied me, warned me against lying. "Are you sure you're not exaggerating, Carla?" she asked gently.

"Did my mother tell you that, too? That I exaggerate? That I make things up? That I lie?"

"She said you had a vivid imagination. Are you lying?"

"No, ma'am."

Mrs. Tipton moved her chair back, stood up, and walked over to a chest of drawers by the window. A shaft of sunlight fell on her shoulder as she rummaged through the top drawer. On the chest was a photograph of her son, almost identical to the painting in the auditorium.

I pictured him flying through thin layers of atmosphere, his portrait smile still innocent on his face. He was high above the earth, where the sky was empty and safe, a cushion of clouds below him. He had the protection of angels—he had wings. I imagined his plane hit—spinning and diving in a halo of smoke, flames curling around him. He could see the curve of the earth coming up to meet him as his plane fell through the clouds, the wind hot and hard against his face. Sound stopped before he was shattered against the ground. I had to give him the dignity of silence; something about his eyes demanded that.

"You can take these and read them," she said, handing me some neatly typed poems. "And I'd like to see some of your writing, Carla."

But I let the school year end without showing her anything I'd written. Whenever I came close, took out some poems to bring to her, I imagined fireplaces and words going up in smoke. The memories turned me back every time.

Late one night during my second year at Tipton, I was recruited by three of my schoolmates to be an accomplice in a venture that would haunt me for years.

It was well past midnight, and the dark breathed with the sound of sleeping girls.

"Carla, wake up—get dressed," Rochelle said. Two other girls stood behind her. Moonlight framed their bodies and their whispers settled over me, nudging me from sleep.

"What? Why should I get dressed?" I said, recalling past treasons. It was night, they outnumbered me, and they were girls. But I was not to be the victim this time. They were including me in a plan they had carried out before. We were going to spy on Mrs. Tipton.

"She dances at night, by herself," I was told in whispers as I pulled on my clothes. "If we climb the tree by her window we can watch. It's really funny."

Tiptoeing across moonlit ground, scrambling up the tree trunk, the others waiting their turn at the bottom, something inside me wanted to turn around, to escape back into sleep as though I had never been snatched from its folds. Hands under my feet helped me up and I hugged the tree as I made my way up to the level of her window.

I peered into a room flickered with candlelight; strains of music filtered through the window and out into the damp night where I lurked like a thief, spying on her sad commerce with a past that had deserted her. It was her bedroom my eyes were invading; I saw an open bottle of wine on the corner table, and two glasses, one full, the other almost empty. Mrs. Tipton was swirling around the room, dressed in a white satin robe, the fabric reflecting the soft light of the room as she turned in her solitary waltz. Her hands held out a photograph of her late husband and her eyes stared at it, as though she could bring him back to life. Suddenly I saw her younger, more slender, her movements fluid and unashamed.

I thought of my mother's determined patrols through our house, through my life—her footsteps clicking down hallways, across floors, into rooms. At that moment, perched in the tree like some alien bird, I wished Mrs. Tipton had been my mother. I hated myself for spying on her. I climbed down from the tree with the weight of her secret heavy as stone in my muscles.

"I'm going back to bed," I said to the others.

"You can't—you have to help us up," Rochelle said.

"Help yourselves up. I don't think this is funny," I whispered angrily.

My arm was caught by her quick hand as I tried to leave.

"Carla, a lot of girls would be honored to be included in this. You just can't walk away."

"I am walking away, Rochelle. I don't care if you fall down the goddamn tree and break your leg. In fact, you'd deserve it. And don't worry—I'm not going to tell anyone. If Mrs. Tipton ever found out we saw her, it would kill her."

Too awake to return to the comforts of sleep, I walked out to the bluffs and watched the sea crashing below. I knew why they had chosen me to accompany them. I kept to myself; I kept secrets. They had needed a fourth person and I was a good risk. But there was no state of grace in silence—I bore the weight of that sad, proud woman's midnight communion. Even years later, I would wish that my eyes had not invaded her room.

Putting one hundred and eighty girls in an ocean-view enclave was inherently risky, and Mrs. Tipton's confidence that she could gently steer us into the avenues of etiquette and propriety was a recipe for disappointment.

Once a month, we had dances with a neighboring boys' school and, if Mrs. Tipton had ever decided to forage through the bushes around the auditorium where the dances took place, her soul would have joined her husband's in a matter of seconds.

I hated those dances. The boys were awkward, had bad skin and overactive sweat glands. But some of the other girls didn't care; they were composing resumés of experience, and there was a lot to learn.

"I'm going to stay a virgin until I get married," Rochelle announced in the locker room one day after gym class.

"Yeah, but she'll give anyone a blow job," someone called out.

"So what?" she answered haughtily. "You can't get pregnant that way and when I get married my husband will know I saved myself for him, and he'll love me even more."

"Until you go down on him and he wonders how you learned to do it so well."

Rochelle tilted her chin up so she could look down on whoever dared to challenge her prescription for the future.

"You guys are just jealous 'cause you don't know how to do it," she said, sitting down on the bench. "I could show you."

"How, Rochelle?" I asked. "You going to drag the gardener in here for a little demonstration?"

She pulled her hairbrush out of her purse and held it by the bristles, aiming the handle toward her mouth. "Okay, this is how you do it." She held her audience as she slowly moved the handle in and out of her mouth, sometimes circling her tongue around it, sometimes letting out a low moan.

"But what about—you know—when the rest of it happens?" a voice asked from a corner of the shower-steamed room. "You don't have to swallow it, do you?"

Rochelle rolled her eyes and slapped the hairbrush down in her lap, looking around at her disciples. "Of course—it's easy—you just open your throat. It's over in a sec."

"Oh, gross!"

"I could never do that!"

"Forget it!"

"I'd puke!"

"You girls are so immature," she said, replacing the brush in her purse and getting up from the bench.

"Maybe you could hire yourself out on our wedding nights," I offered as she walked by me, trying to freeze me with her eyes. "Or you could help us decide who to marry, you know? Sort of interview them first."

"Shut up, Carla," she hissed. "You don't know the first thing about boys."

She was almost right, but I wasn't interested in learning from any of the boys who shuffled through our school dances in their dark blue suits. Their pants were usually too short, their neckties too tight, and they tried too hard to make jokes. I had nothing in common with boys anymore; their humor and snide remarks sounded forced and childish to me. Unlike Rochelle, I had no intention of preserving my virginity for marriage; it seemed like a long time to remain ignorant. I was sixteen, restless, and too curious for my own good. I wanted a teacher, and when it was my turn to help clear the dishes one night after dinner, I decided I'd found one.

It was a mark of Mrs. Tipton's naïveté that she assumed she could hire a young, attractive man to work at her school and still preserve the innocence of her girls. The gardener was one thing—he was elderly and didn't speak English. But the man stirring pots in the kitchen was in his late twenties, tan with hazel eyes; he had the lean confidence of an athlete. I wanted him to notice me, but I knew there was only one way that could happen.

Getting to work in the kitchen was easy. At Tipton, misdemeanors were punished with hours of work, usually in the kitchen before dawn, while more obedient girls were rewarded with sleep. I hid inside a classroom one afternoon, lit a cigarette, and waited for a teacher to walk by.

It was so obvious, I was surprised they didn't punish me for stupidity. But since I didn't smoke, I wanted to ensure I got caught the first time so I wouldn't have to repeat the experience.

At five-thirty in the morning, five days a week, I reported to the kitchen. It was so still at that hour of the morning, I could hear waves breaking below the bluffs, clattering over the rocks, and wind stirring the branches above me. The air smelled like pine and salt spray as I walked across campus, my footsteps soft as a thief's in that black predawn hour.

Eric would already be there when I walked from the dark into the fluorescent light; sometimes we were the only ones there for the first half hour. I learned that he lived upstairs in a single room filled mostly with books. I started to see his life as solitary and nomadic. He had driven across the country, taking odd jobs along the way, spending days and weeks camping out by himself in mountains and parks. I was envious of his freedom, of the restless wandering of his life, and I understood his solitude.

The books that he brought down from his room—that he huddled over during his breaks—almost distracted me from my original purpose. Within days, he had loaned me a dog-eared copy of *Lady Chatterley's Lover* and a collection of Dylan Thomas's poems. Soon, those early, black hours became filled with conversations about writing.

"A little more work, a little less talk," the matriarch of the kitchen would call out—a plump woman with steel-gray hair and cheeks reddened by hours spent over a stove.

I kept Eric's copy of *Lady Chatterley's Lover* for more than a week, reading it under the covers at night by flashlight. By the middle of the second week, I had read it twice. I imagined Eric as the gamekeeper and myself as Connie, awakening to feelings that would at first seem strange and frightening.

"He lay there with his arms around her, his body on hers, his wet body touching hers, so close."

I would shut my eyes and try to imagine the dampness of a man's skin against my own; I would run my hands over my breasts and imagine them as someone else's hands—rougher, calloused, a heavier weight traveling down between my ribs, over the hollow of my stomach. I knew it would hurt the first time. But I would be different afterward. I wanted to be different, to know things that the other girls didn't, to keep it as my secret and laugh inwardly at their ignorance.

I imagined how the muscles of a man's body would feel under my fingers; it seemed mysterious and forbidden, the contours and lines concealed by clothes. My hands were desperate for education. I had watched Eric's arms while he worked, charted the movement of muscles in his back as he lifted boxes and crates. It was strange to think that the skinny, awkward boys at our monthly dances would someday grow into this.

"And it seemed she was like the sea, nothing but dark waves rising and heaving, heaving with a great swell, so that slowly her whole darkness was in motion, and she was ocean rolling its dark, dumb mass."

I wondered how many times it would take before I would be overcome by feelings like that. I supposed I would just have to endure the first time, think of it as an initiation.

"I wish I could be like Lady Chatterley," I said to Eric one morning. I leaned against the doorway to the walk-in freezer, watching him pull loaves of frozen bread from the shelf.

"Here—carry some of these, will you?" he said, handing me a few loaves. "Why do you want to be like her?"

"Because she had someone to teach her about sex, to make her feel beautiful."

"So you're looking for a teacher?"

"Yes."

"Could be risky," he said, smiling at me.

"So what? Things that are good usually are. I'm just trying to get a well-rounded education."

He met my eyes as he walked past me, shutting the heavy metal door on the rush of cold air, and on our conversation. But I'd gotten my answer.

May Day was the celebration of Mrs. Tipton's fantasy that her girls were pure and virginal, appropriately dressed in white with flower wreaths in their hair. There was a May Queen and her court, and dances around a Maypole. It was widely ridiculed by the students, but it was a day off from classes and a chance to show everyone's parents what they had paid for when they put their daughters under Mrs. Tipton's tutelage.

Some of the girls' parents came for the afternoon to watch with brimming eyes this display of purity. Flowers were scattered on the ground and girls held onto strips of white sheet, skipping around the Maypole which Rochelle had dubbed "the tallest penis in the world."

"It'd be kind of difficult to get your mouth over it, wouldn't it, Rochelle?" I said to her.

She turned away and didn't answer; she was the May Queen that year—she didn't have to speak to anyone beneath her station.

No parents watching the ceremony saw a phallic symbol, though. They were there to be reassured of their daughters' chastity, to go home content in the knowledge that their money had been well spent.

Thankfully, my parents were not part of the audience that year, leaving me with very little supervision. It seemed like an appropriate day to lose my virginity. I waited until Rochelle was crowned and the dance around the Maypole had begun.

The day was heavy and overcast—not fog, really, just a low gray sky, stretched taut, with no wind beneath it. It was like a vapor lock—motionless, with the air thick and warm. Despite all the preparations, rehearsals, instructions, the day was chaotic. It was easy to get away unnoticed.

I slipped through the back door of the kitchen and started up the stairs toward Eric's room. The door was open; pale daylight met me on the dark stairway. I could feel it already—a heat starting in my body, hard and determined, refusing to go away. I was sweating under my white cotton dress with its scalloped sleeves and lace-trimmed hem.

I stopped outside the open door, reached in, and tapped my fist on an edge of peeling paint.

"Come in."

I looked around at a small dresser, an orange-crate nightstand, and a single bed pushed against the wall where Eric sat wedged in the corner, a book in his lap.

"What—no dance around the Maypole for you?" he said, smiling at me, his eyes taking it a step further, almost to laughter.

"No. I didn't bring your book back either." I sat down on the bed beside him. The window was open, but the air was stubborn and windless; the room felt like it needed oxygen. I realized I wasn't scared. I looked at his legs, crossed Indian style, the knees of his Levi's faded to white and his bare feet smooth against the scratchy surface of a gray army blanket. And I knew that what was foreign was about to become familiar.

I had not come there with hesitation; I had come like an animal tracking a scent. It was written in blood even before I had climbed the stairs to his room.

He got off the bed, springs creaking a little, and closed the door, sliding the bolt and looking back at me with an answer I already knew. He sat down beside me and reached around my neck to the zipper of my dress.

"This might mean you'll never be able to wear white again," he said, sliding the zipper down.

I didn't answer; I didn't want the distraction of words. It was like a needle had slid into my vein, emptying hot liquid into me, and that was the only thing I wanted.

He stretched me out on the bed and took off my dress and underwear, and then lay down beside me.

"Undress me," he said, his eyes playing again on the edge of a smile. I looked at every part of his body as I uncovered it—a strange new terrain that I had only imagined before. My mouth moved down from his neck, across his chest, between his ribs.

He guided my hands over him, allowing them to stop and explore when they demanded it. It was like hunger, I suddenly realized— raw and insistent, gnawing at parts of me I didn't even know existed.

At first his hands were soft on my skin, light as blades of grass. He didn't try to talk anymore. He knew now that words didn't belong— just the quick sound of breaths tripping on themselves and the pressure of his hands increasing, and the rhythm of blood pumping through veins that felt like they would burst.

He was trying to enter me gently, but I pulled him in, wanting the pain then. I felt the breaking—heard it, almost—and the release of blood as my veins flattened and the heat turned to a dull ache. I saw my blood on him when he rolled over.

"Are you okay?" he asked, words finding their place again in the still, small room.

I nodded, looking at the red stain on him, like a brand.

He got up and went into the bathroom—the sound of running

water—and then he came back clean, unbranded, carrying a damp towel. He put it between my legs and held it there while he kissed me, his mouth apologizing for pain he thought I minded. But he didn't know that it wasn't really pain; it was just something breaking, a tiny sound like a twig snapping. . . and then knowing you'll never be the same again.

I went back to a scene that seemed surreal—girls and parents standing around on a green stretch of lawn, sipping lemonade from paper cups and eating pinwheel cookies with colored sprinkles on them. I knew blood was still leaking out of me, staining my thighs. It made me want to laugh, knowing that beneath my white dress, tiny drops of blood were telling the real story.

16

Eric returned to Tipton the following year, and several mornings a week, I crept out of the dormitory, across campus to the kitchen and up the back stairs. The third stair creaked; I learned to step over it on my way to his room. I also discovered the night watchman went off duty at four o'clock, apparently under the misguided assumption that any delinquent acts would be carried out before that hour. I became a student of that still hour of morning; I knew the smells, the call of a lone owl whose tree I passed under, the deeper layer of silence.

At four-thirty, I would slip through Eric's door and we would have an hour together before the sky started to lighten and he had to go downstairs to the kitchen. I would race back to my room, steps ahead of the dawn, and sleep until I had to wake up as a schoolgirl again and blend into Mrs. Tipton's illusory world, pretending that I fit in, pretending I was still a virgin.

"Why are you so angry?" Eric asked one morning after we had made love. We were lying on his small bed as the moon was starting to fade outside.

"Am I?"

"You know you are—even your lovemaking is angry." His hands slid over my breasts, moved across my stomach to my hips, and followed their curve to my thighs—as if anger were on the surface of my skin and he could smooth it away. "Sometimes I wonder if you're angry at me."

"No—not you. How could I be angry at you?" I said, kissing him, tasting his mouth.

"Who, then?"

I hesitated, shuffled through the people in my life, and only one emerged. "My mother, I guess," I said softly.

"But she's not here," he whispered, his breath close to my ear.

"Yes, she is. She's always close by, telling me I'm not pretty, telling me I'm wrong. I actually like the wrong part—it lets me know I'm right. But the other..."

"You don't feel pretty?" Eric asked.

I shook my head no, feeling tears start to fill my throat.

"Come here." He stood up, took my hand, and led me from the bed to the narrow mirror on his closet door.

"Look at yourself," he said, standing behind me, hands tracing the outlines of my body. "Look at yourself with your own eyes, not your mother's."

But my eyes were crying and the image in the mirror was blurred. It was his hands, though, that pressed the message into me, and I would re-create the feel of them later—even years later—whenever my mother's judgment made me forget what the mirror told me.

Eric taught me to read my own body, to understand its cycles and rhythms. I learned when I could get pregnant and when I couldn't; it became a source of wonder to me, like the transition of tides.

"Someday you'll be thinking of it in the opposite way—when you *want* to get pregnant," he said one morning, with the covers fallen to the floor and his body still on top of mine. It was winter and outside the air was black and sharp. Through the window, I could see the moon like a knife-slit in the sky.

"I'll never want to get pregnant," I told him, my cheek against his shoulder.

"Why not?" He rolled off me then and studied my face in the thin light.

"I don't want to be a mother. I'm too afraid I'd turn into my mother. I'd rather die than treat a child like she treated me."

"How do you know you would?"

"How do I know I wouldn't? What other role model do I have? I'm just never going to, that's all."

I got up and started looking for my clothes.

"Carla," Eric said, his voice drifting over to me like a dust ball in the darkness.

"What?"

"Suddenly it seems kind of crowded in here. Have you let your mother in again?"

I went back to the bed and curled my body into his. "Yeah, I guess so. It's hard to keep her out. She always seems to find a key. See—if I had a child, she'd find a key to the nursery and by the time I got it together to throw her out, there'd be another wounded person limping through life."

Eric's leg wrapped around me. "I've never noticed you limping, Carla."

"I just put on a good act."

That year, for the first time, Lily started writing to me—short, casual letters at first, full of inconsequential details about school and life at home. But gradually the letters got longer, more revealing.

"I feel like there's so much pressure on me to be good," she wrote. "No one really knows me. Especially Mother—she tries to mold me, and I don't argue. I let her, I guess, because I have nothing else. You always had your writing, something that was yours, a private thing. There's nothing in my life I can hide and keep to myself."

But you have been hiding something, I wanted to tell her, but didn't. You've been hiding this side of yourself. It was emerging in her letters; it was being offered to me, but I wasn't sure how to answer her. I wasn't sure how to have a sister.

In another letter she wrote, "Every time you come home for a holiday, as soon as you leave, Mother searches your room. I guess she's looking for any writing you might have left behind. She thinks everything you write is about the family."

"I know," I wrote back. "I played around with the idea of hiding blank sheets of paper around my room, just to let her know I was on to her, but I decided it would only stir up more trouble."

Lily's letters began arriving every week. My answers to her were cautious and often vague, but I began to feel that I now had an ally in a family where there had been none. I'd grown accustomed to my isolation, to floating through a dark galaxy like a planet that didn't belong in that solar system. It was strange to think there might be someone floating beside me.

Lily and I had been closer once, and those childhood memories had remained untarnished by the distance that had grown between us. And now she was returning, bearing gifts—offerings of feelings she needed to share.

I thought back to the child she had been; I saw again the wonder on her face as she watched Central Park turn white with snow, and the tears that fell for hours when our mother wouldn't let us keep a stray cat we'd found in the park.

Just after we moved to California, we discovered that, on nights when the moon was full, it shone through Lily's window like a spotlight and moved across her floor in a slow, graceful passage. It was a new phenomenon to us. In New York, the moon had moved furtively behind skyscrapers and never visited our bedrooms.

We invented a ceremony that Lily called moonbathing; it was the closest I ever felt to my sister. I would tiptoe into her room and we would sit on the floor, baptized by silvery light. Holding hands, we moved as the light moved, always staying within its beam—a union of small hands illuminated by a moon that had graced us by falling through our window.

I don't remember when this ritual ended, or why; I only know it did. We never spoke of it again until, in one of Lily's letters, she mentioned it:

"The moon came through my window last night, and I got out of bed and sat on the floor in the center of the moonbeam. I imagined you were there with me, like when we were kids. Remember how we used to sit there and hold hands?"

I had taken Lily's letter down to the bluffs; I sat on the largest rock and read her words, feeling them tug at me across the miles. And in my empty hand I could almost feel hers—tiny and delicate and pale as the moon. I knew it was just the wind brushing my palm, but it was the closest I had come to holding her hand since those luminous nights, light-years ago.

I wanted to return her trust, share some small confidence with her. But the only secret I had was Eric. Sharing that would have diminished its magic, and I wasn't even sure she would understand. I couldn't picture Lily with a man, and I didn't want to be the one to introduce the subject to her. And, after Graddy, I wasn't sure I should trust her at all.

There were things I couldn't have explained, even if I'd wanted to—changes in the way I saw Eric as he moved around his small room, taking clothes from the drawers or sitting on the edge of the bed pulling on his socks. He was no longer a figure from a book who had emerged from the pages as a mysterious, shadowy lover in the black hours before dawn. I could watch him rummaging for his clothes and see him as he was in childhood, a small boy getting dressed for school. Or I could turn time ahead and see him older, forgetting where he put his sweater and grumbling at his own absentmindedness.

Part of me was sad to see the mystery go. It was gradual—shadows peeled away in layers. But another part of me knew it was being replaced with something more real—with the vulnerabilities and tiny, everyday tasks of being human. It became part of the magic.

In May, the gardener started planting impatiens and primroses around the campus. Walking between classes became a passage through color. Along the path leading to the bluffs, white azaleas shivered in the spring breeze like snowflakes out of season. Dawn was arriving earlier, chasing me down as I left Eric and raced back to my room. I ran with night at my back and the gray morning light waiting ahead to expose me.

It was raining the morning Eric told me he would be leaving before the end of the school year. I walked through the warm downpour and left a trail of rainwater on the stairs that led to his room. My clothes were soaked through. I peeled them off and slid into bed beside him, laughing when he shuddered at the dampness of my body.

I could tell by the way he kissed my forehead and drank rainwater from my skin that something was wrong.

"What? What is it?" I asked, the outline of his face faint in the darkness.

He didn't answer me at first; rain drummed on the windowsill, filling the room with its steady, even sound.

"I'm gong to be leaving in a couple of weeks—leaving the country, in fact," he said finally. "I got my draft notice."

"You're going to Vietnam?"

By December of that year, there would be a lottery and boys across the country would wait to see if their numbers would be drawn. But in May, there were still student deferments, and Eric didn't have one.

"I'm going to Canada," he said. "I can't fight in a war. It means I'll never be able to come back to this country, but it beats getting blown to bits in some rice paddy."

I looked past him to the tracks of water streaking the window. Until that moment, it had been a faraway war. We were in an ivory tower at Tipton—a select group of girls who didn't have to worry about being sent to a country that was unknown to us before American blood started spilling into rice paddies and jungles.

I remember something cold drifting into the room that morning, a sad breeze from some distant place. It didn't carry the light fragrance of just-bloomed roses and carefully tended flower beds. The bell-like sound of girls' laughter didn't travel on its currents. I listened carefully to that breeze, blowing in like a messenger of death.

By the time the rain ended that afternoon, I had decided I was going to go to Canada also. It wasn't the idea of joining Eric as much as it was the idea of escape.

I only had about fifty dollars. All the girls were given weekly allowances, sent by their parents to be distributed by Mrs. Tipton. I was very frugal with mine, counting the dollars as they piled up as if they were a measure of my freedom. I also had a bracelet that had been handed down from my great-grandmother; I thought I could sell it on the way to Canada. It was a fragmented plan at best, almost innocent in its simplicity. I would wait until graduation day when everyone was busy and disorganized. I would walk off campus and start hitchhiking to Canada—to Vancouver where Eric said he was going. Beyond that, I didn't know.

For a week, I said nothing to him about my plans. I became silent and vague during the early hours when we hid together in the dark. I heard time draining away; the sound rushed against me like wind and quickened my heartbeat. Talking could go unremembered; I wanted to fill my memory with the weight of his body on mine, the heat of breath in my ear, the feel of sweat gluing us together skin to skin. I started waiting until afternoon to shower, wanting to leave his scent on me as long as I could.

After too many mornings like that, I knew I had to tell him.

"Do you know where you're going to be in Vancouver?" I asked him.

The window was open, and a fast, warm breeze spread over us, bathing us with the perfume of flowers.

"Not yet. I'll just get a cheap motel room for a while until I get something lined up."

I realized that I didn't even know where he was from originally. But it didn't matter; I was trying to escape the burden of my own history—I didn't want to learn about his.

"Will you let me know when you get there?" I said. "It's important."

"Why is it important?" I could hear the smile in his voice.

"It's not what you think." I propped myself up on my elbow and stared down at him. "I'm going to run away, and Canada sounds like a good place to go."

"What?"

"Not just because you're going there, Eric. You just gave me the idea, that's all. I don't ever want to go home again."

"Carla, you're still a minor—it's crazy. How do you think you'll manage?" he asked.

"I don't know, but I will. I'll work, I'll get a job. I'm not suggesting that I'm going to live off you."

The sky was getting pale and I got out of bed and pulled on my clothes.

"Carla, this is crazy."

"I know," I said. "Please don't try and talk me out of it—you'll just waste your breath."

I kissed him quickly and raced down the stairs and across campus, the dark lifting around me.

It was the one secret I would share with my sister—a thread woven loosely into a fragile piece of fabric. And the unraveling would teach me a lesson that I had never wanted to learn. Our history was the single bond that Lily and I shared, and it would always beckon me back to its most heavily mined territories.

17

Four days before the end of the school year, I was in literature class, listening to the teacher describe the various legends about the search for the Holy Grail. My thoughts were on Lancelot, whose adulterous love for Queen Guinevere condemned him to only see the Grail winging through his dreams, always out of reach. I was daydreaming, wondering if anyone would ever love me as much as Lancelot loved Guinevere, wondering if I could ever love like that. Maybe it was only in legends, never in the real world...

My daydreams disintegrated when Mrs. Tipton walked into the classroom. She glanced briefly at the students and whispered something to the teacher.

"Carla Lawton, will you please go with Mrs. Tipton?"

I felt eyes turning toward me from all corners of the room. Mrs. Tipton had walked out without waiting for me; I came into the hallway and was bruised by her stare.

"Your father is here to see you, Carla," she said.

"Why?"

"I think you know. I'm very disappointed in you. I never would have expected this from you."

"You'd have expected it if you knew everything," I felt like saying, but didn't.

"If something was so wrong that you thought you had to run away," she said, "couldn't you have talked to me about it?"

"I would have, but...it...I couldn't. I didn't know if you'd understand."

"You might have given me a chance," she said, turning and punishing me with the distance her stride put between us. I trailed behind, reading sadness in the muscles of her back.

On the way to her office, I looked up at the sky, hating the white clouds drifting across it. I wanted thunder, tornadoes, tidal waves. I knew Lily was responsible for this; no one else could have been. She'd shot down my dream of escape, but what hurt more was her betrayal. I had offered her a secret, handed it to her like a wounded bird, but instead of nurturing it, she fed it to predators.

By the time we got to Mrs. Tipton's office, my head felt thick and there was a deep ache starting behind my eyes. My father stood up as we entered the room.

"Hello, Carla," he said, making no move toward me, his voice rigid enough to keep me from approaching him.

Mrs. Tipton walked past both of us and sat down at her desk. She motioned us toward the two chairs facing her.

"Lily told you, didn't she?" I asked my father.

"Carla, you don't see this now," he said, "but your sister did you a big favor. You were going to throw everything away for some crazy, childish idea. What in the world were you thinking of?"

I looked at my father, sitting less than three feet from me, and saw only the distance between us. I glanced at his hands, resting in his lap; they had never struck me as my mother's had, but they had never reached for me either.

"Carla," he said. "Answer my question."

"I didn't want to come home—that's what I was thinking of."

He shook his head slowly. "Why on earth would you feel that way? We're a family—we love you. Why would you want to run away?"

"How can you talk about love and then turn a blind eye to Mother searching my room, destroying my writing? You just don't want to see those things, do you?"

"Now, that's simply not true," my father said. "Why do you insist on making these things up? You just haven't learned the difference between imagination and lying."

"Right. I'm always the liar, aren't I? Christ—"

"Carla, dear," Mrs. Tipton said, "I haven't taught you girls to speak like that. There's no call for profanity."

"Yes, ma'am."

My father directed his words to Mrs. Tipton. "We've had this problem with Carla since she was a child. She's very creative with her imagination and she makes things up."

My eyes burned with the effort of holding back tears. Refusing to cry had become my stock reaction to pain. But in some corner of my soul, tears were collecting in deep pools.

"You're never going to believe me, are you?" I said. "Things are different in that house when you're not there. You don't get the real story. You get a twisted version of it..." My voice trailed off. There was no point trying to explain; it wouldn't change anything. I had been caught, my plan for escape had been exposed, and the only thing I was grateful for was that I hadn't told Lily about Eric.

"When did Lily tell you?" I asked quietly.

"She brought us your letters when you first came up with this crazy idea," my father said. "We waited to see if you would come to your senses, and when you obviously didn't, well—here we are."

My mind felt unconnected; too many thoughts were going through it. I would have to write to Eric and tell him. And I wondered why my mother had missed this confrontation, sending my father instead. I wondered if I would be returning to Tipton the following year, or if my parents would go shopping for a girls' military academy. I thought about my sister, tried to picture her face, her eyes, but I could only see her handwriting filling up the pages of letters. And I could feel myself stumbling over her duplicity, unable to walk around it.

"Mr. Lawton, could I speak with Carla alone for a moment, please?" Mrs. Tipton said.

She waited until he was out of the room before she spoke to me.

"Carla, I'll have to give some thought to you coming back next year. This was quite serious, what you were planning."

I felt tears rising up again, and tried to push them down, but they defied me. With no parent in the room, they had no reason to hide. Mrs. Tipton watched me, calm and curious, waiting for me to gather myself together.

"I'm so tired of being called a liar," I said in a weak voice, when my throat finally cleared. "And I'm so sick of having to defend myself against other people's lies."

"Whose lies?" she asked, her tone convincing me that she sincerely wanted to know.

"My mother's—mostly—she has a way of luring people over to her side."

"Your mother has always seemed very sweet and concerned every time I've talked to her," Mrs. Tipton said. "I've gotten the feeling that she's quite worried about you, about how angry you seem sometimes. I think she just wants to be closer to you."

"How often do you talk to her?" I didn't really need to hear the answer; I already knew.

"Every couple of weeks. She calls to ask how you're doing."

"Uh-huh." My tears were gone then, they'd given up. And they'd been replaced by an exhaustion that made me want to sleep for days. "Mrs. Tipton, my mother can be the sweetest woman in the world. She can charm anyone, warm anyone's heart. But you'd better watch your back. Because I've seen the other side of her character and, the problem is, I'm sort of a lone witness to this transformation. So, if I seem angry, there's a reason for it. You know what the biggest lie of all is? That the truth will always win out. Whoever made that up should live in my house for a few months."

Mrs. Tipton reached across her desk and touched my hand. With that gesture, my tears returned, falling into my lap. I put my hands over my face, but I could feel her still watching me.

"Sometimes I've wondered if they were right," I said, struggling with the words. "I wondered if I was crazy, if my mind played tricks on me, if my ears heard things that were never said. But I'm not crazy—I'm not. I just have an annoying habit of saying things they don't want to hear."

"I know, dear."

"You do?"

"Yes, I think so," she said, which was all I needed to hear.

"I really want to come back here next year, Mrs. Tipton."

"Well, I do have to give this some thought, because of the seriousness of what you tried to do. But I'll consider what we've talked about today."

My parents had stayed at a hotel the night before, which is where my mother had remained, sending my father out as a reluctant ambassador.

I kept silent throughout lunch at the hotel restaurant, and my mother aimed her own brand of silence back at me.

During the long drive back to Los Angeles, I sat in the back seat, listening to the sound of the tires and the wind, watching night swell in the air. I imagined myself as part of the darkness—a soft current floating under the stars, invisible to the naked eye.

For most of that summer, Lily and I moved past each other like strangers—ships on different seas. I wanted to be angry at her, but I was unable even to feel that. I'd turned numb. It just seemed like too much trouble to feel anything.

Before the end of August, my sister revealed to all of us—with stunning clarity—the depth of her own anguish. Our family would take yet another vow of silence, find another chance to turn away from something too painful to look at.

For over an hour, I had been waiting for Lily to finish taking a bath so I could get into the bathroom that we shared. She was taking an unusually long time, but there was something else that made me pass by the door several times—a strange feeling inside me, cold and foreboding, that I could neither identify nor ignore. I heard nothing on the other side of the door—no splashing, no sounds of movement. Finally, I knocked.

"Lily, how much longer are you going to be?"

Silence seeped out from under the door.

"Lily—" I felt my voice rising in pitch. Still she didn't answer.

I could taste fear in the back of my throat. I went out to the yard, slid the doghouse under the bathroom window, and climbed on top of it so I could see into the room. The first thing I saw was a river of red moving across the white tile floor. My eyes followed it to Lily's wrist, dangling over the edge of the bathtub, and her pale body, slumped in the water. I felt veins bursting deep inside me, blood leaking out of my heart. My throat opened to scream for help, but no sound came out. I don't know if I saw her move, if I imagined it, or if I was trying to will her to move. The window was open; I slammed my hand against the screen, sending it clattering to the floor below, and I hoisted myself through the window and slid down the wall into the bathroom. I could smell the blood—sweet and thick—my sister's life running across the floor in a slippery red stream. I tried to move quickly, but everything felt too slow. A thin stream of breath was coming out of her mouth. Only one wrist was cut; I wrapped a towel around it and opened the bathroom door, praying that my throat would open, that my voice would return.

"Mother!"

I heard my shriek race through the house, bounce off walls. When only its echo came back to me, I screamed again, my voice sounding unfamiliar and foreign.

My mother came around the corner and when her eyes focused on my blood-soaked hands, they registered an expression of horror I had never seen before.

"Lily—" I said, pointing to the bathroom. She pushed past me, and when I turned around, she was lifting my sister out of the tub. Water and blood dripped from Lily's limp body and my mother's face hardened into grim resolve. It looked as though Lily weighed nothing.

"Go get my keys and bring the car around," she said.

When I stopped the car at the front door, she was waiting outside, holding Lily in her arms like a broken doll. She had wrapped a bathrobe around her body; the towel around her wrist was already soaked through with blood. I ran around to the other side and helped my mother put Lily into the passenger seat.

"You stay here, Carla," she said.

"But I want to go with you."

"No. You stay here."

The tires screeched when she pulled away and I looked down at my hands, still covered with blood. I wasn't sure if I would ever see my sister alive again.

When my father came home hours later, he found me scrubbing blood from the bathroom tiles. My clothes were splattered red and my knees were raw from kneeling on the floor. He filled up the doorway, staring down at me with a look of such sorrow I thought Lily must have died.

"Lily's going to be all right," he said, in a flat, toneless voice. "Your mother called me at the office. I was going to go to the hospital, but she said I didn't need to."

I wasn't surprised. My mother was going to deal with this herself. I saw it on her face as she held Lily in her arms.

"How could this happen, Carla? I don't understand—" my father said.

"I don't know." I kept scrubbing the floor; my arm wouldn't stop its determined effort to clean away all the evidence of my sister's death wish. "We're all strangers to each other in this family. Why is anyone surprised when something like this happens?"

"That's not true—it's not fair to say that." His words resonated in the room, sounding loud and hollow.

"Not fair? Take a look around. Lily's blood is all over this room. She sat in the bathtub and sliced open her veins." But he wasn't looking; he never would, and I wanted to shake him, force his eyes to see her blood, put his hands in it, make his feet slip on it. "What the hell does fairness have to do with it? There's something wrong with this family—are you ever going to realize that? We put up this false front to the world, and behind it are emotions no one wants to acknowledge—they're too painful. And Lily, your perfect, obedient child, obviously didn't see her life as being so perfect. Why don't you try to understand what she was saying?"

My father's eyes filled with tears. Silent, he turned and walked away, leaving me with a pail of bloody water and the stains of my sister's suicide attempt clinging stubbornly to the white tiles. I didn't care that my words had taken deadly aim at my father's heart. The image of Lily opening her wrist with a razor blade was the wound that wouldn't heal.

My mother came back from the hospital that evening and said nothing to me. She and my father had dinner in their bedroom, and the soft murmur of their voices drifted through the closed door.

I spent the night balanced on the rim of sleep, afraid of what I would dream if I let myself go.

The next morning, my parents were dressed and at the breakfast table earlier than usual.

"We're going to the hospital," my mother said when I came into the dining room and sat down.

"I'd like to go, too."

"No, I don't think so," she answered, grazing me with her eyes and looking down at her plate again.

"Why not?"

"Just... because I don't think it would be a good idea. She'll be home in a few days. She needs to rest now."

"What does needing to rest have to do with me visiting her?" I asked, knowing that one had nothing to do with the other, but determined to make my point, or force my mother to make hers.

"She shouldn't get upset now, Carla," my father interjected.

"So, I upset her? Is that what you're saying?"

My mother dropped her fork on her plate. " 'No,' is what we're saying. You cannot go visit Lily with us today. And when she comes home, I don't ever want you to mention what happened. Is that clear?"

"We're not going to talk about this? We're going to pretend it didn't happen?" I asked, directing this to my father, hoping he wouldn't go along with this plan, although nothing in our history suggested that he wouldn't.

"Your mother's right, Carla. It's best not to bring it up."

I got up from the table and started out of the room. "Right. I probably imagined the whole thing anyway."

Before school started in September, my parents bought Lily a wide gold bracelet. There was no doubt which wrist it was meant for; the unspoken message was chillingly clear. She still wears it; it catches the light sometimes, offering a distraction from the thin scar beneath it.

But it doesn't distract me.

18

The nurse answers the door at my mother's house when I ring the bell. I know without asking that Lily isn't there. She doesn't come until the afternoon; I've deliberately timed my visit to miss hers.

"I want to talk to my mother," I tell the nurse, a slender, grayhaired woman whose expressionless face offers no hint to what she's thinking. Her grim surface suggests that there's a lot beneath it, but there could just as easily be nothing.

"Talk to her?"

"Uh-huh. Don't worry, I don't expect her to answer."

She shrugs, indulging a whim that must seem senseless to her, and points me in the direction of my mother's bedroom. I'm tempted to try and explain myself to the nurse, coax a response from her, but I'm not sure I understand my own reasons for being here like this.

My mother is in bed, propped up on pillows, her face looking pale, bloodless almost, against the backdrop of uncreased white cotton. I sit on the edge of the bed and position my face in front of hers. I want her eyes to focus, to see something other than the veil that covers them. My stare asks her for some tiny ember of recognition, but she gives me back nothing.

"You know what I'd like to understand, Mother? Why things got so distorted in this family, why there are so many lies and pieces missing. Haven't you ever wondered what Lily was trying to say when she tried to kill herself? She was being more honest than anyone else, but you wouldn't hear it. You just bought her a bracelet to cover the scar and thought you'd taken care of it.

"There are so many memories that confuse me, but you know what I remember perfectly? That it wasn't always like that. I have good memories—they're old, but they're good. Remember when we lived in New York, when Lily was still a baby? You said, years later, that it was only Father who told me stories, but that's not true. You told me the story about the rainbow—that God painted it when He was very happy and He liked the colors so much that He used those colors for flowers. He painted the petals with a tiny brush. Father told me stories about magic and fantasy, but yours made me look at the sky and the earth differently.

"The magic dust—remember that? You sprinkled it on me to chase away bad dreams. Why did the stories turn mean, Mother? Even the one about my older sister turned from a sweet, sad story about a baby dying into a weapon. I tried to be like the image you painted of her, but I could never be that perfect."

I hear the nurse's footsteps approaching the bedroom.

"It's time for your mother's medicine," she says, coming into the room.

"What medicine?"

"To help her sleep."

"Can it wait just a little while?" I ask her. "I don't want her to sleep yet. I need to talk to her for a few more minutes. I'll give it to her when I'm finished."

"All right," she answers, handing me the pills and giving me a puzzled look. She leaves me in charge of dispensing my mother's medicine.

"I don't understand why fear had to be such a strong presence in this house," I continue, turning again to the film of her eyes where I know anger still hides. I want it to surface, to stand in front of me like the assassin it always was. Maybe now it will look smaller. "Do you remember when I kept asking you about the lady with the nylon stocking over her head, Mother? The one who chased me around the house one night? You laughed at me, you told me I must have dreamed it. But I don't think it was a dream.

"I want you to remember, because that night still terrifies me. I was young—probably eight or nine, and a woman was chasing me through the living room and into the kitchen. She had a nylon stocking over her head, like bank robbers wear, and I was screaming and crying. I hid under the kitchen table, but she crawled under there too and started tickling me until my crying sounded like laughter. But it wasn't laughter. I remember that it seemed to go on forever—I felt like I couldn't breathe. Finally, I got away and ran toward my room, and I ran by the maid standing in the doorway. She had seen it all. Two days later she was fired. You said she had threatened you with a knife, but I didn't believe you. She threatened you with the truth, didn't she? She was the one witness, the one person who could argue with you when you told me later that I was confusing reality with a nightmare. Who was that woman chasing me? You know the one detail that sticks in my mind? Her bedroom slippers—they were yours. Why did you always try to make me feel like I was crazy, Mother? You don't even have to answer me with words—you can answer me with your eyes. I'd be satisfied with that."

But nothing changes in her eyes. There is no darkening, no message forming in their vacant stare.

"You were so angry at me for growing up into a girl, weren't you? You thought if you could just scare me enough, I'd stop. But I didn't stop— I want you to know that you didn't destroy that in me—" My voice breaks and I realize that tears are in my throat and I am, once again, refusing to cry. Even now, even when she is blank and unresponsive, imprisoned in her own silence, I won't allow myself to cry in front of her.

"You know what the cruelest story of all was? That you were dying because of me. Remember that one, Mother? You were going to have a nervous breakdown and die because I was such a bad child. I had nightmares for a year about that, and no one came to sprinkle magic dust on me then. Did you know about the day Father showed me a manila envelope and told me it contained your medical records— records that confirmed how precarious your health was? Of course, he wouldn't show me the contents, and looking back on it, I assume there was nothing in that envelope. But it worked at the time. You recruited everyone for that story, didn't you?"

My mother's eyelids are dropping. I watch them flutter open and then fall again.

"You don't need these fucking pills—you go to sleep whenever you want, anyway." I put the pills in my pocket, adjust her pillows, and close the door softly behind me.

"Did you give your mother her medicine?" the nurse asks, intercepting me at the front door.

"Yes."

I drive away from my mother's house, winding through familiar streets still bordered by hedges of honeysuckle, just as they always have been. The aroma resurrects childhood images that shuttle through my thoughts, moving between light and shadow. I stop at the lot where, years before, I was stripped naked and abandoned—a casualty of Halloween. There is a house there now—vacant lots are a thing of the past—but I listen for the echoes of girls' laughter, the thin trail of voices hanging on the wind like vagrant ghosts.

Maybe it's better that I hear nothing, I think, as I put the car in gear and pull away. I've heard enough for one day. I've heard the deafening message of my mother's silence, letting me know that she is the caretaker of our history and she will seal off its darkest passages if she chooses. She will vanish into death with armloads of secrets, and I am defenseless against her piracy.

I'm left with the resonance of her silence in my ears, like the ocean sound in the hollow of a conch shell. It is the sound of emptiness, of dreams that seem too real, of memories that waver in the distance. And it will always be there.

I stop at a pay phone in a supermarket parking lot and call Beck's number, expecting his machine to answer and tell me he's not there. But, instead, his voice says, "Hello?"

"What happened, Beck? Did your machine break?"

"I knew it was you, Carla, so I picked up."

"Really?"

"No. I was taking a break, and I thought I'd be civil and answer the phone."

A delivery truck rumbles past me.

"Where the hell are you?" Beck asks. "On a freeway call box?"

"At a pay phone by a supermarket. If you need bread, the truck just brought a fresh load. Beck, I just left my mother's house, and I did something very strange while I was there. I sat and talked to her as though she would answer me."

"Did she?"

"No, but that didn't deter me," I tell him, thinking again of my mother's unfocused eyes.

"I'm not so sure it's strange. I'll have to think about it. Listen, I need to get out of here—let's go get some coffee."

We meet at a restaurant on the Coast Highway and sit at an ocean-view table. Beck has come in carrying some written pages; I want to ask him about them, but I wait for him to bring it up.

"I thought about your one-sided conversation on the way over," he says. "I think it was probably a healthy thing to do. Would you have talked to her like that if you thought she'd answer you?"

"No."

"So, consider it therapy. Speaking of which—can I read you something?"

"Where does the therapy come in?" I ask him. "In reading it to me, in my feedback, or in the fact that you wrote it at all?"

"All of the above."

A waitress comes up to the table and we order coffee and bran muffins.

"Let's wait until she brings our order and then I'll read this. It is kind of dark, are you sure you're in the mood?"

"Sure—that's a mood I can always tap into."

The waitress returns and puts the coffee and muffins down in front of us. After she leaves, Beck leans forward and starts to read.

"'Come with me,' the dream says, 'follow me down. I will take you to the dank regions at the river's edge, dive with you to its bottom, show you the black sludge oozing with the poisons of your civilized world. Go ahead, wade in it—it belongs to you. It came from you; it is your blood, your semen, the juice of fruit that dies before it ripens.

"'They will call you mad for following me. They will lock you away with others who hear the same call, thread wires into your brain and turn you into a sleepwalker who hears only the thud of doors behind him. There is a reason for the black labyrinth of my world—it is where the truth hides. It's the other side of the moon, the other side of rage—white-hot and scalding in its fury.

"'You remember that rage—it came to get you years ago, but they told you to quiet its voice. "We know better," they said. "We have shaped countries from open land, scored history with bullets and blood, conquered the sea with exploding harpoons, lifted bloated, gasping bodies up toward the sky as emblems of our conquest. Listen to us—we are the future, we are the destiny of the world."

" 'No,' the dream says, 'listen to me. You tried to forget me, but you never did. I was always there, coiled under the weight of night, moaning beneath the rush of wind. They said I was madness, but you've always known I was truth. I am the cold trickle of sweat down your back, the thin strains of music playing in your ear when everyone else hears nothing. I will be all that's left when forests are scorched and the hills turn to dust, when women's breasts dry up and babies go hungry, when the sky rains fire and the seas become barren. I will always be the darkness they didn't want to see. But you can see me now. I can show you how far it goes down, how black the deepest fathoms are. Don't be frightened—you can dip your hands in it. It's only death.

" 'You don't want to listen, do you? You'd rather believe them that this is madness. They can cure you, give you pills in paper cups and slip long needles into your veins. But at night, just beyond the threshold of sleep, my voice still calls you. I am your guide, it's a downward journey. It feels like falling, doesn't it? Only you never land. There is no bottom; the journey is all there is to this game.

" 'Think back. You remember—think back centuries ago, when elephants roamed the plains of Africa and the sky was blue and noisy with the flapping of wings, when whales traveled beneath ice flows, heading for warmer seas. They tell you it's not murder, as tusks are sawed from bullet-torn carcasses and the skies become deadly quiet and the seas bubble with blood. They tell you it's progress—it's the growth of civilization. Remember when night turned the desert to black velvet and shy, nocturnal creatures left thin trails across the sand? That was before headlights sliced through the darkness, caught their startled eyes and tires ran over their soft bellies, before cities were paved over the sifted floor of their world and metal and glass rose to blot out the sun. Remember storms rumbling down from the mountains, before the mountains were burned and bulldozed, before the sky surrendered and the clouds evaporated?

" 'Can you feel the rage returning now? Licking the flesh off your fingers until your hand is skeleton white? Follow the rage down—it will lead you to me. They will all have to meet my eyes eventually. But you can go first. Does it matter that they call you mad? Tell you your dreams are only hallucinations woven from threads of a night darker than it should be? In the end, all there will be is the strafe of wind and the moon bleeding blue light on a dying planet . . . and the dream taking you down.'"

Beck stops reading, looks up at me, and takes a sip of coffee that's turned cold.

"Is this your character's dream or yours?" I ask softly, not really sure that I want to know.

"A little of both—sometimes the lines get crossed. Maybe, if I keep writing it, I'll stop dreaming it."

I look away from Beck and the cups of cold coffee between us, out across the water at a boat tilting on the horizon. It's not that different, what we're both doing—chasing dreams into latitudes where ships vanish and men are lost forever. But we keep returning with treasure chests full of old, painful memories and wounds that never seem to heal. I wonder how long we can do this before there is so much strewn around us that we can't find each other. Or maybe, by that time, we won't even be looking for each other anymore.

19

I was accepted back at Tipton for my senior year, but I could tell, from Mrs. Tipton's eyes, that my acceptance didn't mean she had forgotten. Her expression, whenever I encountered it, reminded me that I had disappointed her, and warned me against trying it again. My answer was to retreat into a world of words, mine or someone else's. I was usually found buried in a book or filling up spiral notebooks with poems and short stories.

Often, I saw the image of my sister's damaged wrist—her thin, blue veins interrupted by the smooth line of scarring. I would return sometimes to sweeter memories, to moments when I felt close to Lily, but the memories had a surreal, dreamlike quality because, in the end, my sister had come to long for the cold finality of razor blades.

I had kept Lily's letters, and when I reread I saw, behind the delicate tilt of her script, a face more open, more vulnerable, than the one she wore when I went home for the holidays. In our parents' home, she was pale, almost ethereal, moving gracefully around the mine fields that were everywhere in that house.

When I graduated in June, I looked across the audience and saw her sitting between my parents, a shy replica of their most carefully constructed dreams. She'd probably lost her attraction for death, I decided—edges of blue steel would be kept away from her veins. She had chosen numb obedience instead. It seemed like a bleak alternative to me, but I had to admit her life was more tranquil than mine.

127

Eric and I had written to each other during the school year, but by June our letters had become shorter, time lengthening between each one. I knew, when I received a letter days before graduation, that it would be his last.

That summer, Lily was sent to a tennis camp, but no offer was made to send me anywhere. I was on probation, apparently—required to stay within a ten-mile radius of home so that I wouldn't be tempted to take flight. It was decided that in the fall I would go to college in Los Angeles and live at home, and one morning my parents presented me with the old Chrysler previously used by the maid for running errands.

There were changes in our house; more people bustled through it, polishing silver, watering houseplants, arranging flowers. Plans were being made to add another wing and, each morning, my father traveled to work in a chauffeur-driven limousine. It didn't escape my notice that his limo driver looked like he wrestled alligators in his off hours, or that there were, occasionally, other imposing-looking men with him.

"If I were playing Sherlock Holmes," I said one night at dinner, "I'd assume you'd hired some bodyguards."

"That's ridiculous," my mother said, too quickly.

"I don't think we should keep this from the girls, Rachel." He looked at my mother for several seconds, engaged in a mysterious, silent dialogue. Then he turned to me and Lily. My sister had just come home from tennis camp two days before, but she looked like she hadn't been exposed to even a minute of sunlight.

"My firm has been extremely successful," he said. "I think that you girls are old enough at this point to realize that there are people who get jealous of anyone who has more than they do."

"And since you have more than the majority of people in America, you've acquired more than your share of jealous beggars nipping at your heels?" I asked.

"Carla—"my mother snapped.

"No, it's all right, Rachel. It's true that I have—we have—more than a great many people. And while it's made our lives extremely comfortable, there are risks that go along with that kind of success."

"So you have a bodyguard," I said, wearying of his circuitous explanation.

"Yes, I do. I've had some threats, Carla, very serious ones. And you should be aware of something else. I've obtained a gun permit and there is a loaded gun in my bedside table. I doubt anything will happen to necessitate using it, but you should know it's there."

I didn't think anything my parents did could shock me anymore, but I was wrong. I looked across the table at my sister, demure in her white, long-sleeved blouse, the cuffs buttoned to cover her wrists, her gold bracelet perfectly in place.

"I don't believe this," I said, letting my fork drop on my plate. "I can appreciate that you are frightened at getting threats and you want to protect yourself. But couldn't you have thought of some other alternative? You have a daughter who opened up her veins in the bathtub and you bring a loaded gun into this house and tell us where it is? I think everyone here has lost their mind. Or maybe you just can't stop editing your memories. In case Lily gets in the mood to die again, she has an alternative method now, doesn't she?"

"That's enough out of you!" my mother shouted, getting up from the table and coming over to me. She slapped me hard across the face and I glared back with no tears, repeating our familiar ritual. Lily sat with her hands in her lap and her head bowed, staring at her plate, waiting out the storm. This was how she survived now; she lived for the lulls in between. But I wondered what would happen if there were no breaks, if the squalls kept coming. Would razor blades sing to her from the medicine cabinet? Bullets whisper their hiding place?

My father had gotten up and was coaxing my mother back to her chair. "Rachel, let me handle this. That was unnecessary, Carla. Why do you always have to lash out and hurt people?"

"We have a little definition problem here. I think all this editing of reality is far more damaging than my attempts to lay the truth out in full view. We never talk about that day—we talk about when Lily got sick. She didn't get sick—she tried to kill herself. I realize it's a subtle distinction, but I think you might agree that it's an important episode in the life of a family. But you won't look at it. Instead, you and Mother push it aside, put a bracelet over her scar, and call it something else. And then, as if it's a perfectly normal thing to do, you get a gun and announce where it's kept, like you're telling us where the lawn mower is in case we want to do some yard work. Do you remember what you asked me that day, Father? You said, 'How could this have happened?' You still don't know, do you? And you never will because you and Mother just shut your eyes to anything you don't want to see."

My mother got up again and said, "I'm not listening to this anymore. Come on, Lily, let's go in the other room." And my sister, her spirit folded into quiet compliance, followed.

"You just can't leave well enough alone, can you, Carla?" my father asked when we were alone in the dining room, anger and the light of candles between us.

"You're right, Father, I can't. But you know what? I'm going to change that as of right now—I am going to leave it alone. Because nothing is ever going to change around here. You'll be playing these charades until the day you die."

If I had known how prophetic my words would be, I would never have said them.

Lily came into my room that night; I woke up to find her sitting on my bed, thin and delicate in the half-light of moon.

"Sometimes I know I love them," she said, her voice light as dust balls floating on the dark, "but other times I think I hate them. I'm just not as brave as you, Carla."

"It's okay—you can feel both those things, Lily—I do. They've made it easy to feel both. Just be brave enough to stay with us, that's all you have to do."

She crept out of my room as softly as she had entered, and I knew we would never speak of that conversation.

Only a few weeks passed before I broke the vow I'd made to my father that I would remain silent in the face of every turmoil that rocked our house. On a rainy night, shortly before Christmas, my silence ended.

The rain had started that morning as I drove the freeway to the college I'd ended up at, nestled in the smog and tangled streets of downtown L.A. The only kindred spirit I had found there was Kyle Portman, my creative writing teacher. He was a short, round man with unruly curls covering his head and wire-rim glasses that always slid down his nose. His daily attire was faded, baggy jeans and a black turtleneck, or a black T-shirt if it was warm. He was unique on that campus where most of the students wore letter sweaters and most of the teachers dressed in button-down shirts and loafers. He introduced me to Sylvia Plath and Anne Sexton, and I became addicted to the raw anger and the torment in their words. I touched the edges of my own rage and started to feel more comfortable with the idea of writing about it. I saw a dignity in my sister's attempt to die.

I had a meeting late in the afternoon with Kyle about my own work, and I started driving home under dark skies with the rain falling relentlessly, and ideas forming in my mind that I wanted to write down before I forgot them.

I raced into my parents' house, my hair dripping rainwater. I knew dinner would be over and Lily would be in her room doing homework. My father had been in New York all week and I had succeeded in missing dinner for most of those nights. Things were more likely to become confrontational when he was not around, and I was trying to stay far away from the front lines.

"Hi," I called out as I headed for my room.

"Come in here, please, Carla." My mother's voice found me in the hallway and pulled me in the direction of her bedroom. I leaned in the doorway, keeping my feet in the safe territory of the hall.

"Hi—I have a lot of homework to do—I want to get to it," I said.

"You can give me five minutes. That's not going to kill you, is it?"

I recognized danger in her tone; it was like a storm warning, and I had an immediate urge to run for higher ground.

"I really want to get to this, Mother. I'll talk to you later—when I finish," I said, trying to keep my voice level and unafraid.

She had been on her bed watching television, but suddenly she bolted up and was in front of me, her hand clutching my arm, pulling me into the room. With her other hand, she slammed the door shut behind me.

"I said come in here, and you just can't resist talking back to me, can you?" Her fingernails were digging into my skin, and her face was reddening. Danger signs that were too familiar.

"Mother, there is nothing you need to say to me right now. I said I'd come in later."

I could feel the ideas that I had wanted to write down escaping, drifting away; sentences were coming unhinged and words were crumbling into irretrievable pieces.

"I want to ask you about your classes. All you ever think about is yourself. The whole world revolves around Carla, doesn't it?"

"Not around here," I said.

I saw her hand coming up to slap me, and unwilling to endure the humiliation again, I shoved her backward. She fell onto the bed, her face stunned and her mouth unable to talk. When she regained her voice, she said, "I'm going to call your father. I'm going to tell him you pushed me down. What if I had hit my head?"

"On what—the pillows? Go ahead—call him. Tell him how it was all my fault, how I instigated this. He'll believe you—he always does."

I got out of her room before she could rise from the bed. If there had been a lock on my bedroom door, I'd have used it, but my parents' room was the only one with a lock. Throughout the night, I would wake up, certain I heard the approach of my mother's footsteps. But she left me alone; it was only the rain lashing against the house, and wind shaking the trees.

Just before dawn, I woke up and listened to the silence of no rain outside. But as the light turned gray, I heard a car come up the driveway; I knew what it was.

When I came into the dining room, my father was sitting at the table drinking coffee, still in his business suit, looking tired and drawn. My mother had her chair pulled close to his; she was in her bathrobe, and morning sun ignited the red waves of her hair.

"Carla, I hired a private jet to bring me home after your mother phoned me last night."

I thought of saying, "You could always bill me for it," but decided my mouth had gotten me in enough trouble.

"How could you do that to your mother?" he asked.

"Maybe you'd better tell me what I did first, since the version you hear is always different from the one I remember."

"You shoved her and knocked her down."

"This is true," I said. "I do have this knee-jerk reaction when someone grabs me, drags me into a room, and then raises her hand to slap me. It's a good thing the bed was behind her, or she'd probably be in traction now."

My mother's eyes burned into me. "There you go lying again. I merely asked if my daughter could spend five minutes with me. I did not use force."

"You didn't grab me? You weren't about to slap me?"

"Of course not."

"Fine. I must be in one of those hallucinatory phases again. Is there some lecture you'd like to give me, Father, or details of my punishment—because I have a class to get to."

I was Alice down the rabbit hole again; things weren't in proper proportion and no one was making any sense.

"You are only to use your car to go to and from school," my father said. "And you are to come home each night for dinner."

"For how long?"

"Until we say."

"Fine."

Broken storm clouds scudded across the sky as I drove away from my parents' house, putting cherished miles between me and their constant distortions of reality. I loved the sound of the wheels along the road—the sound of movement. It occurred to me that I could just keep driving; they had overlooked this opportunity for escape when they gave me the car. But I wasn't brave enough; Lily was wrong about that. My words were more courageous than I could ever be.

20

Tell me a secret," I say to Beck, our footsteps marking the sand behind us and a pale orange sun moving down the sky. "Tell me something you wish for or dream about."

His arm tightens around my shoulders.

"I'm not sure you'd want to know any of my secrets. Tell me one of yours first."

"Okay." I pause and rummage through the possibilities. "I used to think that if I could find a high enough mountain, and if I could reach up at just the right moment when a star was falling, it would touch my fingertips and shoot magic into me. And then no one would ever be able to hurt me again." I look out at the water, at a wave rolling toward shore. "Silly, huh?"

"No—it's beautiful," Beck says. "How old were you?"

"Twenty-three."

He looks at me quickly, a split-second delay on his laughter.

"Seven or eight," I tell him. "Something like that. Young. So...your turn. Tell me a secret."

Gold light is playing across Beck's face; salt wind whispers through his hair.

"Sometimes I think I have too many secrets," he says.

"Tell me one."

"This novel I'm working on is changing me."

"That's not a secret," I say softly, as a wave splashes over our feet and leaves again.

"Probably not, but there are other secrets buried in it."

"There are times when I feel so far away from you, Beck. It's like I look around and wonder where you've gone—I hate that feeling."

We are in front of my house, facing the ocean, watching the sun drop, slick and orange, behind the sea.

"Come on," he says. "Let's go inside."

We go into the bedroom and Beck takes off my clothes slowly, like he did when we were first together and still exploring each other's bodies. His tongue travels down my neck, across my breasts, leaving a damp trail on my skin.

Our lovemaking is hungry, and there is a desperate edge to it that may be coming from him, or me, or both of us—I'm not sure. His eyes are open, looking at me; I feel the heat of his stare on my face. I have to close my eyes against it—I don't want sight right now. I want to sink into the feeling of him moving inside me; I want to disappear into it. But even through my closed lids, I can see his face above me, watching me when I come. Still inside me, he rolls me over on top of him and holds me tight, his heartbeat thundering in my ear.

My mouth moves up to his neck, travels to his ear. "I love fucking you," I whisper.

"It was fucking—not making love?" he asks, his voice worried.

"I didn't mean it in a bad way. I didn't mean it comparatively."

His arms pull in around me and his leg angles across the back of my thighs. As though he's afraid I'll move away.

"I'll tell you another secret," I say to him, propping myself on my elbow and staring down at him. "Then you'll owe me two in return."

"Tell me."

"When Lily tried to kill herself, there was a moment—afterward—when I thought she probably had the right idea. There was this part of me, deep inside, that was so tired—so tired of fighting. It looked like an easy way to surrender. But there was another part of me that thought, if I can stick it out, if I can make some sense of it, then someday wonderful things will happen to me."

His fingers rake my hair, pushing it off my face. "And have they?"

"Yeah, I think so. This feels pretty wonderful. A lot of what's between us is wonderful, and then there are the vacant parts."

"The parts when you look for me and I'm not there?" he asks.

"Yeah—those."

The stars are out by the time we get around to thinking about dinner. We fix sandwiches, open a bottle of wine, and go out to the deck. The air feels like autumn; the wind blowing off the ocean is light and cold.

"Why don't you ever tell me about the hospital?" I ask him. "Your draft-evasion hospital stay. That's a lot of what's feeding your novel, isn't it?"

"Uh-oh. We're back to the secrets again."

"Did you think I'd forget? You owe me, remember?"

There is a long pause and I know he's turning it over in his mind, weighing the costs. I wonder if somewhere a star is falling; I want Beck to reach up and let it graze his fingers so nothing will ever hurt him again.

"Okay," he says finally. "I guess it's probably something I should tell you about.

"They had the wards divided up according to type of disturbance, and degree. But the people who had voluntarily committed themselves, like I did, had grounds privileges and could walk around. There was one area cordoned off with chain-link fence where they put all the severely disturbed patients. I would look at these people sitting in the dirt, playing with themselves, screaming out things that weren't even words—it was like some horrible zoo.

"What frightened me the most was, after a while, I started to see that it wouldn't be that difficult to end up like that—like some subhuman creature pawing at the dirt and talking in tongues. Your mind starts to see possibilities that it didn't consider before. It gets frayed—you feel it unraveling, and every day becomes a struggle to stitch it back together to close up the holes.

"I was afraid, also, that even though I had committed myself, I might not get out. Paranoia started coming into it. What if I had entered this world, and the doors had closed behind me? How long would it take for madness to set in when there was madness all around, in varying degrees?

"The men on my ward weren't too bad. Most of them spent their time bumming cigarettes or stealing them from each other. Some would smoke them down so low that their fingers were permanently brown.

"There was this one guy on my ward—he said he'd been having acid flashbacks, so his family committed him. But he kept getting worse. I noticed they were dosing him with Thorazine three times a day, and the more they drugged him, the more he lost control of everything, even his bodily functions. Sometimes he'd shit in the shower room and the attendants would come in and yell at him and make him clean it up. It kept happening, you know? And one day I saw him in the shower room, walking around in circles naked, with shit all over him—just sobbing. He started acting out scenes from plays— his favorite was *Rosencrantz & Guildenstern Are Dead.* It was amazing—he had most of the play memorized.

"One night, he came over to my bed and started whispering it to me. I still remember part of that passage: 'You die a thousand casual deaths, with none of that intensity which squeezes out life, and no blood runs cold anywhere. Because even as you die, you know that you will come back in a different hat. But no one gets up after death. There is no applause—there is only silence—and some second-hand clothes. And that's death.' I was on Thorazine, too, although not as high a dose as he was on, so I didn't know at first if I was dreaming. But there he was, kneeling there in his pajamas, reciting this death speech to me, and I realized how badly he wanted to die, because he was never getting out of there and he knew it.

"They ended up transferring him to another ward. The next time I walked around the grounds, there he was behind the chain-link fence, pawing at the ground like an animal and crying. You want to hear something really bizarre? In some ways, he made more sense than anyone else in there. He just saw it all too clearly and it pushed him over the edge. I think of him a lot lately."

I move closer to Beck, slide my arm around him, but I feel other things breathing in the dark beside us, whispering memories and quotes about death. I want to be alone with him, but lately I feel like I never am; ghosts hang on trellises and call out his name. But then I have my own ghosts, so who am I to blame him?

It's past midnight, black and moonless, when Beck gasps and sits up in bed. His breathing sounds quick and frantic, like someone who has been badly frightened.

"Beck?"

"It's okay—just a dream. I was falling, and I had to stop. It was like falling down a tunnel."

He gets out of bed and grabs his robe.

"Where are you going?" I ask.

"I need to write some things down."

"Right now?"

"Yeah."

Through my sleep, I hear him typing in the other room, and feel him get back into bed sometime before dawn. When I wake up, he is still sleeping, but now he looks peaceful, far away from nightmares.

"I'm going to stay in bed for a while," he mumbles.

I kiss him on the forehead. "Okay."

His hands pull me back down and his leg slides over me, pulling me into him. "Don't get up yet."

"You were up late writing," I say, my cheek against his chest.

"Yeah—I had this dream, it was like I was dreaming my character's nightmare."

"Which was?"

He moves a little, pulling away to look at me. "This man is getting killed—beaten by the side of the road. I saw the road so clearly last night, as if I was there. The asphalt was cracked and there were tufts of weeds along the gravel shoulder. And I saw the man's face, his teeth stained with blood—he was getting hit again and again, with a piece of wood. I saw the fear on his face . . ." Beck stops talking and I see tears pooling in his eyes.

"Beck, who was hitting him?"

"I don't know," he says.

But I think he does.

21

My parents believed in lengthy punishments; they went for quantity, not quality. For the crime of shoving my mother, I was forbidden to use the car for the duration of the Christmas break, and for a month after that I could only use it to travel to and from school. But I was allowed to take walks, and that's how I spent my days—walking around the neighborhood, loitering around houses where I used to play, staring at trees I used to climb, brushing past childhood memories and feeling older than I'd ever thought I would.

I hiked in the hills behind our home, but the one spot I used to run to when I was a child had been taken over by a house. I felt like a wild animal, migrating to what was once familiar territory only to discover that strange invaders had transformed the landscape. The mountaintop had been mine once; I had buried treasures under rocks and had lain on my back watching clouds sail across the sky.

On Christmas morning, I joined Lily and my parents around the tree for the ritual of opening presents. Since I hadn't been allowed to drive, I'd been forced to go through my own things to come up with presents—earrings for Lily, and an art book for my parents.

Lily gave me a gold pen and pencil set; as I thanked her, I tried to read in her eyes the message behind the gift. Was she telling me to keep writing, to ignore our mother's wrath? But her eyes wouldn't answer me.

I unwrapped the large box from my parents, knowing it was clothes and dreading what I would find there. Underneath the tissue paper was a bright orange dress with short sleeves and a full, round skirt— a pumpkin dress.

"Thank you," I said softly, hesitantly, wishing suddenly that California hadn't outlawed incinerators.

"I want you to wear that today," my mother told me.

"I'd rather save it for—um—another time." I was trying to avoid the confrontation that was barreling toward me, but I knew it was hopeless. I was in its path, tied to the tracks.

"Carla, this was a very expensive dress," my mother said, growing larger as Lily and my father shrank into the distance. "I don't want you looking like a hippie today. I want you to wear that dress."

"So I can look like a pumpkin instead? I'm going for a walk—I'll be back later." I got up and walked away, but I should have known the argument would follow me.

I didn't make a clean getaway; my father cornered me in my room as I was putting on my shoes.

"Carla, let's not have a fight on Christmas," he said, a one-man peacekeeping force.

"I was trying not to."

"That's not how it looked to me. Now, your mother put a lot of effort into choosing that dress for you."

"On that point, I think we agree."

"She just wants you to look nice," he continued. "I don't know why you have to resist at every turn, why you have to make it so difficult for her. Do you know that she's been having difficulty breathing at night?"

"I'm sure this is going to come around to me somehow."

"Well, I'm afraid it is, Carla. It comes from being upset. Her throat closes up, her breathing passage gets blocked. It's terrifying to her, and to me. If one of these attacks lasts too long, I'll have to give her a tracheotomy. Do you know what that means?" He took a step toward me and pointed at my throat, his finger grazing my windpipe. "I'd have to make an incision here, and—"

I stepped back from his hand, his accusation, from the guilt I was feeling even though my mind argued there was no reason for guilt. "I think I know the mechanics of it. Father, don't you ever get tired of this? If I could have used the car, I'd have bought you a medical book for Christmas so you could look up some more ailments to blame me for."

He turned to leave and stopped in the doorway. "I should have known you'd revert to sarcasm."

Of course, I thought, what else do I have? The truth has no place in this family. A part of me knew I had to leave him with the lies; they were, in the end, easier for him to deal with than reality.

"I'll wear the dress, okay? Will that make everything all right for the moment?"

"It'll make your mother happy."

"Uh-huh."

I walked out the front door into sunshine and dry desert air, longing for the Christmases we'd left behind in New York. I wanted to lift my face to a cold, white sky and see my breath like a tiny cloud in front of me.

There was only a thin trail winding into the hills. Behind me, the city looked small and insignificant, the Pacific a blue mirage. I thought of not turning back, of vanishing into the parentless world of mountains and, when after more than an hour, I turned around and started back toward my parents' house, I hated myself for not having that much courage.

I endured the rest of the long day, sat on the sidelines in my pumpkin dress, feeling restless and angry at a life that seemed to be closing in around me, a world I wanted no part of. Guests arrived, expensive gifts were exchanged, and eggnog was served in silver cups. But all I could think of was running—to anywhere or anything that would feel different. If going to college meant living at home, I'd sacrifice college. I decided to quit at the end of the year—travel, join a circus, start a cult—anything that could be defined as changing my life.

When my punishment finally ended, I became adept at looking my mother in the eye and lying to her. I invented friends I was staying overnight with—safe, conservative girls. I even invented a sorority girl in whose room we gathered to drink tea and do homework.

The reality was, I was sleeping on the floor of Kyle Portman's tiny living room with a few other students from our creative writing class. Occasionally, other friends of Kyle's would drift in to get stoned and talk about poetry and music. We played Bob Dylan and Leonard Cohen albums and read aloud the poems of Lawrence Ferlinghetti and Gregory Corso.

Often our late-night conversations turned political. The Pentagon Papers had been published and Daniel Ellsberg had been indicted for unauthorized possession of secret documents.

"Ellsberg is probably the biggest hero in the whole fucking country," Kyle said. He encouraged us to politicize our writing.

"As writers, you have a responsibility to recognize the power of words and to use that power. Rilke said, 'I live not in dreams but in the contemplation of a reality which is, perhaps, the future.' Think of how you might affect the future with your writing."

And we, his loyal listeners, would nod and return later with poems and prose about Vietnam, or racism, or the oppression of women.

I noticed that Kyle loaned out his bedroom sometimes to hastily formed couples; he would join the rest of us, sprawled on the floor of his living room in sleeping bags or under blankets. Couples were interchangeable and no one seemed to mind. We were above emotions like jealousy or possessiveness. We were tough and open and free of the constraints of our parents' generation.

We wore beads and leather sandals and enjoyed the sideways looks we got as we walked past hair-sprayed girls in color-coordinated outfits and boys in letter sweaters. We were proud of ourselves for being the one group on campus with enough conscience to ignore football games and frat parties and dwell, instead, on the jungle war that was snatching up boys by the thousands and tossing them into a death pit. We laughed at the couples with pins and rings and other emblems of possession. We were beyond that. We shared our writing, our thoughts, our drugs, and ourselves, and we were addicted to our freedom.

I went home just enough to keep my story plausible. I didn't want to jeopardize my new life.

One night, a friend of Kyle's showed up—a quiet, bearded man with shoulder-length dark hair, carrying a duffel bag and a guitar.

"This is Dane," Kyle announced. "The wandering minstrel. I never quite know when he'll blow into town."

Dane sat quietly for most of the evening, taking joints that were passed to him, listening intently to whoever was talking or reading, but saying nothing himself.

When it got late and eyelids were starting to get heavy, Kyle said, "Dane, why don't you play us some tunes? Looking around at this group, I'd say lullaby music would be appropriate."

Only then did he speak to us. When he took out his guitar and started playing, the melodies that filtered through the room were like a strange, soft language. I watched his fingers move across the strings and looked at his face, partially hidden in shadow, and I imagined his hands, his mouth, on my skin. These were not generous feelings; I didn't want to see Dane disappear into Kyle's bedroom with anyone except me.

I slept that night in one of the sleeping bags Kyle always had lying around. If I had stretched out my arm, I would have touched Dane, lying on his back, head resting on his duffel bag, with a blanket pulled up to his neck. Looking at him sleeping, I wondered if his dreams were as gentle as his music.

The next morning, I woke up before anyone else. The day was overcast and pale, and it was cold in the apartment. I leaned over Dane and touched his face lightly.

"Hi, want to go get some breakfast?" I whispered when his eyes opened. In the dim light the night before, I hadn't noticed that his eyes were a pale shade of hazel, a color I'd never seen before.

"You don't have classes?" he asked.

"Nothing I can't skip. Dane, what do you put on your driver's license for color of eyes? They should invent a new color for what your eyes are."

"Hazel," he laughed, sliding out of the sleeping bag. "It was either that or a question mark."

Kyle was in the kitchen when we were on our way out.

"Taking Dane to class with you, Carla?" he asked.

"Actually, I was going to miss some classes this morning, but I'll show up for yours."

"Make sure you do."

We left Kyle's apartment and walked toward the coffee shop, past business-suited men and students hurrying to class. The morning sky was white and flat, and cars honked and inched down the street. I saw Dane looking around furtively, an unaccustomed visitor to a cement and asphalt world.

"Too much city for you?" I asked, as we approached the glass doors of the coffee shop.

"Yeah, it's always sort of overwhelming to me." His voice sounded apologetic, embarrassed that he'd been discovered.

Over omelets and coffee, I asked him questions, trying to figure out how he was able to drift around the country with a guitar and a duffel bag. My questions sounded like curiosity, but they hid another motive—I wanted a formula that would give me the same freedom Dane had.

"When I graduated from high school," he said in a voice so soft I had to lean in to hear him, "my uncle gave me some money and told me to take some time before I went to college—you know, kick around, see the country, figure out what I wanted to do."

"So... have you figured it out?"

"Yeah, I've figured out that I want to keep kicking around the country," he said, laughing softly. "It's probably not what my uncle had in mind."

"Where are you from?" I wanted to imagine him at some starting point, some place from which he had wandered.

"Bend, Oregon," he said. "It's like most small towns—a great place to grow up in, but suffocating if you stay. So I bought a used van and drove to New York. I got culture shock as soon as I entered Manhattan, but I had some friends there—Kyle was one—and I stayed around for a while, playing guitar in a couple of clubs in the Village. Then I started back across the country, went through the South, which is an interesting experience when you're driving a beat-up van and you look like I do. You start getting real nervous about guys with gun racks in their trucks and chewing tobacco in their cheeks."

"So what are you looking for, traveling around like you do?" I asked him.

"I just like the freedom. I always have to get back to the mountains, though. When I'm traveling across country that's flat and endless, I dream about the mountains at night."

"Your music doesn't have lyrics."

"No—I guess because I'm used to traveling alone and not talking too much. I just let the melodies speak for me."

I left him later that morning, sitting in Kyle's living room alone, playing guitar. I drove home to shower and change clothes. And to convince my mother that I had to spend another night studying at school.

"You need to study down there two nights in a row?" she asked, when I said I wouldn't be home that night.

"I have a test this week. It really helps to study with these other girls."

"In what subject?" she said, a little too absently. We were in the kitchen; she was arranging red and yellow roses in a cut glass vase, and wasn't looking at me, so I couldn't read whether or not there were danger signs in her eyes.

"History," I answered casually. "Not my best subject."

"What is your best subject?"

I was trying to inch my way toward the door, but her questions kept stopping me. "Excuse me?" I said.

"I haven't heard you mention what you plan to do with your life. What exactly are we paying for in terms of your education?" She looked up at me then, her eyes boring into me.

"Mother, this is a big subject, what I'm going to do with my life. Could we discuss it another time? I have to get back to campus."

I showered and changed clothes at record speed, trying to avoid any further interrogation. I didn't know how long Dane was going to be around, but my guess was that after a few days he would head for the mountains again. I wanted to spend as much time with him as I could, and that meant walking wide circles around my mother and her talent for detective work.

When I went back to Kyle's apartment that evening he and Dane were there alone, sitting on the couch talking.

"Sorry, am I interrupting?"

"No, not at all," Kyle said. "Actually, we were just talking about getting something to eat. Why don't I call and order a pizza and you two can go pick it up." He glanced at me as he walked to the phone and I understood from his look that he knew how I felt and it wasn't coincidence that he was sending us out on an errand together.

It was dark and a light rain was falling when we got into Dane's van. With the windshield wipers pushing drops across the glass, I studied his face as the white glow of streetlights misted through the rain. Something about his eyes always made me think his mind was somewhere else.

"How long are you going to stay in L.A.?" I asked him, feeling hesitant about interrupting whatever was going through his thoughts.

"I don't know. Not long, probably—a week is usually my limit."

Later that night, after Dane's music had lulled us into silence again and people were reaching for blankets and curling up with pillows, I unrolled a sleeping bag next to him, closer than I'd been the night before.

And sometime during the night, when the rain was falling harder and the street outside was quiet, when the room was dark except for a thin beam of light slanting through the curtains, our hands touched and held on until morning.

I was confused at how differently I felt toward Dane. I had been living with the same attitudes as the others who frequented Kyle's apartment and formed a tight band of idealists on a campus that was best known for its football team. Sex was not something we approached with reluctance, yet I hesitated whenever I thought of inviting Dane into Kyle's bedroom. The idea of making love with him was a frequent distraction. Entire decades would be discussed in my European history class while I was imagining the various ways my mouth could explore his body. I was enjoying the fantasy so much, I was almost afraid to make it real.

Two days passed and I could see a growing restlessness in Dane. It was Friday, and there was no story I could invent that would enable me to stay at Kyle's apartment through the weekend. I wouldn't have another chance to be with him until Monday, and I wasn't sure he'd stay around that long.

There was no one else lingering around the apartment that evening; the three of us went to a club near campus and listened to a group sing Dylan songs and bad renditions of Beatles material. We drank beer and tried to ignore them. In the red-light glow with the music burying my voice, I whispered to Kyle, "How do you feel about loaning out your bedroom tonight?"

"How does Dane feel about it?"

"I don't know—I haven't asked him yet."

Kyle laughed and leaned into my ear. "I was wondering when you'd get around to this."

When we got back to the apartment, Kyle took some of his class papers into the kitchen and left me alone with Dane in the living room.

He took his guitar out of the case and went over to the couch. I sat on the floor facing him, wondering how I was going to handle a moment I'd been thinking about for days.

"Dane?"

"Yeah?"

His fingers kept playing the strings; soft sounds filled the room, and I realized I had to speak in his language—a language of silence and harmony. I stood up and held out my hand; when he put down his guitar and took it, I led him into the bedroom.

We'd gone from lamplight into darkness, and I was grateful for the lack of visibility when I put my arms around his neck and kissed him. I was unsure of what his response would be, but his mouth told me I wasn't the only one who had been thinking of this.

"Let's lie down—you're making my knees weak," I whispered to him.

He was slow and unhurried in the way he undressed me, in the ways he touched me. It was as though long hours of traveling alone had taught him to explore each moment, to move at a slower pace. I could taste the city on his skin, but years of climbing to high cliffs were there, too, in the strength of his muscles.

I wanted more than just that night—more than the shivering of going slow, his whispers telling me not yet. I wanted to be part of the world he carried with him, that he spun into songs and long days alone.

22

Clouds still hung over us the afternoon Dane left; the sky hadn't shown itself for days. It was the type of weather I would always associate with him.

"I'll come back in two or three weeks," he said, sliding the door of his van shut. "I just need to recharge myself for a while. I'm going to go back to Oregon and see my family, and then go to Washington—to Mount Ranier. I'll call you along the way."

"I wish I could go with you."

"Maybe you'll decide you want to," he said, holding me against him, a cold wind stirring around us and the noise of traffic at our backs.

"Actually, I have decided. I'm quitting school at the end of the year. Will you take me with you then?"

"What are your parents going to say?"

"A lot, probably. Which is part of the point. But it's what I want to do. So will you?"

He squeezed the back of my neck and kissed me. "You got a deal."

Dane came back to Los Angeles a few times before the end of the school year; we looked at maps and marked off routes.

"I'd like to head into Canada," he said, his red pen marking the journey as it moved across the country. "Banff is supposed to be incredible—I've wanted to go there for a long time."

"Yeah—Canada has always been appealing to me."

"It has?"

"Uh-huh. It's a long story."

When Dane wasn't there, I would lie awake some nights, listening to footsteps on the sidewalk beneath the window, the sound of sirens screaming through the streets, and I would imagine Dane sleeping between mountains, listening to the call of coyotes, wild and defiant in the silvered dark. Two different worlds, and his was the one I wanted.

I waited until the end of May to tell my parents. I gave myself a specific night when I knew they would both be there. It seemed appropriate to bring it up at dinner, since that was when most of our confrontations took place. I began as the maid was clearing the dishes from the main course.

"I have something I want to tell you," I said. "An announcement of sorts."

Lily lowered her eyes, retreating from the first sign of danger. My parents waited, and I suddenly felt like a criminal, caught in the beam of a searchlight.

"I'm not going back to college next year."

"Oh? And what exactly do you think you'll do?" my mother snapped. "You don't expect to live here and have us support you as though you're still a child, do you?"

"Well, Rachel, we could give her some help until she decides—" My father's offer was severed, midsentence, by a look from my mother.

"I'm going to travel around with a friend—a guy I met recently. He's been traveling around the country in his van—hiking in the mountains and camping out. He's seen some of the really beautiful, untouched areas of this country, and I'm going to go with him."

My mother took a deep breath and let it out slowly. "We did not raise you and provide for you and educate you so that you could drive around in a van with some . . . park ranger." She slapped her hand on the table for emphasis and a fifty-dollar water goblet almost tipped over.

"Could we just get the basic facts straight, please? He's not a park ranger, he's—"

"That's true," my father interrupted. "If he were, he'd be employed, and my impression is that he's not."

I noticed the maid had not returned with dessert; I envisioned her hiding in the broom closet, waiting out the storm.

"I'm a little confused here," I said. "What's the most disturbing aspect of this to you? That I'm going to be with an unemployed person, that I'm traveling in a van, or that I'm dropping out of college? Surely my absence from this household is not going to cause anyone to go into mourning."

"Everything," my mother snapped. "I'm almost afraid to ask what your sleeping arrangements are going to be."

"Well, since both of us are unemployed, we can only afford one sleeping bag, so you figure it out."

"Carla, can we dispense with the sarcasm?" my father said.

"Sure, but do you think we could have some logic here? I expected you to be upset about me dropping out of college and traveling around, but we seem to have gotten sidetracked onto whether or not my traveling companion has a job. Either this is irrelevant, or I'm missing something."

The maid finally appeared, looking like she'd rather be facing a camp of armed terrorists, and served fresh raspberries in small crystal bowls. An uneasy truce greeted her arrival and remained until she was back in the kitchen, presumably out of earshot.

"I suppose there's nothing we can say to change your mind," my father said.

"I can't think of a thing. It's what I want to do with my life right now."

My mother laughed, and it was a sound that sent me shuddering back through time to a small girl who heard that laughter as a storm-warning that violent winds were headed her way.

"I'm going to finish college and maybe go to graduate school," Lily said softly. I had almost forgotten she was there, and at that moment I wished she weren't.

A few days before I left, my father handed me a check for fifteen thousand dollars.

"This is between you and me," he said. "Your mother doesn't have to know about it."

"Thanks—I'm sorry if I'm letting you down. But I guess I've never been too good at being what you wanted."

He looked as though he were going to answer me, but I waited and he said nothing. In that moment, I suddenly understood that he had never known what to say to me.

On the Friday that Dane and I left, I called a cab to pick me up at my parents' house and take me to Kyle's apartment so we could leave from there.

"Why doesn't your friend come here to get you?" Lily asked, watching me carry my things into the hallway.

"I was afraid he'd get chained to the dinner table and interrogated about why he doesn't have a job."

I heard the cab coming up the driveway and I turned quickly and hugged my sister, squeezing her between my arms as though, in that one fierce gesture, I could communicate all the love and sorrow and anger I had ever felt toward her.

I had wanted to take the coast route, but Dane wanted to go to King's Canyon; we compromised and drove up the coast to Santa Barbara before turning inland. Once we left the ocean, the heat was heavy and relentless. We drove past orange groves and stopped at a roadside stand for bags of oranges. At night, we sat under the stars with bread and fruit and wine, the sound of Dane's guitar serenading us in the warm darkness.

One night, after we had fallen asleep, our bodies wound around each other in sleeping bags we had zipped together, the wind came up, scraping across us and covering us with dust. We got up and moved into the back of the van, laughing as gusts attacked our bare skin.

"See, it's never boring," Dane said, closing the door on a rush of dust. We slid into our sleeping bags, and wind rocked the van, making it feel like a train being jostled along the tracks.

"I'm glad you're here," he whispered, his hand finding me in the dark. "I'm glad you came with me."

He was already hard when I moved on top of him. "I always want to be with you like this," I told him, and I didn't wait for his kisses, for the soft stroking of his hand along my spine. I pulled him into me as the wind screamed outside and rattled the sides of the van.

Long after I thought he was asleep, he started talking to me. Beneath the howl of winds, his voice was soft as ash.

"I love this so much, being out here with the wind blowing like this. I feel like it's the most cleansing thing in the world. I go crazy when I'm in the city too long, you know? It's like being addicted to something."

"A mountain addict," I said.

"Right. I know when I die, it's going to be in the mountains, as close to the sky as I can get."

The night before we got to King's Canyon, we slept near the Kern River in a grove of trees. A clear, full moon hung in the branches, its light splintering down on our faces. In one of the trees above us, an owl sat calling into the darkness.

"That's good luck," Dane said.

"What is?"

"The owl. It's a message of luck when he stays near you, calling out like that."

I would wonder later how the owl and the moon and everything that felt so perfect under that clear, dark sky could let us down. But that night, with the weight of Dane's body next to me, the river flowing along the course it had carved over centuries, and the pearl-soft moon bending over us, I thought our lives would always be that good.

A steep road took us above the river into the green world of King's Canyon. Black granite mountains towered above us, and Dane was like an animal returned to its habitat after months of captivity. Clouds were moving into the sky and the weather had turned colder.

"Dane, it's already two o'clock. Maybe we should get a campsite before you go scrambling up some mountain—which I know is the only thing on your mind right now."

"We'll have time."

He pulled off to the side of the road and got out of the van. I followed him to the foot of a dark mountain and watched his eyes scan the jagged face, which, at the top, was already obscured by clouds.

"Let's go up this one."

"Dane, it's going to start raining any minute. And you don't even know if this is a trail that people are supposed to take. We should at least look at a map first."

He was so enraptured, he was making me nervous.

"It'll be fine—we'll just go partway up," he said.

We locked the van and started up the face of the mountain. Dane was like a mountain goat, and I wondered if he even remembered that I was behind him. I yelled to him at one point to slow down and wait for me; he let me catch up, but within minutes, he was ahead of me again. I had to concentrate on the jagged rocks so I wouldn't slip, but when I stopped to look down, I saw tiny lakes far below and a wide green meadow in the distance.

The rain began like a mist, drifting over my back and coating the rocks. My foot slipped, and in that second I saw the danger we could be in.

"Dane, it's raining!" My voice bounced off the rocks and sounded thin in the high, damp air.

He turned around and worked his way down to where I was standing. "You can go back down if you want and wait for me at the bottom," he said. "I just want to go a little higher."

"Dane, please, it's getting slippery. It's cold and you don't have a jacket on. Look, this is really a bad idea. Let's go back down and we can do it tomorrow if it's not raining."

I knew, even as I talked, that I wasn't going to be able to coax him down. The rain was still a mist, but the sky was as dark as the mountain.

"Please don't go up too much higher," I said.

"I'll be fine. Here are the keys to the van. I'll be down in a little while—don't worry."

I watched his back as he climbed up the steep rocks, and I wished an owl were hovering nearby, carrying prayers and luck on its wings.

I slipped once on the way down and cut my hand on a jagged piece of rock, but I was so intent on getting to the bottom that I didn't feel it until blood started running down my fingers.

When I got down, I looked back up the mountain and Dane was a tiny figure, heading for the clouds. It was raining harder. I went to the van, got a poncho and binoculars, and went back to the foot of the mountain. As I put the glasses to my eyes I wanted to see Dane coming down the rocks; I prayed for his image to look large and close and safe. But I saw him climbing higher; his head was almost inside the cloud that was hugging the top of the mountain.

I waited for hours until daylight was fading and the rain was coming down hard. I had thought that Dane might have gone around to the other side of the mountain, and that any minute he would come up behind me, smiling and drenched with rain. But every time I thought I heard footsteps behind me, I would turn and see nothing; it was only the cold drumming of rain behind me.

I had to get help, but if Dane did come down, I wanted to be there.

I ran to the van and drove to the main road, planning to flag down the first car I saw. When headlights appeared, I pulled over and ran almost into the path of an oncoming truck.

"I need help," I said to the man. "My friend is in trouble—he's up that mountain. Can you get someone? I don't want to leave for too long in case he makes it down."

"Okay, I'll go find someone with a C.B. and have them radio the rangers."

I pointed out the mountain that had swallowed Dane in its cover of clouds and showed him where I would be. I had to trust that this stranger would return with help...and I had to wait.

Almost thirty minutes passed before he came back, followed by two ranger trucks. The rain had let up, but clouds still hid the sky; I looked desperately for a cluster of stars to signal the end of the storm, but none appeared.

"How long has he been up there?" one of the rangers asked.

"Since this afternoon. I couldn't see him anymore, he climbed so high. He disappeared into the clouds."

He stared up at the mountain and at the thick black sky.

"We have some search and rescue guys here," he said, "but I don't know how far they can go in the dark when it's wet like this. And I think sending a helicopter up is impossible in this weather. I can radio them, though."

He went back to his truck. I stood listening to the new silence that had fallen over the canyon, the settling of cold night air. It was so quiet in that moment that I heard my own heartbeat, but then I heard something else.

Through the black air, the thin echo of a man's voice traveled down the cliff and stabbed me. I held my breath and listened again. It was a scream spiraling down the rocks.

"I heard him—I heard him screaming!" I yelled, running over to the ranger's truck.

He walked back with me, and we stood looking up, as though Dane would follow his voice, appear on the side of the mountain. The scream came again—a faint, low call from somewhere inside the clouds.

"He's way the hell up there," the ranger said. "Look, I have to tell you—we can't send a helicopter up tonight in this weather. We'll have to wait until tomorrow and see how it looks. I can let some of the guys go up part of the way, but it's dark and it's slippery—I can't ask them to risk their lives."

I started crying—warm tears that turned cold on my face. Beneath that, there was a shivering in my muscles that had nothing to do with tears or the cold.

"He's going to die, isn't he?"

The ranger put his arm around my shoulders and said nothing.

"He knew he would die in the mountains," I said. "He told me that. But I don't want him to go like this—alone up there—frightened."

His arm tightened. "What's your name?"

"Carla."

"Carla, I'm Steve. Why don't you sit in the cab of the truck and we'll turn the heater on for you. It's going to be a long night. We're going to do everything we can, but you have to understand that we're limited in the dark with this weather."

Sometime during the night, I fell asleep, and in my dream, I saw Dane sitting in a grassy meadow playing his guitar. He was smiling and his eyes were closed—lost in his music, like I'd seen him so many times. Behind him, a dark gray mountain was bending over him as if it were going to topple and bury him.

At dawn, the sky was still gray, but the clouds were higher. Steve said the helicopter could go up and try to pinpoint where Dane was.

The news came back that he must have fallen from high up on the mountain to a ledge below. The problem was, he was between two mountains then, and the space was too narrow for the helicopter to get close enough and drop a rope.

His screams were getting fainter and less frequent. By afternoon, the search and rescue team had found no way to get to him by climbing; the rock above and below was smooth and vertical.

"The only way we're going to get him is if the helicopter can drop a longer line than the one we have," Steve said. "But we're going to have to get one somewhere."

It was starting to rain again, a light, gentle rain. I felt numb; I couldn't cry anymore, and I couldn't hope. I'd heard two of the men mention hypothermia and I wondered if Dane would survive even if they were able to rescue him.

Just before dark moved in, we heard another scream, but this one was moving closer to us, falling from the sky in a long arc of sound.

Then it ended—so softly. It just slid into the air and suddenly there was nothing but silence. No one said anything; even the rain seemed to stop.

In that moment, before the ache carved out its place in me, I thought how perfect the silence was and how Dane would have smiled at the canyon holding its breath and the rain drifting away like a whisper, and the mountains standing mute and timeless—witnesses to his death.

23

I called Kyle from King's Canyon and told him what had happened. I didn't know how to contact Dane's parents; it was a task I left to Kyle.

The task left to me was identifying Dane's body. Steve drove me to the ranger station, and I wondered why I wasn't more frightened at seeing his body. It was as though I had already seen it a thousand times during the hours when I stood in the rain listening to his screams. Death was already standing behind him, and I had seen them both balanced on that slippery ledge.

"This isn't going to be easy," Steve said as he led me into the station. "You can just stand across the room and basically identify the clothes, all right?"

"It's that bad?"

"Yes."

Black plastic was unzipped and I felt Steve's hand gripping my arm. "Just look at the clothes quickly," he said.

I glanced up and saw Dane's work shirt and jeans, covered with blood and sagging where his body was shattered inside them. I avoided looking at his face, but it registered, on the edge of my field of vision, that there wasn't one.

"Yes," I said, and turned away.

I moved toward the door, and the wind outside suddenly sounded like music.

"His hands," I said, turning back again. "I need to see if his hands got broken."

Steve grabbed my arm. "Carla...I don't want you to look again. Come on, let's get out of here."

"But I need to know."

"He fell a long way, Carla."

We were standing outside under a sky that had only a few clouds left in it.

"For whatever it's worth," Steve said, "he probably wasn't even aware of what was going on toward the end because of hypothermia. He might even have passed out before he fell. I just wanted you to know that, in all likelihood, he didn't suffer for too long."

"Thanks."

"Are you going to be okay? I don't like the idea of you driving back alone."

"I need to be alone. It'll help me be okay," I told him.

I put Dane's guitar among our clothes in the back of the van; each time I looked back at it, sweet melodies leaked out of the wood and strings. I took the shortest route back to Los Angeles, only stopping when I needed to. Memories were chasing me down the highway.

I got in on a Wednesday, feeling like I'd been away for a long time. The buildings looked dirtier and more imposing, the streets more littered, and the summer air hung like a cloud of brown smoke. I found the key to Kyle's apartment under the mat and let myself in, walking into a room of stifling heat and shadows. Kyle hadn't lifted the shades when he left that morning to teach his summer classes, and the room had simmered for hours in the half-dark heat. I raised the shades, opened all the windows, and turned on a fan.

I could see Dane, leaning in the doorway to the kitchen, steam from a coffee cup curling around his hand, or sitting on the couch where yellow sunlight was baking the dark leather. I let myself cry then, washed away the images with tears.

Kyle found me asleep on the couch when he got back; I didn't even remember lying down. He held me for a long time without saying anything—just letting me cry—and when I looked at his face, it was streaked with his own tears.

"It hurts so much," I said to him, knowing I didn't need to but wanting to put words to the pain. "It's like my whole heart is hurting—there's no room for anything else."

Kyle dried his face with the palm of his hand and then brushed his thumb across my cheek. "I know. We just have to go through it. I held it together until after I talked to his parents, and then I fell apart. They don't have any other kids..."

"I should have made him come down, Kyle. I shouldn't have let him keep going like that. He'd still be alive."

He took off his glasses and rubbed his eyes, shaking his head slowly. "Don't do that to yourself. What could you have done— thrown him across your shoulders and carried him down? Because that's what it would have taken. It was an accident, Carla. He made a bad call, and there was nothing you could have done to stop him."

I slept that night with city noises coming through the walls and windows—footsteps, the hum of power lines, the stop and start of traffic. No owls visited this darkness, where lights crossed out the stars and the moon dangled unseen behind skyscrapers. I knew the city nights would never feel the same to me, because Dane had left me with a piece of his world, where nights are laced with silver and the wind tells stories.

I forced myself, the next day, to drive to my parents' house—to tell them I was back, to tell them why, and to tell them I wouldn't be staying there.

At the door, the maid started to tell me where in the house my mother could be found, but her footsteps came down the hall—high-heeled and determined.

"Carla—" she said, surprised. "I thought you were camping out somewhere."

"I had to come back early—I—" The words wouldn't come, not in front of my mother's cold stare. "Can I see Father for a minute?"

"He's in the study," she said, turning away and clicking back down the hall.

My father looked up from his desk when I walked in.

"Dane died," I said, before he could ask why I was there. I wanted to show him my wound right away so he wouldn't rub salt in it.

He hesitated, watching me—waiting for tears to fall, probably— not realizing that I didn't cry within the walls of his house.

"Sit down," he said finally. "What happened?"

"He fell. We were hiking, and he went up too high, and... they couldn't get to him in time."

"I'm sorry," he said awkwardly, not knowing how to respond, not able to reach out and offer comfort. But the blue of his eyes darkened with emotion, and I took comfort in that.

"I just wanted you to know I was back. I'm not going to be staying here, though. I don't really know what I'm going to do. Right now, I—"

"I would say getting a job might be a good idea," my mother's voice intruded from behind me. I turned and saw her standing in the doorway. I hadn't heard her approach.

I glanced at my father; he had given me money without her knowing it and I was bound by secrecy. "Right. Maybe I could go to work at Newberry's or something."

"Well, I'm sure you think something like that would be beneath you," my mother answered, moving into the room, her footsteps drawing the boundaries of another battlefield. "A salesgirl is not a bad job to have."

"You'd like that, wouldn't you, Mother? Because all the time I would spend selling hairspray and Keds and bubble gum, I wouldn't be writing."

"Carla," my father interjected, "don't talk to your mother like that. I realize you're upset, but—"

"Do you? I wonder, because the only things that seem to matter in this family are the things that involve the two of you. I just watched my friend fall to his death, I stood in a park ranger's office and watched while they unzipped the body bag. And all Mother is concerned about is how I'm going to make enough money so I won't have to take any from you. It's a strange set of priorities you have around here. I guess I should be used to it, but then I'd worry about myself if I were."

My father opened his mouth to say something, but I didn't give him a chance. I was on my way to the door, to the driveway, to the road— someplace where I could cry without their seeing me.

24

For a week I stayed at Kyle's, sleeping most of the time, until something in my body tugged at me. I checked the calendar, counted days, tried to figure out how late I was. But I'd lost track of time; the only thing I was certain of was that I was late.

I went to the campus infirmary for a blood test and, when I called later that day, I got the answer I already knew.

"Would you like to see a counselor?" the voice on the other end of the line asked.

"No, I—uh—I don't need a counselor. Thanks anyway."

I hung up and thought about the anonymity of the phone. I was a name on her patient list, and she was just a voice on the other end of a line that ran across streets and neighborhoods, crackling with messages that might or might not change someone's life.

The late afternoon sun had moved behind a building, softening the light in Kyle's living room. I sat on the couch thinking about the tiny life inside me, growing in my womb. I stared at the shadows moving across the wall, followed them as they slid toward the floor.

Dane's child—I could see him as if he were already born—the same pale, hazel eyes, the same smile snagged at some halfway point, as though he might take it back before it could break through completely. A child of stars and mountain winds. I could see his face tilted to the sky, to the rain, to the flight of birds who'd been born with the wings he wanted.

I could see the child, but I couldn't fit myself into the picture. If I tried to place myself beside him, I could only see my own mother, and I had to push her away—for his sake. I had to protect him from the glare of her eyes and the confusion of her seasonal moods. He was young and open, and her words would cut across his softest places.

There had been moments in my life when I'd started to speak and had heard my mother's voice instead of my own, when my eyes had suddenly felt cold and sharp, making me run from my own reflection. Those moments were infrequent and fleeting, but I was afraid that they were telling me something about a hidden part of my personality, a part that could rise up and wound a child, if I ever let a child get that near.

The breeze had turned silky and the light was fading around me. A key clicked in the lock and footsteps followed the sound.

"Carla, are you okay?" Kyle said.

"I'm pregnant."

He sat down on the couch beside me and put his arm around my shoulders.

"I can't have it, Kyle." My voice was a dull monotone in the gray-blue room. "I can't have this baby. I don't think I can have anyone's baby. I don't want history to repeat itself—particularly not my history."

"You're not condemned to that, you know. This is not an immutable law," he said gently.

"But the risk is there. And it's a big risk. My only example of motherhood hardly qualifies as a healthy one." I wanted him to understand why Dane's child was never going to be born.

"You're going to have an abortion?" he asked after several minutes.

"Yes."

"Maybe I can help. If you don't want to deal with the risk of an illegal abortion, there is another way," he said, getting up to switch on a lamp.

"Forget it, Kyle. I'm not into coat hangers."

"There are herbs that will do it."

"And you just happen to have some lying around, huh? Jesus, Kyle, this is a side of you I didn't know about. I thought you were just into writing. You're moonlighting as an herbalist?"

"Carla, I'm glad everything that's happened hasn't diminished your acidic sense of humor," he said. "I'd have worried a lot more about you if it had. There's an Indian who lives up in Topanga Canyon—he helped someone else I know. If you're interested, we can take a drive up there, and if you're uncomfortable with it, I'm sure we can find someone willing to do the job with sharp instruments."

In the thick heat of that Saturday morning, we braved the traffic on the Coast Highway, and then turned inland at Topanga. The hills were dry and brown and a beige cliff of jutting boulders leaned over the winding mountain road. My stomach felt queasy on some of the curves—a reminder of why we were taking this drive in the first place. As we climbed higher, the air started to smell like summer-baked earth; despite my queasiness, it was a relief to be out of the gray cement city and the ever-present stench of buses and cars idling bumper-to-bumper on melting asphalt.

"It's sort of an appropriate place to end this, isn't it?" I asked Kyle.

"I'm not sure I understand—"

"I mean, Dane would have liked it here—the mountains, the creek, the trees. It doesn't seem like as much of a betrayal."

Kyle turned left at a sign marked Old Topanga. "Carla, you can change your mind, you know."

"No, I can't. Please understand—it's even more important because it's Dane's baby. If I fucked it up, Kyle—and it's a pretty good bet that I would—I couldn't live with myself."

"Okay. I just want you to be sure," he said.

Trees canopied the two-lane road and, on the left, along the creek, small houses were perched precariously on the banks, rickety wooden bridges connecting them to the road. We turned right onto a dirt driveway, gold dust billowing up around us. There was a corral with a tired-looking horse in it and several cars in various stages of dismemberment. I couldn't see any house.

"So where does this guy live? In the trees?" I asked Kyle.

"Close—the house is hidden behind those trees on the hill."

A dirt path led up to a tiny wooden house. The door stood open and we walked in to a cluttered space that was both living room and kitchen. Three men were sitting around a wood-stove that substituted for a table. One of them had gray-white hair tied back in a ponytail, and I hoped that he was the one we were there to see, because the other two looked like they were in their twenties. Age and wisdom were suddenly prerequisites if I was going to go through with this. The two younger Indians got up and left the room, and we were motioned over to the chairs they had vacated.

"Henry, this is Carla," Kyle said, and my peripheral vision saw him retreat after this introduction. He had brought me here, put me on a raft, and pushed me out into a wide river. He would stand on the banks and wait for me to choose my course.

Henry was fixing me with a deep brown stare that was making me nervous. He was uncovering things inside of me; I felt tears streaming from places I thought had been mended, pain tumbling out in front of him. I tried turning my eyes from his, but they pulled me back, as though they hadn't finished studying me, as though there was more they needed to see.

"So, you don't want a baby?" he said finally in a deep voice that floated through the small room with the air barely moving and the day so quiet I could hear the horses pawing the ground in the corral down below.

"No—no, I don't. I just can't," I said, words piling up behind those few, wanting to be spoken. But I wasn't sure how much I should tell him. I glanced at Kyle, but he was far away and I was in the middle of the river.

"And the father?" Henry asked.

"He's dead."

His eyes hadn't left my face; I wasn't even sure if he had blinked. My cheeks felt flushed and hot, and sweat was running down my sides.

"Would you want the baby if he hadn't died?"

"I don't know. It doesn't really matter, does it? He's dead."

"It's something you should ask yourself, I think," he said in a low voice. "Babies are important, and I have the feeling you've thought beyond this one occasion."

He got up and walked over to the stove. A blue flame licked the bottom of the teakettle as he took three plastic bags filled with herbs from a drawer.

I studied his back as he spooned the herbs into a cup and returned the bags to their hiding place. I was trying to determine his age, but his body held contradictions; his back was wide and strong, but his legs and hips were thin, as though the muscle had shrunk with time. His jeans hung loose, held up by a leather belt with a large turquoise and silver buckle. When the water boiled, he poured it over the herbs and stirred it slowly before pouring the potion through a strainer into another cup. This is what he brought to me, steaming and smelling of mint and other plants I couldn't identify.

"Let it cool a little," he said, "but not too much. It will be better if you drink it hot."

The taste was so bitter it made me grimace.

"Just drink," Henry told me. "It's supposed to be bitter." I wasn't sure if he was talking about the tea or the reason I was drinking it.

I got it all down, fighting waves of nausea, and when I finished, Henry said, "You should go home now and lie down. Rest as long as you need to. There will be some pain."

The pain didn't wait until we got back to the apartment. It began on the Santa Monica Freeway, with the Pacific Ocean far behind us and, up ahead, downtown a smog-coated mirage.

"Kyle, it's starting to hurt," I said, as cramps gripped my uterus and sent pain traveling along the nerve paths of my legs.

"Hang in there—we'll be home soon."

I felt something damp between my legs and I knew I was starting to bleed.

By the time we pulled up to Kyle's apartment, I was dizzy with the pain. I ran into the bathroom and watched as thick blood poured out of me into the toilet. The tears I had swallowed earlier came up to remind me that somewhere in that red mass was a tiny part of Dane, and this time I didn't fight their message; I let it choke me and spill out of my eyes onto the bare skin of my thighs as I sat doubled over with cramps.

Kyle put me to bed and sat beside me for a few minutes holding my hand.

"I guess it was better this way," I told him. "The other would have been worse."

"Probably," he said. "But it's not easy any way you do it. I'm sorry, Carla."

I drifted into sleep as if bouncing over rocks in fast-moving water. But I landed in the soft fleece of a childhood memory. My mother and I were in the snow in Central Park. I was barely four, small and padded with baby fat, zipped into a red snowsuit. I had not become her enemy yet. That would come later, when years shaped me into a girl and she saw before her a replica of the youth she could never recapture. As my breasts grew and my shape changed from straight lines to curves, my mother would feel time bending its orbit to suit me. We were planets changing places in a galaxy over which she had no power. She would never forgive me for becoming the mirror of her aging.

But on that day, with snow glistening around us, I was still innocent—years away from blame. We built a snowman the same height as me; my mother found stones for his eyes and nose and she broke a twig into small pieces, forming them into a gentle smile on his full-moon face.

"He'll melt, won't he?" I asked, anticipating sadness down the road. "When the sun comes out, he'll be gone."

"But it won't matter," my mother told me, "because you'll always have him in your memory."

I woke up and realized that the cramping had eased and had been replaced by a thick, dull ache. I looked at the dream as it was moving away, becoming dimmer. I have a lot of things in my memory, Mother, I thought—I remember how your face looked then, when I was small—before your eyes pushed me away and your words aimed arrows at me.

25

October has brought the Santa Ana winds; hot gusts blow through the house and the air smells like brushfires even though there haven't been any yet. It's a bad month for me. I glance over my shoulder, thinking I hear girls' voices calling to me, teasing me, feeling again their hands pulling off my clothes as I lie on the hard ground staring up at a Halloween moon. During the day, I scan the hillsides across the highway, on the alert for plumes of smoke, wondering if this will be the year that flames will spill down, jump the highway, and incinerate Malibu. It's not improbable, it's happened before, although not in my section of Malibu.

I hear Beck come through the front door, and something in the way he closes it tells me to brace myself.

"That fucking asshole got his whole nose redone and now I'm supposed to pay for it," he says as he strides into the living room where I'm proofreading some pages I've just finished.

"I assume we're talking about the man you hit? What was he supposed to do? Leave it the way your fist rearranged it?"

"They could have just set it. Some tape and a Popsicle stick would have done it. Jesus, some doctor on duty in the emergency room could have done it." He was pacing up and down the floor, and between his anger and the dry wind crackling with the threat of fire, my patience was running low.

"Beck, unless you have a medical degree that I don't know about,

167

you have no idea what damage you caused or what kind of treatment he needed. Why don't you count your blessings? The guy's not taking you to court—he's trying to settle this between your two lawyers. There's a lesson in this situation and I don't think you're getting it."

"Oh, and what's that, Carla?" he said. "Enlighten me."

"That maybe you should tie your fucking hands behind your back until you can learn to control them. You can type with your toes in the meantime."

I leave him still pacing the floor and go down to the beach. I'm not sure if I'm trying to walk off my own anger or the residue of Beck's, but I'm determined to walk until I lose one or the other. Tully doesn't care why we're walking as long as there are birds to chase and waves to run through... I envy his contentment.

We walk down to the Malibu Pier and then turn back as the sun moves down, oily and orange, into the haze of smog that desert winds have blown out to sea. I look inland at the beige and gold hills—dust and dry brush thirsty for rain.

I am halfway to the house when I see Beck coming toward me, jogging along the tide line, his jeans wet up to his knees.

"I'm sorry," he says when he catches up to me, his breath coming hard and his face shiny with sweat.

I put my arms around his neck and press my forehead against his shoulder. "Okay—I guess I'm a little short-tempered today, too."

Tully brings Beck a plastic bottle and drops it at his feet, waiting for him to throw it.

"Why don't you buy this dog some toys so he doesn't have to play with garbage," he says, tossing the bottle up onto the sand and laughing as Tully scrambles after it. "On the other hand, it's a pretty good way to clean up the beach."

We go out to dinner and sit across candle flames and glasses of wine, and everything Beck does feels like an apology. We are hesitant and polite with each other—almost unfamiliar—and I can hear doubts and unresolved questions whistling between us.

The hesitancy is still there when we get into bed and Beck rolls over and touches me as though I'm new to him, as though he doesn't know what I like and what I want from his body. His hands are quick, reluctant to stay on any part of me, and even his body feels lighter—suspended on air. The night is so warm, I have left the sliding doors open and it's as if the wind has room to blow between us, even though our bodies seem to be pressed together. When Beck comes he still feels like he's apart from me—holding back—and then he's gone, turning away to his side of the bed, his breath already changing rhythm, lulling him to sleep.

I lie still, listening to the crashing of the surf and Beck's slow descent into sleep. Red numbers on the digital clock flick time away, but the passage of minutes does nothing to ease my restlessness.

It's familiar, this feeling of aloneness, even with someone else close by. I let Beck move away from me because I'm used to it that way. Thinking back over my life, I realize that I've always seen it as a solitary journey—a passage that, at moments, might brush the borders of someone else's life, but will continue on its way, separate, comfortable in its isolation. When someone like Dane inhabited my life and took away some of that solitude, I was surprised, as if I'd received an unexpected gift.

Beck is lying on his side, hugging the edge of the bed, tempting gravity to topple him to the floor. I peel the sheet back and open my legs to the wind that's streaming in through the doors, let it fill the space between my thighs. My hand finds its way through the wind, and my breath catches, as if Beck had not been there less than an hour before—as if no one had touched me there in months. I put my arm across my mouth to silence my breath and deaden the sounds that want to escape from my throat. As my hand moves faster, I bite into the flesh of my arm, the sound of Beck's breathing moving farther away as I'm reeled into a world of my own.

There is only the weight of darkness on top of me and the wind churning between my legs. The orgasm that rocks my body takes me oceans away from where Beck lies balanced on the side of the bed in blind sleep.

I take my arm away from my face and the wind brushes my mouth. Mingled with the smell of the sea is another scent, different from the one Beck and I leave in the bed after our bodies pull apart. It is lighter, sweeter, and it hurries out the door on the next gust of wind.

26

It hasn't rained in so long, the animals are starting to come down from the hills in search of water. A few blocks from my mother's house, I see a coyote loping past a tall hedge that conceals a white-pillared mansion from the street. It's one o'clock in the afternoon, but he's so thirsty he hasn't even waited for nightfall. I'm tempted to trespass on someone's property and turn on a hose, just so he'll vacate this wealthy neighborhood. On the other hand, I like the incongruity of it. I imagine his paw prints denting manicured lawns, his eyes peering through shrubs at people walking poodles in sweaters.

Lily opens the door, looking older than her years, severe in a straight linen dress, her hair pinned back from her face. The temperature inside is only slightly warmer than that of a walk-in freezer.

"Did the thermostat get stuck or are you keeping ice cream in the living room?" I ask, putting my purse on the antique bench that's always occupied a decorative, nonfunctional place by the front door.

"Careful not to scratch that, Carla," my mother used to say whenever I ran through the entryway. "It's valuable."

I sat on it once, just to try and understand the reason for its placement. My feet didn't quite reach the floor and I sat forward, realizing that if anyone opened the door, they would bash into my legs.

Lily and I go into the den where our mother's wheelchair is placed in its usual spot, facing the window so she can watch the day drift by.

"We turned up the air-conditioning because Mother was too warm," Lily says, following behind me.

"How can you tell?"

"Because I spend time with her, Carla. I know what's going on with her—intuitively, I know," Lily answers, tilting her chin up the same way our mother used to do when she wanted to make it clear she would tolerate no dissension. It's her emphasis on the word *I* that triggers my response.

"Lily, I spend time with her, too. I'm here every week. Why do you make it sound like you're alone here all the time?" I ask my sister, hating it that she has managed to put me on the defensive.

"But sometimes I wonder why you come here, Carla. It's as if you have your own agenda. You're watching and waiting for something that will benefit you instead of being here out of love and a desire to be supportive. I guess I shouldn't be surprised—you've never been terribly concerned with how you were affecting this family. You just insisted on rebelling at every opportunity."

What about the effect your suicide attempt had on this family, I want to say but, as usual, don't. I try to observe a code of silence when it comes to my sister's damaged veins.

Lily is on a roll now, our mother's vacant stare stretching like a wasteland between us. "Remember that summer when you came back from high school, after you'd tried to run away? Mother was so distraught—and embarrassed—with you flouncing around the house looking like a slut." She spits out the last word like something bitter in her mouth.

It was the summer after my parents had escorted me back from Tipton, my escape plans ruined, my anger on the rise.

It was the summer I stopped wearing underwear. I didn't just stop wearing a bra—everyone was doing that—I stopped wearing all underwear, taking immense pleasure in the look of horror that crossed my mother's face. I would pass her in the house, the outline of my breasts visible through thin cotton tops or T-shirts. I also refused to shave under my arms, prompting her to banish me to my room if guests were expected.

All I could think about was where I wanted to be—in Canada with Eric—and I was furious that I was in my parents' house instead. I wanted to be touching him, making love with him—I'd torture myself thinking about it. And I would walk past my mother, feeling the wind under my loose, Indian-print skirt, brushing me like a lover's fingertips, and I'd smile at this secret arousal.

Or I'd sit across from her in Salvation Army jeans, the denim coarse and rough against my crotch, and I'd think, "See, you didn't win. I turned into a woman despite your best efforts to scare me away from it. I'm sitting here in front of you thinking about fucking and you have no idea." In those moments, my anger moved over to accommodate a feeling of victory.

I stop remembering and return to Lily. "How do you know what went on that summer? You were away at tennis camp—learning to serve."

"Mother wrote me about what was going on around here—you parading around braless. She had to turn to someone. And I saw it for myself when I came back. You looked like some hippie who had no morals at all. They should have just shipped you off to Haight Ashbury."

"Jesus, Lily—how did you get so old?" I ask softly, more to myself than to her.

The maid interrupts us, coming into the den with a silver tray and three glasses of iced tea, one with a straw in it. She is completely unfamiliar to me.

"Is she new?" I ask Lily after the maid has silently left the room.

"Yes. I had to fire Mary—she wasn't working out."

"Lily, are you sure it isn't just that there's an allotted time period for maids in this house until they're canned?"

"I had a very good reason," Lily says, placing the straw gently in our mother's mouth and then watching to see if she'll drink or just sit there with it dangling from her lips. "Mary was not good with Mother. She was too rough."

"Well, it's good to know there's justice in the universe."

"Carla, that is uncalled for."

"Oh, come on. Mother treated maids like most people treat disposable cups. Why are you so charitable?"

"Why are you so mean?" my sister asks.

"Survival instinct, probably. Although on the other hand, it could be a genetic trait. If you think about some of the things that went on in this house—like Graddy—Mother wouldn't even give me a forwarding address for her so I could write. But you don't see any of that as mean, do you, Lily? It's just part of managing a household to you, right? They're servants. They don't really count...Oh, what the hell, why am I getting into this with you?"

"You just take these positions to be contrary, Carla—to stir up trouble."

"I don't need to stir up trouble in this family. It's an integral part of our lives," I tell Lily, standing up to leave.

I look for the coyote on the way home, telling myself it will be a sign of luck if I see him. Something wild ought to be able to survive in this neighborhood.

27

Dane's death was still tangled in my dreams, waking me up to the taste of tears in my throat. It was getting difficult to walk past places that reminded me of him; the memories weren't turning dim, they were getting sharper. Finally, I decided to leave California and go to New York.

Kyle had a friend who lived in Greenwich Village, a singer who performed her music in clubs at night and waitressed during the day. She always needed money, and taking on a roommate was one way to get it. Carrying my typewriter and one suitcase stuffed with clothes and a few books, I walked up two flights of creaky stairs, loving the mildew smell of the torn green carpet, just because it was different and far away from California.

Renée was tall and thin, with straight blond hair, parted in the middle, and wide blue eyes that always looked surprised. She had a sofa bed in the living room, which became mine, and an empty refrigerator, which she said I could fill with whatever I wanted.

"I don't usually eat at home," she said, although it didn't look like she ate at all.

I still had most of the fifteen thousand dollars my father had given me; I opened a bank account and pledged to make it last as long as I could. My fledgling New York life was divided into two halves—the hours I spent writing and the hours I spent playing. During the day I was left alone in the apartment while Renée was at work; I filled up pages while the city changed to autumn colors outside the window.

Sometimes, I would take a cab uptown to Central Park where I would walk between the flight paths of crisp leaves, look up at the sky wedged between buildings. And I would remember. I had left something in this city—tiny splinters of my spirit, and I had returned for them. I'd come back as though coming back to a lover, pressing myself against the city's heartbeat and breathing in its smells as if there were no sweeter elixir in the world.

At night, I left the solitude of my private world and went out with Renée and her friends, sometimes to a club where Renée sat perched on a stool with her guitar, singing into a smoke-filled room.

Her friends all had jobs that had nothing to do with their aspirations. They were waiters or store clerks on their way to becoming actors or painters or musicians. I wondered how long my father's money would hold out before I would have to take a job I resented. Some of the women had thick, wavy Janis Joplin hair, some looked like Renée—narrow, elongated; they dressed in black and decorated their necks with beads. As usual, I kept a cautious distance. The men wore army jackets and smoked Shermans, and I was more at home arguing with them about politics or existentialism. I went home with a few of them for herb tea or bad coffee, and quick, uninspired sex. There was no romance in it; it was more an act of revenge.

On those nights, my mother would float through the room, enraged but unable to stop us. I needed her there; her presence fed my anger, and her revulsion confirmed my victory over her.

In the watery, early morning light, I would slip out of their beds and spend a few minutes tiptoeing through their apartments, through the clutter and keepsakes of their lives. I'd look in their refrigerators, in their bookshelves, take inventory of what was on the walls. I learned their secrets. One who considered himself avant-garde and chillingly intellectual had his baseball trophies on the bookshelf next to his high school yearbook. One who wore leather and talked street-tough had an abundantly stocked kitchen and gourmet cookbooks next to his toaster.

I liked them more after I'd uncovered some of their secrets, some of their vulnerabilities, but I didn't like them enough to let them get too close to me. I had secrets, too, and the only time I let them out was when I was alone writing. An angry, defiant child would take the pen sometimes and insist on telling her story, but then I would step in after her and soften it, disguise it, take the edge off the truth that the child was trying to tell.

I was writing short stories, and I started sending some back to Kyle in California. He called and said he was sending them on to a publisher he knew in New York. My words were winging back and forth across the continent, miles above the reach of my mother, although that didn't stop me from worrying that she would eventually discover them.

Before winter moved into the city, my father called and said he was flying in on business. With some trepidation, I agreed to meet him the following afternoon, for tea, in his suite at the Plaza.

In the lobby, cold stares bounced off me, nicking my skin. In my scuffed, secondhand boots, long skirt, and leather jacket, I looked like an impoverished street urchin among fur coats and color-coordinated outfits dripping with gold jewelry. My hair was long and usually hung in my face—a protective shield I was unwilling to surrender.

"Carla, you look... different," my father said when he opened the door, uncertainty painted on his face.

What I noticed, though, was that *he* looked different; his skin was pale and his eyes were ringed with shadow. I had wondered, on the way over, if I had been summoned out of parental courtesy, since his schedule had taken him to the city that was now my home, or if there was a more disciplinary reason. Judging from past history, parental courtesy had played no role in this late-afternoon summons, with a tea tray on the table, complete with tiny cookies and crustless sandwiches. I sat on the couch and watched as my father put careful distance between us, choosing the armchair opposite me. It seemed like his movements were slower, more tentative; maybe it was just time moving in on him, but it looked like something more.

"How are you doing, Carla?" he began, awkwardly, like a teenage boy on a first date.

"Fine. I'm writing a lot," I told him, measuring out my words. I was picturing my stories, safe in a mail pouch in some airplane.

"Have you talked to your mother?"

"No."

"Carla, why are you so intent on hurting her? She has devoted her life to being a good mother and you have caused her nothing but anguish. You've even affected her health," my father said, his eyes earnest and full of concern for my mother's fragility.

"Oh, please, can we stop with that story now?" I asked. "Mother is strong and healthy. There is nothing wrong with her."

"You're what's wrong with her. You have caused her a lot of stress that has definitely weakened her."

I tried to let him know what had gone on in his absence, how our house had turned into a battleground when he left town, and how the story was altered upon his return. I was convinced, if he knew the truth, he would no longer think of me as the villain.

"I'm not the reason for the discord in our house," I told him. "I've just been the most convenient one to blame. Mother picked fights with me every time you left. How was I supposed to react when my room was searched, when my work was destroyed? Was I supposed to hang my head and slink away into the shadows?"

"Your mother never did that, Carla."

"How do you think she found my writing, then? Do you think the pages flew from my room into hers? I couldn't do anything right, Father, can't you see that? There was no way I could win—I couldn't even compete with a ghost. 'The wrong child died,' remember? I was listening that night—I heard Mother say that to you."

Something darkened on my father's face, as if a shadow had passed through the room. I wouldn't understand it until years later, but I noticed it on that gray, shadowless afternoon.

"I tried to avoid the fights—I really did, but it was impossible," I continued, feeling my throat tighten as tears pushed their way up. "I tried being quiet, like Lily—Jesus, I would have become invisible if I could have. When you got home, you were always told a completely different version of what had happened. I was always wrong, and you never questioned that. You never even gave me a chance to tell my side."

"I didn't need to hear your 'side', as you call it. I saw how your mother was suffering, and I knew she'd have no reason to start fights with you. You must have provoked them."

"Oh, she had reasons, but I don't think we can even begin to unravel that one. Don't you think I might have suffered too, over always being the one criticized, the one who didn't match up to Lily or to your first child, who somehow attained sainthood by her untimely death?"

"No one has been unfair to you," he said emphatically. "And no one has made a point of criticizing you."

"Excuse me?"

"You heard me."

"Father, you just refuse to even consider what I'm saying, don't you?" I said, knowing I was already losing ground.

My father looked at me with eyes that had never seen me. "Because it's not true, what you're saying," he answered. "Why do you have this addiction to lying? Carla, I'm beginning to wonder if you were just born to be the bad seed."

I learned something about New York that day—if you are feeling broken and splintered, the city will rise up like a dragon jolted from sleep and trample you. I walked out of the Plaza into the gray, dying light, the headlights of cars looking large and distorted through the tears that were welling up in my eyes, streaking my face. I went a few blocks until I felt composed enough to deal with a cabdriver, but I couldn't get a cab. I walked a few more blocks and a business-suited man bumped into me and yelled, "Watch where you're going, cunt!" I tried again to hail a cab but, as soon as one stopped, a man ran in front of me, jumped in, and slammed the door.

I ended up walking all the way back to the Village, with my father's words slowing me down, scraping along the sidewalk like shackles, loudly announcing my sadness to every passerby.

Something had died in that hotel suite—a fantasy that I had kept tucked away for years, waiting for the right moment to bring it out. The fantasy was that, if I could just find the right words, if I could just find the courage to tell my father the truth, he would believe me.

But he had called me a liar, a bad seed, and I walked through the streets of Manhattan feeling like the failure he said I was.

28

I spent almost two years in New York, turned twenty-two in a noisy club with Renée playing guitar and blue smoke curling under the lights. I had stayed locked into my routine of writing during the day and, at night, plunging into the lights and noise. Renée and I sailed past each other every few days; we had different schedules, and she had a boyfriend who occupied most of her time. With the apartment to myself, I wrote for long, undistracted hours, grateful for days when snow or rain would press against the windows and seal me into my own world.

My short stories had been accepted by the publisher Kyle had sent them to; pieces of my life were going to be bound and sold. I imagined my mother seeing them in some bookstore, pictured her face turning to fury. On the rare occasions when I called home and spoke to her, I carefully avoided this piece of news. It sat in the center of our conversations like a time bomb, ready to explode when its moment came. But those phone calls had taken on a calm, suspended quality, like a day when the wind stops.

I avoided newspapers because their pages frequently contained news of my father's burgeoning wealth. Occasionally, when I passed a newsstand, his face would corner me, accost me from between columns of print, and I would be forced to a standstill on a crowded sidewalk, staring back at him. I would notice a tiredness, a loosening around his eyes, that I first saw on the afternoon I went to his hotel suite. But the world saw only his wealth. Every investment, every deal, seemed charmed.

I got pregnant again, just as winter was melting and spring was moving in. But it was easier to deal with the second time around; by that time, there were clinics offering legal abortions.

Renée took me and brought me home, letting me sleep in her bedroom until I felt better.

"Whose was it?" she asked as I lay in bed, groggy and aching, a Kotex stuffed between my legs.

"I'm not sure—I've narrowed it down to two possibilities," I said. "But it doesn't really matter now, does it?" I was proud of my New York cynicism; I wore it like a disguise against a city that looked for soft spots on those who traveled its streets.

But it struck me that, unlike the first time, it really didn't matter. I didn't give a damn whose seed had been scraped off the walls of my uterus. What mattered more was that I'd let it happen again. There was something more than carelessness going on. I knew how to prevent this; Eric had taught me years before in our dark, refugee hours. But I had gotten careless.

"Carla, it's not that I don't like having you around," Renée said one morning after I'd vacated her bedroom and returned to my makeshift bed in the living room, where I sat with sleepy eyes, staring into the steam of a coffee mug. "But you got some money for your book. Don't you want to have your own place now? Don't you want a bedroom?"

I also still had some of the money my father had given me when I took off with Dane. But I was getting tired of New York—of the city's din of cars and people, and the glare of lights blotting out the stars. I'd started to dream of skies that looked the way they should, of trees growing out of earth, not bending thin and sad over cement sidewalks. I had started to look forward to sleep so I could visit land again, smell wet soil and eucalyptus trees and alyssum blossoming on hillsides.

Sometimes, in my dreams, wolves howled to each other from steep mountainsides, but I knew this was only a figment of dreams. The wolves who used to roam the land had been poisoned and shot, strung up along barns and fences, slung across saddles when the country was settled by men who killed whatever got in their way. But I wanted to at least be closer to their spirits; in the city, even the faint sound of their ghosts was lost in the noise.

I left New York in August, when the city was sweltering and

humid and the smell of garbage drifted up from the sidewalk and into open windows. I returned to California where it was also sweltering, but dry as paper: everything looked like it was either melting or dying. Neither coast seemed very appealing.

I wondered if I would feel sad when winter came, like I did when I was a child facing the sunlight of my first California Christmas. Would I feel the loss again of cold white days and people bundled up in coats and mittens, taking small, careful steps on snowy streets? There was anonymity to New York winters—faces hidden behind scarves, heads covered by hats. I knew I would miss that.

For a few days I stayed at Kyle's apartment where Dane's van had remained in the garage while I was in New York. Kyle had started it up sometimes, but it took five hundred dollars to a local mechanic to make it sound like it would survive.

In the summer heat, I drove up to Topanga Canyon to look for a place to live. On the steep road, I thought back to my first visit, to my first pregnancy, and to Henry's dark Indian eyes as he handed me the cup of bitter herbs that would end it in a rush of blood and pain.

It took only two days before one of the phone numbers I got off the health-food store bulletin board led me to a tiny house perched on the side of a hill. It was on Inspiration Trail, which made me want it before I even saw it. The wood floors were rough and uneven and the only sources of heat were two wood-stoves. Through the windows, only sky, hillsides, and a few rooftops were visible. I could let daylight slide into darkness without having to close curtains and hide myself from the night. There was a bed in it, a kitchen table, a stove, and a refrigerator. I moved in the next day with my typewriter and clothes.

New York was peeling off me in layers, and in some deeper place I was relearning the language of the hills—the blue silence of dawn, the night calls of coyotes. I moved my bed into a corner of windows and the moon sailed across my face. Each day, a rooster down the hill alerted me to the approach of morning. Sometimes Dane's memory rose up on the wind and slipped into bed beside me. With him was the tiny spirit of a child, and I found myself whispering "I'm sorry" to the flocked sky and the distant call of an owl.

I thought of going to visit Henry, but something stopped me. His eyes had seen things I wasn't ready to look at, and although there were days when I drove past his house, I never stopped.

The only other person I knew in the canyon was a girl who worked at the health-food store, whom I had met during my two days of house hunting. Rainbow advertised her name with color-streaked clothes, earrings shaped like tiny rainbows, appliqués on her jeans, and a few decals on her car. I wasn't sure which came first, her name or her habit of decorating herself and all her possessions with bands of color, but it all fit.

"Want to know what my real name was—before I changed it to Rainbow?" she said one night. We were sitting on the used couch I'd just bought from the canyon midwife, working our way through a screw-top bottle of Gallo wine and half a bag of grass.

"Sure," I said, a dozen ludicrous names running through the grass-haze of my mind.

"Margaret-Anne. I don't tell too many people that, but I trust you with this embarrassing artifact from my personal history."

"Rainbow, you've probably spilled this to everyone you ever got stoned with, and you just don't remember. But I promise I'll keep your secret... mostly because I won't remember it tomorrow anyway."

Rainbow wiped some ashes off the couch and said, "I hope she cleaned this before she sold it to you. I mean, maybe she used it when she was delivering babies. I don't see any stains or anything..."

"I would assume she usually goes to the person's house who is having the baby—think about it," I said, giggling at the thought of a midwife expecting a woman in labor to leave her own home and drive over to a neighbor's to have her baby there. "Anyway, can we not talk about fertility, please?"

But we did talk about it, swapping abortion stories like soldiers exchanging war stories, and somewhere between midnight and two A.M., Rainbow told me something I not only remembered the next day, but thought about for weeks afterward.

"I met this girl who had an operation where they snip your tubes so you can't get pregnant. She was back at work three days later."

"I thought they tied them," I said.

"This is better, I think. It's permanent, and she didn't have any scars. I met her at the beach—she was wearing a bikini so I would have seen if she had any scars. They went in through her navel. Kinda tempting, huh? No more pills or IUDs or... accidents."

That was how I ended up at a county hospital in downtown Los Angeles, part of a group of six—four abortions and two sterilizations, all scheduled for the same morning. Assembly-line surgery.

There were others who were there to make fertility a thing of the past, but they were scheduled for different days. We all ended up together at first, though, for two sessions of instruction—lectures and blackboard diagrams detailing exactly what was going to be done inside our bodies.

"The doctor will use a laparoscope," our instructor explained. "A small incision will be made in your navel and another just below the hairline. We'll then pump air into you, so your stomach will sort of inflate like a balloon." She laughed at this, but the humor escaped me. "That way, the doctor can see everything clearly. Then, each tube will be cauterized. Now, one possible risk is that sparks could hit other organs..."

I tuned out at this point. I had made my decision, and the list of possible complications was not something I wanted to hear. I looked around at the others and they all looked like their minds had checked out, too.

Most of the women were in their forties, and my youth didn't escape anyone's attention. One of the nurses, a Chinese woman with a ponytail down to her waist which I immediately envied, took me aside after the first session.

"Carla, because you're so young, you're going to have to be evaluated by a psychologist," she said. "As you can see, these other women are older and they've already had children. You've never had a child. We have to make sure you know what you're doing."

"Do I seem like I don't?" I asked.

"Actually, you seem pretty levelheaded about it to me, but I'm not a psychologist."

"What about the girl who's scheduled for the same morning as I am? She looks young."

The nurse shook her head. "She's thirty, and she had a baby that she gave up for adoption two days after it was born."

"So, basically, one has to have a more colorful past than mine to qualify for this surgery without seeing a psychologist?" I said.

"If you call age and having babies colorful."

Clutching a piece of paper that had the name Dr. Marsden and a suite number written on it, I took the elevator to the fourteenth floor of a downtown medical building. As I sat in the waiting room thumbing through out-of-date magazines, I wondered how I was going to come up with a brief, concise explanation for why I wanted to get sterilized at the age of twenty-four. The risk was, I might open up a locked attic full of childhood debris, stir up dust that would organize itself into the shape of ghosts. I could imagine the doctor advising me to save the money I was going to spend on surgery and commit myself to a lifetime of therapy instead.

I was called into an office that had a view of the neighboring buildings and the layer of smog that seemed to link all of them together like a sheet of brown mesh.

"Carla, I'm Dr. Marsden," the short, gray-haired man said, eyeing me from behind black-framed glasses. "Please sit down."

I noticed a couch, in just the style one would expect to find in a psychologist's office, but I opted for the chair by his desk.

"This is a rather serious decision for a twenty-four-year-old to make," he said, sitting down and looking at my file. "I notice here that you've had two abortions—were these difficult experiences for you?" He was searching for tears, for emotions that would disqualify me, make my decision appear irrational.

"No—not really," I answered casually.

"What makes you sure that you won't want a child in the future?"

"I've always known I didn't want to be a mother. Well, maybe not always, but since I started writing, which was before high school. That's all that's important to me."

"Oh, so you're a writer?" he asked, leaning back in his chair and fingering the pen that he was apparently going to use once he made a diagnosis.

"Yes, and I feel that my stories are my children. I create them, I nurture them, then I send them out into the world."

He smiled at that analogy, and I didn't tell him that my memory jumped back to stories that would never be able to travel into the world—the ones devoured by flames after my mother found them. That's what motherhood means to me, I wanted to tell him. Stories being burned at the stake, drifting into the world as ashes.

"Many artists feel that their work is their act of creation," he said. "It's quite common. But that doesn't necessarily mean you can't have both."

"I don't want both, though. Stories are a much safer thing to create, to mother—they don't disappoint you. They're exactly what you want them to be because you control them."

Dr. Marsden leaned forward and put his elbows on the desk. "You think children are a disappointment?"

"I was," I said. "My sisters weren't, but I was."

"How many sisters do you have?"

"Two. One living and one dead. But the dead one still lived with us," I answered in a calm, even voice.

"Excuse me?"

"She lived with us—like a ghost, you know? My mother talked about her as if she were still alive. She was the perfect one. I was always a disappointment."

It was four-thirty on a Friday afternoon and Dr. Marsden looked like he'd already had a rough day. I could see a decision forming in the creases of his forehead; he could continue asking me questions and perhaps stretch his day out for another couple of hours, or he could just okay the surgery and say good-bye to me.

"Well, it seems you've thought this through, Carla," he said after hesitating for a minute. "I'm comfortable in saying that you know what you're doing and can go ahead with this."

It's the white light I remember, like a frozen eye staring down at me, and the music, piped into the operating room, that made me think Lawrence Welk was going to be performing the surgery, or at least attending.

It seemed like only minutes later when I fought my way out of anesthesia sleep to see Rainbow on one side of the bed and the doctor on the other.

"Am I healthy?" I asked, remembering the complications I hadn't wanted to hear about, hoping I didn't fall into that small percentage of casualties.

"Yes, you're fine," the doctor said. She was young, dark-haired, tan, and I had only met her an hour before surgery.

"How are you feeling?" Rainbow asked, touching my shoulder lightly. Her voice was gentle and low, the tone people frequently adopt when they're coaxing someone back from sleep.

"Okay . . . sleepy . . ."

I noticed the doctor had disappeared and in her place a nurse was there, saying my name in a loud voice.

"Carla, Carla, come on—wake up," she said, her white shape moving into my field of vision. "You're going to have to go home soon."

Rainbow turned and glared at her. "They just brought her out a few minutes ago. You short on beds or something?"

"She's an outpatient."

"I know that. She's also just had surgery. Do you mind if she sleeps it off for a little while?"

I heard the nurse's shoes squeak as she turned quickly and walked to the next bed, preparing to rouse another patient. Someone else was wheeled in and I lifted my head just enough so I could count the number of prone bodies in the room. Six—they'd finished everyone in a little over two hours. I sank back into the pillow again.

"Carla," Rainbow said, her voice forcing my eyelids open, "you're going to have to wake up soon, sweetie. Nurse Ratchet is on the prowl, looking for empty beds she can short-sheet."

Rainbow helped me into my clothes and steadied me as I walked toward the door. I threw up on the way out, and I hoped that the drill-sergeant nurse would either step in it or have to clean it up.

The day was warm and heavy; heat waves rippled across the road. I dozed off on the long ride home, retreating from the brightness into a dark zone of sleep, telling myself, as I drifted off, that I no longer had to be afraid of becoming my mother.

29

There is something different in the air of my mother's house; I feel it when the maid opens the door—it washes over me with the chill of a snowdrift.

"They're all in the bedroom," she says.

My mother is lying in bed, with her doctor and Lily standing over her.

"What happened?" I ask no one in particular.

"Mother may have pneumonia," Lily answers. "Her breathing is very labored and her lungs sound congested. We're going to have to put her in the hospital."

"I want to get a chest X ray so I can see what's going on," the doctor adds. "But I don't like the way she sounds. I'll call for an ambulance."

Something vague and cold wraps around me, clinging to my shoulders like fog around a mountain. I look down at my mother and, in my mind, I can already hear the siren coming for her, see the hospital corridors and the doctor's grim face, smell the disease and death that disinfectant can't conceal.

This could be the end, I think. But I don't know how to lose her. I've grieved for the mother she was when I was small and her arms reached for me. But in time, battle cries took over and they are the only sounds ringing in my ears. I don't know if I'm generous enough to grieve for the opponent she turned into.

Lily and the doctor are moving toward the door, leaving me alone with my mother. I sit down on the bed beside her, listening to her breath, slow and gurgling in her chest. Her eyes are almost closed—it's the almost that makes me look again to see if they're focusing on anything, to see if they're watching me.

The drapes are half-drawn, giving the room a shadowy gray cast, as though the day is later than it is. A shaft of light falls between us; it glitters with dust particles and I imagine it as something solid that my hand can't pass through. But my hand doesn't try; I don't reach out. Instead, I remain on my side of an ancient barrier.

The sobbing begins as though coming from someone else; I hear it before I realize it's me who is crying. By then, it's too late—I'm given over to it. I don't even know, really, why I'm crying. It may be because there is a part of me that should cry, but can't, so the rest of me is making up for it.

"Why did you have to make it so impossible to care about you? Why did you stop being my mother?" I ask the mute woman lying pale and still below me, a stranger who only seems familiar because she's always been around. My voice is choked and hoarse; mingled with the sound is the rasp of her breathing.

Finally crying in front of my mother is like raising a white flag, signing a peace declaration, ending the war. I've held my tears prisoner for so long, they eagerly escape my eyes.

She looks so tiny and frail—lost in the wide bed—I wonder how she could ever have frightened me as much as she did. Was she always this tiny? In my memory, she looms over my life, able to reach across whole continents.

I put my hand over hers and notice how much larger it is. My hand is wide, with long fingers and a writer's bump on one that's been there as long as I can remember; I can hide her hand under mine, make it disappear.

"Carla, what are you doing?" Lily's voice slices through the room. I pull my hand back quickly.

"Nothing. I was just... thinking."

"You're crying," my sister says, surprised.

I wipe my face with my hands, liking the feel of them, their pressure on my skin, glad that they're large and strong. "Yeah, I am."

Lily is dry-eyed, in control. "We have to take Mother now," she tells me. "The ambulance is here."

"I didn't hear it."

"There was no siren, if that's what you mean."

"Right—I guess there wouldn't be."

Two men come in, lift my mother onto a gurney, and strap her down. I watch silently as they wheel her out to the ambulance.

"Carla," Lily says, taking my arm, "it might not be serious. We won't know until they do X rays and tests and . . . you know. We're just being cautious, but there's a chance that it could be something very minor."

My tears start again and I don't fight them. "Yeah—I know. It's not just that . . ."

I'm confusing her; I know that. I'm confusing myself, too, because I'm still not sure where the tears came from.

"I just wish I understood," I tell my sister.

"Understood what?"

"All of it—I don't know. I have to go, Lily. I'll call later."

I drive into Santa Monica, remembering that I have some errands to do, thinking that the ordinariness of this will settle me. But the blur of tears is making it impossible to see the road. I pull over and sit in my car, crying. I am in front of a bakery and people are walking out, their mouths full of sugary pastries, trying not to glance at a woman slumped over the steering wheel, sobbing. I hear their footsteps on the pavement, feel their self-conscious stares, their curiosity.

I wipe my eyes, pull away from the curb, and blend into traffic that's heading toward the ocean.

Heat clouds rim the sky and the air is humid and thick. But my thoughts spin backward, to other seasons. To a gray, overcast autumn just days before my tenth birthday. My mother took me to the hairdresser with her and had him cut my hair so short I could have applied to a military academy. It was the first time, but there would be more. Each time my hair started to grow over my ears, it would be cut again despite my tears and protestations.

I remember fleeing into the safe world of my bedroom when I got home, standing in front of the mirror and staring at my butchered hair. My eyes were already red and swollen from crying.

"Why do you hate me so much?" I said, wishing I had the courage to ask my mother instead of my own reflection.

Maybe I'm still asking that, I think. Maybe I need to just give it up.

I'm not sure where I'm driving to. The car rolls down the ramp onto the Coast Highway, adhering to habit. But I don't want to go home yet, I argue with the tires spinning along the highway. I turn off at Sunset, putting the ocean in my rearview mirror and watching it get smaller as I go up the hill into Pacific Palisades, toward Beck's small, book-cluttered house.

It's his cocoon, a place I rarely visit, hidden behind a towering eucalyptus tree. The house needs painting and some diligent land-scaping, neither of which will be attended to by Beck.

I know, as I wind through the narrow streets, that he is at his desk, his reading glasses balanced on his nose, his body curved over the black slope of words as he fills page after page.

It is one of our many unwritten rules that I don't show up at his house unannounced while he's writing, which he always is. I'm not sure how all these rules evolved, but they're there—tiny flags dotting the landscape of our relationship. I treat them like land mines, stepping gingerly to one side or the other, but this time I'm walking right into one.

Beck answers my knock with a pen in one hand and a cup of coffee in the other. He is in a white shirt and jeans, and I suddenly have the same rush of desire I had the first time I saw him standing behind a podium, fumbling with his reading glasses. Sadness is still gnawing at me, ghosts are flitting around my shoulders, blowing cold breath on my neck. And, as inappropriate as I know it is, wanting to fuck Beck has come over me so suddenly I feel myself getting wet as I stand in the doorway, looking at his face for some sign of how he's going to react to this unexpected intrusion.

"My mother is in the hospital," I say, as much to remind myself of why I'm here as to explain it to him.

He puts his coffee cup on the bookshelf and folds me into his arms. "When?"

"They took her a little while ago. They think she has pneumonia."

I press my face into his chest—against the triangle of skin where his shirt is unbuttoned. There is comfort in the familiarity of his scent, the ridge of bone and the cushion of muscle. He leads me into the house, arm tight around my shoulders, into the chaos of books pulled from shelves and left on the floor, and mail he hasn't gotten around to opening.

"It's so confusing," I tell him. "I don't know if I'm upset because I feel guilty that I don't hurt more than I do, or—I just don't know. I feel so strange."

"I know."

But he doesn't know everything; he doesn't know that, along with this weight of confusion that I've carried into his house, I've brought another feeling that has now turned white-hot and is snaking down to my knees, making them too weak to stand any longer. I turn and kiss him, probably too savagely because I can feel the surprise on his mouth.

"Carla, are you sure—" he starts to ask as I pull him down to the floor. I hear the pen fall out of his hand and roll across the wood, but it's a tiny sound, buried in the weight of our breathing. Or maybe it's just my breathing, I'm not sure. I leave his shirt on him and go for his jeans. There is nothing gentle in this; it's a desperate, hungry attempt to distance myself from illness and hospitals and death. It's the most alive thing I can do, and there's a part of me that needs to prove I'm alive, that I won't die even if all the secrets that I will never understand die with my mother.

It's over in minutes, and the clothes we didn't bother to take off are soaked with sweat. I look down at Beck, pinned to the floor between my legs, and I half expect to see confusion on his face—bewilderment at this untypical reaction. But his eyes are looking into me with the precision of lasers. I climb off of him, uncomfortable with what they might be seeing.

"It's okay," he says. "I don't think it's strange."

"You read my mind too easily."

"That's because it was very loud. Maybe it all ends up coming from the same place—the feelings we don't understand and the ones we do."

I lie back on the hard floor, my head almost touching a stack of books, my skirt sticking to my legs.

"Brings back memories for you, doesn't it?" Beck asks, moving to the couch and pulling on his jeans. "Your father?"

"Yeah—part of me is scrambling around for what I'm supposed to be feeling and is coming up empty-handed."

"And the other part?"

"It's wondering why I don't know better by now," I tell him. "I'm searching all around for a map to the treasure, and I should have learned a long time ago that there is no treasure."

He kneels on the floor beside me and bends over me, his mouth meeting mine.

"Will you come out and stay with me tonight?" I ask.

"Uh-huh. Let me work a little longer and then I'll be out."

I close my eyes and let his voice float over me. I want to stay there, with the floor against my back and Beck's shape bending down, protecting me from a sky that has a bad habit of falling on me.

30

In my dream, my mother has died. It's not the first time; she has entered my dreams before like this, dangling her death in front of me until my fingers close around it and I wake up with it beside me, curled on the pillow, its breath in my face.

But this dream is different. I am not a small child in this one, lost and frightened amid a sea of black clothes, running from adults whose fingers point at me, follow me, chase me down. This dream is white—hospital white—with wide corridors and sounds drifting out from rooms that are closed to me. I am wandering through the corridors, looking for my mother, although I know it's too late. There is no hurry—she is already gone. But I need to find her.

People pass me in crisp white uniforms, with soft shoes that squeak across the floor. But they won't meet my eyes. I'm just another visitor in a place where it's common for heartbeats to stop. The world goes on, they know that. They assume I'll find my way, so they don't stop for me. They disappear down other corridors.

I find her door and my hand freezes on the knob, unable to turn it, unwilling to enter the territory of her death.

But I know, if I wait, she will come to me—slide out from under the door and talk to me in a different voice—one I haven't heard in years. I can take her home with me then, the way she once was— kneeling down and zipping up my jacket against the cold November

193

winds, walking me through the white-snow days of a New York winter.

In my dream, I know I can take her home with me this way; I can permit her entrance into my life. I will put vases of tuberose in every room, so the perfume will lure her and make her feel at home. It doesn't frighten me, this new way of having her in my life.

I wake up and open my eyes carefully, not sure of what I'll see beside me. My dreams have a way of following me into the morning, crossing their borders into the foreign country of day where they're not wanted. But my eyes open on Beck, his face composed and calm, far away in sleep.

I get up and call Lily at the hospital; I don't even have to wonder where she is.

"How is Mother?" I ask when the operator puts me through to the room.

"Much better. It's not as serious as we thought it might be. She's resting much more comfortably and her breathing's getting a little better. Are you coming by?"

"Of course."

"They're giving her antibiotics and they seem to be working already."

Lily recites this diagnosis in a professional, comfortable tone; she is soothed by specifics, definitions. My sister loves orderliness, I think, as I look around my living room at stacks of magazines that should be thrown out, and a wastebasket full of crumpled white pages, each one signifying a change of mind. There are too many pictures on the walls and too many books—more than will fit on my shelves. I need the clutter; it fills up the lonely spaces in my life.

I don't know how long I can delay going to the hospital to see my mother, but I know I'll try. Beck was right—it stirs up memories.

I didn't dream about my father's death before it happened; I didn't need to. It was etched on his face. I saw it before I admitted it to myself. I saw it in New York, when the gray light fell through his hotel room window and nestled in the new creases that had appeared on his skin. I saw it in his eyes—the way they were already leaving, looking past what was in front of him.

I saw, but I didn't want to admit it. Until my mother called and I could no longer pretend.

"Your father has to go in for some medical tests," she said. I was sitting in bed, writing, still recovering from my sterilization. It wasn't that I was in pain, it was more a matter of lying around, thinking about what I'd done. Sterilization—I even liked the word. It meant that I would never become like my mother; all the unborn souls were safe from that legacy.

"Tests for what?" I asked. Her voice was softer that day, frightened.

"Well, he hasn't been feeling well for quite some time. He's been fatigued and he complains about nausea. He has been working very hard, so it could be that. I'm just not sure. Of course, he's also been under a great deal of stress, what with all these rumors..." Her voice trailed off as though there was no need to complete the sentence.

"What rumors?"

Her breath came out in a short burst. "Apparently you don't read the newspapers."

"Actually, this is true. I figure that I know enough people who do read the newspaper that, in the event of an impending nuclear holocaust, one of them will have the decency to call and alert me."

"Carla, I really don't appreciate your humor in light of what's going on," my mother snapped. I could see her floating along the line of telephone wire into my house, her mouth set in a hard line.

"You haven't told me what the hell is going on—am I supposed to be telepathic?"

"And I won't tolerate your swearing."

"Okay, I apologize. Now, could we please backtrack to Father's health and these rumors you mentioned?"

"Oh, it's just silliness," my mother said. "People invent things because they're so jealous."

"What things?" She was forcing me to pull it out of her.

"The things they're saying—that your father may be facing an investigation, that he might have made his money by getting information he shouldn't have had, that he paid people to get him tips." Her tone dismissed the charges.

"I believe it's called insider trading, Mother," I said, trying to absorb the full impact of this. If the rumors were true, my father had broken the law, he could stand trial, be found guilty, go to jail. My father... For a minute, my mind struggled to bring his face into focus. I searched for the fear that should have been gathering inside me.

"What about his health?" I asked.

"Well, it's no wonder, with all the stress he's been under. And you know, he's terrible about getting checkups. I tell him and tell him to go but he just puts it off. This time, he's not getting out of it. I'm taking him myself tomorrow. I spoke with the doctor on the phone and he wants to do some tests, mostly because your father's lost so much weight recently."

"Mother, are there any other symptoms that you haven't mentioned? You're parceling out this information again." It was one of her most infuriating habits.

"I'm telling you about your father's condition," she answered.

"Okay, so you'll let me know what the results are?"

"Yes, if you'd like," my mother said, with just enough hesitation to suggest she thought I didn't care.

A day and a half went by before she called again. Several times, I started to dial my parents' number, but stopped; a part of me didn't want to know. I thought of the afternoon in New York when my father looked gaunt and tired, and some instinct rose up and told me that his body had been betraying him for a long time, waging a secret war that he'd refused to acknowledge.

"Your father has pancreatic cancer," my mother said when she finally called. I could hear tears pulling at her voice and I knew she'd already been crying. But she was readying herself, too—looking around for weapons to slay this new dragon that had the audacity to trespass into their lives.

"I think we should get a second opinion," she said. "You just can't trust doctors these days."

"Mother, isn't this the doctor you've had for fifteen years?"

"Yes, but they all make mistakes, you know. He didn't operate—he didn't actually *look* at the pancreas," she said, getting more insistent.

"How many tests did they do?"

"A lot—hours of tests," she conceded. "The thing is... there's no cure. It's fatal."

I let the word rest in front of me for a minute, turning it over, examining it like a scientist studying a specimen.

"Well, whatever you think, Mother," I said. "Second opinions are important, I guess. How is Father holding up?"

"He doesn't know and I don't want you to tell him."

"Jesus Christ—are you going to wait until he's at death's door before you break the news to him? It's his life—he has a right to know this." I was standing in my living room, looking out across hillsides that had just started to turn green after a recent rainstorm. I turned away from the view and faced the wall, uncomfortable with the sight of new life sprouting up.

"I'm doing what I think is best," my mother said in a voice sharp and unyielding as steel. "I thought, if you had the time, you might want to visit your father."

Driving out of the canyon was always a strange feeling; it meant relinquishing the protection of the mountains, exchanging the tranquility of a small, cloistered community for a world teeming with strangers and brimming with unseen risks.

The day after my mother's second phone call, I drove down the hill with even more reluctance than usual. I had been avoiding newspapers for so long, I didn't know how my father was going to look. I imagined bones outlined against skin, hollowed cheeks, and dark-circled eyes. Despite growing up in a house full of secrets, deception was not my strong suit. I doubted my ability to conceal from a dying man the fact that he was dying.

My mother led me into his office, stopping once in the hallway to admonish me.

"Remember, don't you dare let on that anything's wrong,"

Her words pushed me through the door.

"Hi, Father—how are you?" I said from the doorway, with a forced cheerfulness that seemed glaringly obvious to me. He looked up from his desk and I could see that his shoulders were scooped out, his neck was thin and lined.

"Carla, this is a surprise. I thought you'd forgotten about us altogether."

I felt something catch in my throat, but I wasn't sure what it was. It should have been grief, or even guilt, but it tasted like confusion.

I sat down on one of the leather chairs, far enough away that I didn't feel pulled by the reality hovering around my father; any closer, I might have surrendered to its power, given it words and transformed it into the truth that my mother was steeling herself against.

"Sorry, I've been pretty busy," I said.

"Oh? What have you been up to?"

"Writing."

"Carla wrote a book," my mother announced, turning a hard-edged look on me. I knew she'd find out eventually, but I hadn't pictured the actual moment of confrontation. Somehow, this seemed like a terribly inappropriate time. "It's a book of short stories, I believe. Isn't that right, Carla?"

"Yes—just fantasy stories—sort of," I said, my voice dropping in volume. I wondered when my mother had decided that this visit would be a good time to introduce this subject.

"Well, I'd like to see it sometime," my father said innocently. "Maybe you'll bring us a copy?"

"Sure." I was counting on him forgetting.

He asked where I was living, and I launched into an exhaustive description of my tiny house, the view of the canyon, the fire station down the road, and the coyotes that came out at night. I was trying to monopolize the conversation so no more questions or bombshells would be dropped, and I succeeded.

"Clifford, I think you should take a nap now," my mother said after about twenty minutes. "He's still a little worn out from that virus," she added, directing this last comment to me, warning me.

"Right—the virus." Familiar angers bubbled up in me and I was glad my allotted time was up.

My mother walked me to the door and turned to face me. "What is the theme of your book?" she said. "These stories of yours?" Her eyes judged me, convicted me. They had never left room for appeal.

"My idyllic childhood," I answered.

"And you're going to bring us a copy?"

"Yeah—I'll line out the offending passages. It should be a quick read for you that way."

"You just can't resist lashing out, can you, Carla? You always did have a sarcastic mouth," she said, her eyes still playing the role of executioner.

"And you always pick the most curious times to launch these salvos at me. You give me the responsibility of keeping Father's condition hidden from him, and then, while I'm wrestling with that one, you bring up the subject of my book. We could have gotten into this on the phone, couldn't we? But you didn't want to get into it—you just wanted to win a point."

"When you have children someday, I hope they treat you with more respect than this," my mother said with a perfectly measured indignation.

I was turning toward the door as she said that, and I turned back and faced her, the amputation inside me suddenly sharp and raw. My womb would stay hollow, I had made sure of that, and I opened my mouth to tell her, to hurl it at her, to wound her. But her eyes caught me—froze the words before they could take shape. And I knew, in that moment, that it was my wound and her victory. She had gotten to me, she had made me turn on myself, punish myself with the clean work of a surgeon's tools. Telling her would only put the crown on her head and the scepter in her hand.

Silently, I walked away from my mother, got into the van, and drove away.

At the foot of the driveway, I had to slam on the brakes to avoid hitting two men—one with a camera, the other with a notepad.

"Jesus, I could have run into you," I said, rolling down the window. "What are you doing standing in the middle of the driveway?"

"Are you the daughter?" the man with the notepad asked, coming over to the van. He had dishwater blond hair and wire-rim glasses, and he acted like he was on his tenth cup of coffee.

"Carla—my name's Carla."

"Can you give me any kind of statement about the accusations against your father? Do you think he's guilty of insider trading? Has he said anything to you?"

"You don't honestly expect me to answer that, do you? What are you going to do, hang around the driveway and stop everyone who comes in and out? I mean, this probably isn't the best way to get a story, you know."

I saw the reporter's eyes move from mine to the driveway behind me, and I glanced in the rearview mirror to see my mother walking toward us.

"If you're smart, you'll keep your mouth shut," I told him.

"My daughter has nothing to say to you," my mother said. "And you're on our property. Get off."

I put the van in gear. "Have a nice evening, guys."

Just before I turned the corner, I glanced back at the three of them, still standing in the driveway, and wondered if the photographer would take a picture. It wouldn't matter, though; it wouldn't tell the real story. Pictures have a way of not telling the truth.

There was a photograph in my parents' bedroom—a family picture taken the Christmas after Lily tried to kill herself. All you see is a family standing around the tree, smiling for the camera; you don't see the wounds, the scars, the rage. The camera captures only what you give it, and the rest remains concealed.

I usually avoided looking at that Christmas photograph. It made me feel the full weight of the secrets I'd been asked to keep.

31

Our steps were being choreographed around my father's failing health. It was like a tribal dance of death, except that the person in the middle of the circle didn't know he was dying. He didn't hear the footsteps pounding around him or see the circle tightening. My father seemed oblivious to changes in our behavior which should have made him wonder if we'd all been lobotomized.

After an absence of more than a year, I began showing up for dinner once or twice a week. After years of offensive strikes on my writing, my mother made polite inquiries about my latest work. Lily, who now had her own apartment but seemed to always be at our parents' house, had exchanged her shy demeanor for a bubbly recital of current events and weather conditions.

I kept waiting for my father to ask, "What the hell is going on around here?" But he floated through it all, as he always did, seeing this harmony as if it were the most normal thing in the world, as though we had not spent years howling at each other and rattling sabers.

Occasionally, he mentioned feeling discomfort in his stomach; he would pick at his food and he was becoming painfully thin. At times, I'd see his eyes turn inward, as though he were trying to understand the mutiny being played out inside his body. I was consumed by guilt for my role in this charade, and for not having the courage to disregard my mother and Lily and tell my father the truth.

There seemed to be a carefully laid-out plan for making my father's remaining time pleasant and light, which meant burying reality in the backyard, and despite an inner voice warning me, there I was, holding one of the shovels, throwing dirt on top of the truth and hating myself for it.

But Lily walked away with the winning hand in this game of deceit. We were sitting at the dinner table; it was autumn and the evening was passing through that blue, magical hour just before dark.

"Lily has a very important announcement," my mother said between the salad and the main course. In my memory, I can almost see her tapping her knife on a glass to get our attention, but I know it didn't really happen that way.

"I'm getting married," Lily said, with the exuberance which had started to define all her communication in those months.

No one said anything for several seconds.

"Well, isn't that wonderful?" my mother persisted. "I think it's the most exciting news. Lily will make such a beautiful bride."

"I hope this isn't a ridiculous question," I said, "but who are you marrying?" I hadn't heard about my sister even dating anyone.

"Everett Norvell," my mother answered, apparently deciding Lily had said enough for the moment.

"Everett Norvell!" My laughter exploded around the sound of his name. "He's a friend of yours and Father's. What did he do with his wife? Ship her off to a rest home and then divorce her?"

My mother's eyes bored into me. "Miriam died a year and a half ago, Carla. Everett has been very lonely and Lily was a great comfort to him. They ended up falling in love. I hardly think that age should be a consideration in matters of the heart."

"Oh, you're absolutely right—it shouldn't," I said. "Just important things like race, religion, and social standing, right? And finances, of course."

"I love him, Carla," Lily said emphatically and then turned to our father, who was, after all, supposed to be the main beneficiary of all this prepackaged happiness. "Don't you think it's wonderful, Father?"

"Yes, yes—congratulations," he answered. But his eyes had retreated again, probably scouring the map of his internal body, trying to decipher the changes.

I managed to quiet my laughter long enough to congratulate Lily, but it was staggering to imagine her walking down the aisle to marry a man who had bounced her on his knee when she was a little girl. Hadn't we called him Uncle Everett then? I thought of him making love to her—I was certain Lily was a virgin—and the picture looked so absurd, I had trouble keeping my mind on it. Lily's pale, smooth skin pressed against flesh that had long ago surrendered to the pull of age.

I remember that evening's dinner as being steeped in sadness, even more so because of the ridiculously cheerful banter of my mother and sister. They were orchestrating Father's last days, and I could only guess how differently he would have lived them had he been told the truth.

The maid came in at one point and told my father he had a phone call. While he was out of the room, the three of us sat uncomfortably, with nothing to say to each other since all our conversations lately were for his benefit.

"I have to meet with my lawyers tomorrow," my father said when he came back into the dining room.

"I read that some of the people in your company were questioned," I said, ignoring the knife-blade looks from my mother and Lily.

"Yes, that's true." His expression was calm and open, as though he were grateful for the chance to talk about it.

"So, is it true?" I asked. "Was there insider trading?"

"Oh, what does it matter?" my mother cut in. "They just don't like anyone making a lot of money."

"I think it matters because it's illegal," I told her. "And it matters if some people have gotten rich at the expense of others."

My father pushed at the food on his plate. "I don't know about anything illegal. I have no evidence of that."

"You don't know about it, or you're sure it hasn't gone on?" I persisted.

"Will you please stop it, Carla," my mother said, her voice growing shrill. "We are trying to have a nice dinner here. Lily's getting married—this is a happy occasion."

I surrendered to my mother's illusion for the remainder of the meal, eating silently and keeping my anger to myself.

The preparations for Lily's wedding were more than I could bear. During those weeks, I decided that, given the choice between oral surgery and marriage, I'd gladly head for the dentist's chair. My mother bustled around the house with lists in her hand, muttering about caterers and flower arrangers. Lily was constantly wailing about some monumental tragedy like not having the right shoes. And I learned that my bridesmaid dress was not under my control; it was up to Lily, which probably meant it was up to my mother.

I was summoned to the house one evening to pick it up. The light was turning purple on the hills as I drove out of the canyon. I had to coax myself into these visits; the false smiles and small talk always wore me down.

Lily led me into what used to be my room and slid plastic off of a pale green dress with puffed sleeves and a long, thickly gathered skirt.

"Well, here it is," she said.

"Lily, it's the color of a surgical gown." I regretted my words as soon as I said them.

Her face crumbled and she started to cry. "You just don't like it because I chose it."

"No, that's not it. Actually, that's the reason I'm going to wear it. But I don't understand—how did you come up with this color?"

"Mother thought it would be pretty."

"Okay, now I understand."

Lily was sitting on the bed, small and fragile.

"Lily, please don't," I said, sitting down beside her and putting my arm around her shoulders. "I'll wear it, okay? I'll look like a surgeon with fashion dementia, but I'll wear it. I won't complain about it anymore, I promise."

"I just want this to be a beautiful wedding—for Father's sake. He deserves to have that memory."

"Do I need to point out that this is not the best reason to get married?" I said.

"No," she answered in a small voice, wiping her eyes with the back of her hand. "But I love Everett—I'm pretty sure I do."

"Lily, maybe you should wait until you're completely sure. I have this feeling that you don't think you deserve to be happy, so you're settling for something that makes other people happy."

My sister looked at me with eyes that told me I was right, even though her words never would.

The location of the wedding, which was discussed in hushed voices, hinged on my father's health.

"I wanted to have it in a hotel—in a ballroom," Lily whined to our mother. "You know, all decorated and regal looking." My sister the princess.

"But dear, your father is very weak. It would be better to have it here at the house so he can go lie down if he needs to."

"I think it would be better to just tell the man he's dying," I offered, not that anyone asked for my contribution.

"I'm handling this the way I think is best," my mother snapped. "Obviously."

"Carla, please don't ruin things," Lily said, and I saw tears starting to collect in her eyes again. "We'll have the wedding here, Mother. It'll be fine—it'll be beautiful."

"Can't you learn to keep things to yourself, Carla?" my mother said.

"You mean like the truth? Sure, I don't see why this should be a problem. I should have a genetic predisposition to this sort of charade."

On the day of Lily's wedding, the house was decorated with so many flowers, they should have included hay-fever warnings on the invitations.

Lily was vacillating between giggles and tears, and my mother finally gave up trying to calm her and just gave her a large glass of champagne.

Most of the guests were my parents' friends; I realized that Lily had become so entrenched in their lives that she had no friends of her own. The living-room furniture had been moved out and rows of chairs faced the fireplace, in front of which Lily and Everett were to take their vows.

There were murmurs and sighs when my sister walked down the aisle in her white satin bridal gown. The long sleeves and high neckline left only her hands exposed, and her face was behind a sheer veil. She walked in on our father's arm and my eyes were on him. He walked slowly, hesitantly, and he was starting to look jaundiced, which was even more apparent next to the startling white of Lily's dress. I glanced around the room, wondering how many of the guests knew. It would be typical of my mother to let everyone else in on the secret she was keeping from my father. Her version of the safety-in-numbers theory—deception in numbers.

It was midafternoon. The air outside was gray and drizzly and I kept looking out the window wishing I were somewhere else. I wanted to be back in the canyon, with mist washing down green mountains and the sound of guitar music drifting up the hill from a house hidden by trees.

I remember fragments of the day—links on a chain, but not the whole chain. What comes back, though, with perfect clarity, is how alone I felt looking out across my parents' living room at the people gathered to see my sister get married. The faces were familiar, although older, and the women's makeup had become thicker over the years. Their smiles were the same no matter who they were talking to.

These were people who preferred to negotiate their lives rather than live them; they had weeded out spontaneity and abandonment in favor of things manicured to perfection. There was nothing raw or wild in any of them, and I remember feeling something move in on me, something that felt like sadness, although it wasn't. I was looking at faces that had come in and out of my life since I was a child. The flat, gray light that came through the windows didn't play across them, it muted them—painted them all with the same brush. And I remember that I felt my own isolation more acutely than I ever had before.

After the ceremony, I drifted over to a corner of the room, nursed a glass of champagne, and watched the careful interaction of the guests. It was like watching a rug being woven—cautiously, perfectly, with no stitch out of line. I was the only loose thread, and I was trying to stay out of the way.

It was when I ventured out of my corner for another glass of champagne that I almost collided with Mrs. Cunningham.

"Carla, how nice to see you looking so lovely," she said.

She was wearing a lavender wool suit with matching shoes and amethyst jewelry. Her chin-length blond hair had been molded into a flip and attacked by so much hairspray, it wouldn't dare fall out of shape. I realized that her hairstyle hadn't changed over the last fifteen years.

"Nice to see you, too," I said, looking around for someone with a tray of full champagne glasses.

"I certainly hope this day has given you some ideas about your own life," she said.

"My life?"

"Well, dear, it breaks your mother's heart, this unconventional life-style you lead. Ever since high school and that rebellious stage. You should have been going to proms and getting pinned. I'm sure she feels that she'll never live to see you get married and settle down. If she did have any hopes, I'm sure your promiscuity has dashed them. It's been so humiliating to her, and to your father."

"Mrs. Cunningham, is there some monthly newsletter that I don't know about? I mean, how are you so knowledgeable about what I did in high school and what I've been doing since?"

"Carla, all I'm saying is that you could give a bit more thought to your parents' feelings. We all want you to be happy."

"I see. All, meaning who? Everyone in this room?" I said.

"For starters."

I decided it would be dangerous to have another glass of champagne. I went back to my corner and counted the minutes until I could remove my surgical-green dress and return to the canyon where no one cared who you slept with in high school, or even if you'd gone to high school at all.

At some point, I noticed that my father was no longer in the room. I studied his absence—how everyone just seemed to move in and fill up the space he had occupied. I wondered if this was how it would be—close the circle, fill in the empty spaces. And I wondered, too, if his coming death was any more real to me than it was to my mother and sister. Maybe the only difference was that I knew how to talk about it. I always was better at words.

32

My mother has been in the hospital for two days, and I haven't visited yet, although I've gotten daily progress reports from Lily over the phone. I asked Beck to stay with me, and he has, waiting patiently for me to stop avoiding the inevitable. My rationalizations have a short life span; he knows that.

So this afternoon, we're finally getting ready to visit her, and while he's in the shower, I stand in the steamy bathroom, wipe moisture off the mirror, and look at my reflection.

"My face is changing," I say to him, loudly enough to be heard over the shower.

"Is this leading up to a conversation about plastic surgery?" His voice sounds loud and wet.

"No—in fact, I'm regressing."

The water is shut off and Beck gets out of the shower, wraps a towel around his waist, and comes up behind me.

"Regressing?"

"Yeah. My mother being in the hospital is taking me back in time— to when my father was there. It wasn't a great time all the way around. I'd just gotten sterilized, I was trying to convince myself I'd done the right thing, but I wasn't so sure. I'm starting to look like I did then. My mouth is tense, my eyes have that don't-you-dare-fuck-with-me look, and my face is breaking out."

"And your imagination is working overtime," Beck says, kissing my neck. "Come on—get dressed. You'll feel better after we get this over with."

My mother is in Saint John's Hospital in Santa Monica. A wide, green lawn shaded by trees and dotted with picnic tables separates the hospital from the street, creating the illusion that it's not really a hospital, that behind the windows people are not ill or dying or pleading for drugs to ease the pain. It's an illusion I've always appreciated as I've driven past.

"They should give our family a discount at this place," I tell Beck. "We've become regular customers."

We pull into the parking lot and I feel sweat starting to pool in my armpits and trickle down my sides; my head feels light and disoriented.

"It'll be over soon," Beck says.

It's walking past other rooms that gets to me—the doors that are ajar, offering glimpses of supine bodies with tubes and jars hooked up to them. I pass by their sicknesses, their pain, in the safety of the hallway, wondering to myself why they are here and for how long. In some rooms, a doctor's white shape is bending over the bed and I hear the muffled sound of his voice. I imagine him giving dire predictions about the patient's hope for recovery; I imagine tears, shock, and the pale face of fear.

We get to my mother's room and find Lily on a chair beside the bed. I'm sure her vigil has been going on since early morning.

"Hi, Carla. Beck—nice to see you again," she says with surprise in her voice, meant to point out that Beck never visits. Lily thinks that everyone, no matter how vague their connection to our family is, should take time to visit our mother—sit at her side and watch her stare vacantly into space. She has trouble understanding why people don't avail themselves of this opportunity.

Beck pulls up two chairs for us and, as I sit down, I try to see my mother lying in this hospital bed. But I only see my father's image; it invades my memory and alters my vision.

"Is she any better?" I ask my sister.

"Yes, thank God. The doctor said she's responding better than he expected. He said she could go home tomorrow, but I want her to stay a few more days, just to be on the safe side. So, Beck—are you working on a new book?"

This is how Lily conducts the few social interactions she has—around our mother's inert eyes. She calls people into a circle around a wheelchair or a bed and then plunges into cocktail party pleasantries.

"I'm about three quarters of the way through a novel," Beck tells her, and I watch him studying my mother, trying to read something on her blank face.

"What's it about?"

"Death, mostly."

I should be annoyed at his answer, but instead, I have to bite back a smile.

"Good one, Beck," I tell him. "Maybe you should pass out copies of your manuscript on the cancer ward."

"Carla!" Lily says. "How can you be so callous as to joke about something like that? My God, look where we are, and you indulge in this gallows humor."

"Lily, you look where we are. Mother's not in here with cancer. She's fine—I mean, in context, of course—she's as fine as she ever is. You've already said she's better and could go home except you want her to stay. I think a good dose of humor, gallows or otherwise, is probably a good prescription for this whole fucking place."

"Why do you persist in using the F-word all the time?" my sister says.

"Because it's so descriptive, and so versatile. It's sort of a multipurpose word. Eliminating it from my vocabulary would be like giving up this great grammatical tool. Without it—well, you get the picture."

I can tell Beck is enjoying this exchange, particularly because he started it, and is disappointed when a nurse comes in.

"And how are we doing today?" the nurse asks, directing this question at my mother. I'm about to ask if she's new on the floor when Lily fills in the blank and says our mother is fine. The nurse stays just long enough for Lily to regain her society hostess demeanor.

"So, you two have been together for a long time now. When are you going to get married?"

"Well, I'd go for it," Beck says, "but Carla refuses. Every time I ask, she rejects my offer."

Since I have no idea whether or not he's serious, and I have no memory of him ever mentioning marriage, I decide he's joking.

"Actually, I have some reservations about the ceremony itself," I tell Lily. "If I were bold enough to wear white, I'm afraid someone would come up and paint a large red letter over one of my breasts. Probably one of Mother's friends who stopped sending me Christmas cards after word got around that I'd become a braless hippie who was planning on escaping to Canada with all the draft dodgers."

"You could just get married in a red dress and save the paint," Beck suggests.

"That's true—or hire a security guard to frisk everyone for cans of spray paint."

Beck nods, as though this is the most serious discussion we've had all week. "And then, to remove all doubt, we could both invite our past lovers and give them name tags with the year and the duration of the affair."

"That's a good idea," I say, laughter invading my voice. "Like— 'Hi, I'm Carol. Two weeks in 1973.' And we could color-code the name tags to distinguish between one-timers and repeat customers."

Our laughter is contagious only to each other; Lily looks stunned and angry.

"Stop it, Carla!" she shouts at me. "Just stop it! You never have forgiven me for getting married, have you?"

My laughter is gone. I look at my sister across ancient battle lines.

"Lily, I hope you're very happy in your marriage. I wouldn't know, of course, because you never say anything about it. But as far as forgiving, the only grudges I hold are the dress you made me wear and the guest list, which looked like a firing squad to me . . . but I think only the dress was your fault."

"You're supposed to be here visiting Mother," Lily says, "not arguing with me."

"That's true, except I've never figured out exactly how to visit Mother. There aren't a lot of avenues of communication available here, which is probably why you and I always end up going at each other. There's nothing else to do."

Beck stands up and walks over to the window. "Maybe the two of you should stop dancing around it," he says, "and get to what's really going on between you—or what's not going on."

I know he's right, but I wouldn't even know how to begin; I resort to my usual solution, telling Lily I have to go and heading for the door.

"Let's take a walk before we drive home," Beck says once we're outside the hospital.

It's late afternoon and the sun has turned filmy behind a thin wash of fog blowing in from the ocean. We've gone a few blocks when a man with long, matted hair and a tattered jacket crosses the street and waves us down with wild, frantic gestures. He's wearing Hawaiian print shorts and no shirt under his jacket. We stop and Beck pulls out a few singles from his wallet. The man takes the money, looks at it, and starts shouting at us.

"What do you think I can buy for three bucks? You can't even eat anymore for this. It's not right! I used to have money—I had a house once and clothes. I used to be able to go into restaurants. Now you know what? They make me leave—because I only have three bucks and I can't eat for that. So they don't want me there. Everything I had is gone. I can't get medicine, I can't get a fucking thing anymore. I was a taxpayer—I had money, just like you."

I know we should move away, but something that feels like shock is keeping us rooted to this one spot on the sidewalk. The man is still yelling, but now the words are running together.

I look over at Beck, hoping he is less shocked than I am, and that's where my eyes are when the man lunges at him and pounds a fist against his chest. I see the arm in my peripheral vision, but what registers is the transformation of Beck's face, from surprise to fury, and suddenly there is another arm in my field of vision—Beck's— swinging toward the man with such force I feel the air rush past me. I hear the impact of knuckles on flesh; it sickens and fascinates me at the same time—the dull thud that seems to linger for too long, as though the sound waves are momentarily stunned. The man reels backward, blood pouring from his nose, and he's still shouting about the poverty of his life, as if he doesn't know he's been hit. Beck closes the space between them that opened up when the man was thrown back by his blow; he is still hitting him—in the face, the stomach.

There are no voices now, just the thud of flesh on flesh, over and over. I want to scream, but my throat feels paralyzed; I've forgotten how to push my voice through it. The man has fallen to the sidewalk and Beck is standing over him, his arm still swinging. But I suddenly imagine that his hand is holding a stick; the sidewalk dissolves into a deserted stretch of cracked asphalt with dry weeds along the shoulder. The dream Beck told me about months ago is coming to life in front of me; he is playing out his own work, becoming the character he invented.

Someone must have called the police. Sirens scream toward us and two cops jump out and pull Beck off the man.

"What happened here?" one of them asks me.

"I—I don't know. Things just exploded." I have an explanation, but if I gave it to him, Beck would end up in a mental ward.

An ambulance pulls up and the man is lifted onto a stretcher; his face is covered with blood and one eye is swollen shut. I look from his face to Beck's—from a red mask of pain to a blank stare. Beck looks as though his eyes are frozen open. He focuses on me as they're pulling him toward the car and, in a surprising moment of clarity, he says, "The car keys—I have to give you the car keys." One of the cops retrieves them from Beck's pocket and tosses them to me, and they put him in the back seat and drive off.

It's only then that I notice a crowd of people has gathered to watch this. I have no idea how long they've been here, but now I'm standing alone, facing a throng of strangers who are staring at me as if I'm their instructor and they're waiting for class to begin.

I *could* give them some instruction, I realize, but my head is pounding, my throat is dry, and there is blood splattered on the sidewalk. Not a good classroom atmosphere.

"This is a lesson in the hazards of being a writer," I could say to them. "You invent a character, open up dark corners in his personality—tunnels that you have to crawl into with him in order to write about them. The trouble is, sometimes they cave in behind you, and you can't get out."

I turn my back to their eyes and walk away, back toward the hospital and Beck's car. I have nothing to teach them; they'll have to figure it out on their own.

33

The day my father called me I was out in my garden, pinching back marijuana plants so the buds would grow thick and close together. I ran inside and picked up the receiver, my fingers sticky with resin, and immediately had an attack of guilt. An irrational inner voice suggested that a spy was lurking in the bushes and that the timing of this phone call was not coincidental.

"Hi, Father," I said, in a voice so overly casual, it alone should have raised his suspicions.

"Carla, your mother is gone for the afternoon—shopping, I think. I wondered if you could come over. There's something I wanted to talk to you about."

"Sure, I can come now if you like," I told him, looking at my fingers and wondering how long it would take to scrub the resin off.

It was midafternoon—a clear December day with air that seemed cold and silvery, glistening with moisture and winter sunlight. It was a day that made death feel like some foolish, dark idea that surfaced at night and disappeared to nothing by morning. But the day lied; I heard death's whistle in my ear. It was there below my father's voice, calling to me, reminding me that it offered no choices.

I drove to my parents' house, dreading the visit, but for different reasons than usual. I played back my father's voice in my head; there had been no blame in it this time. I heard need and it was so unfamiliar it scared the hell out of me.

The house felt strangely quiet to me when he answered the door. I wondered if the maids had vacated the premises, too.

"Hello, Carla, thanks for coming," he said, with the formal manner that I had come to associate with him.

I had to force my eyes to look at him; he was withering right in front of me. What was worse, I had to force my eyes to lie to him—conceal the knowledge that I'd pledged to keep secret.

He led me into his study, motioning me to one of the two chairs bordering the fireplace. As he sat down opposite me, I noticed that for all his frailty there was something serene about him. It was as though the disease ravaging his body was far below him, and aside from glancing down at it occasionally, he was paying no attention to it. He was floating above the flames, hovering on high currents in a sky as blue as he wanted it to be.

"I thought I could trust you with this—that's why I wanted to talk to you," he began. His eyes left my face then, moving away to some far point. "Carla... I'm not going to be around much longer. Your mother doesn't want me to know, and it would hurt her if she learned that I do know. But I'm dying."

I didn't say anything for a minute or two, I let the words tumble around between us.

"Yes, I know," I said softly, glad that I could finally say it.

"I'm not sure why your mother is trying to keep it from me. Perhaps she thinks I'll get better—I just don't know. But I want to allow her her reasons, whatever they are. I don't want our conversation today to go any farther than this room."

Ropes were tightening around me, pulled by many different hands. I was being sworn to secrecy by each parent, with my sister taking the side she always chose, and it was the same secret.

"Why don't the two of you just talk about this?" I asked.

My father looked at me as though the idea had never occurred to him, which it probably hadn't. As far as he was concerned, I might as well be speaking in tongues.

"Did you talk to your doctor?" I asked.

"Yes. You and he are the only two who know I'm aware of this. I know it's pancreatic cancer and I know my time is short."

I suddenly felt bonded to this doctor whom I had only met a few times over the years. I wondered if he knew how long this game of bartering secrets had been going on in our family. Secrets were our currency; we bought things with them—victories and favors, and sometimes silences full of anger or sadness.

"I just don't understand why I have to be the depository for all these things that the two of you want to hide from each other," I said.

"Well, I'm afraid I'm about to give you another one," he answered unapologetically. But then how could he apologize? He was only repeating patterns of history—our history that we all seemed condemned to repeat again and again.

"Great, I can't wait."

"I had a—uh—friend when I was in college," my father said. "She was older than I was by about four years, which seemed like a lot then. We were involved for about two years and then I broke it off. Sometime last year, she got in touch with me at the office—just out of the blue, after all this time. She wanted to see me, so I left work early one afternoon and went to her apartment."

"Father," I interrupted, "am I going to need a drink to hear the rest of this story?"

He looked confused for a second. "No, no—I don't think so. Nothing happened, if that's what you mean."

"Yes, that's what I meant. Okay, continue the story—I was a little worried there for a minute."

"Well . . ." my father studied the floor, letting minutes slip by. "I went to her apartment and the entire place was covered with pictures of me. She'd cut out photos from magazines and newspapers. It was like a shrine or something. She'd never married. She had just spent all those years following me and my career, and documenting it in her home. I felt so badly for her—she seemed so lonely—I visited her several more times, weekly, in fact, before I got sick."

"Can I ask why you're telling me this?" I said gently, not wanting him to think I didn't appreciate this confidence.

"Because, when I'm gone, if this ever comes out—if your mother finds out somehow—I want you to make sure she knows that nothing happened."

"But until then, you don't want me to say anything, right?"

"Right."

"Here's a bold suggestion," I said. "Since we're being honest here, wouldn't it have been easier if you had told Mother what you just told me? At the time it happened? It was perfectly harmless."

My father hesitated. "I guess I thought she might not believe me."

"This family should think less and talk more. It would be a hell of a lot healthier."

I don't know if he heard that. He was already up and shuffling through the papers on his desk. He picked up one, held it at arm's length, looking at it as he came back to his chair. It suddenly seemed appropriate that, with age, the eyes get farsighted, preferring distance over things close to them. My father was holding everything at arm's length—his cancer, his legal problems, even his life—looking at all of it with vision that shut down when things moved nearer.

"Part of the money I'm leaving you in my will has a condition attached to it," he said, his eyes squinting at the paper.

"Condition?" I imagined required shopping trips with my mother, weekly dinner engagements.

"I want you to buy a house. It's the only way I can think of to lure you out of this nomadic life you seem drawn to. So this money must go to a down payment on a house, and whatever is left can be applied to monthly mortgage payments. Is that understood?"

"Yes," I said, trying to absorb too much at once—death, taxes, and real-estate agents.

My mother came back just as I was getting ready to leave. She greeted me with a mixture of surprise and suspicion; she was never comfortable with conversations that took place outside her jurisdiction. She was the empress of dialogue in our house, and any independent interaction put the violators into the arena of treason. Lions were poised behind the gates, ready to sink their teeth into brazen Christians.

"Hi, Mother. Father and I were just visiting," I said on my way out, on her way in. I enjoyed her lack of control over what had already transpired. It was a war of secrets and I had just scored a victory.

Tell him the truth, I commanded my eyes to say to her, since my voice had proved cowardly. I'm just as guilty as she is, my logical, left-brain voice said. I hadn't told him the truth either, and it was a guilt I would carry around in my pocket for the rest of my life.

I drove back to the canyon that evening, angry at the lies and wounded by the image of my father's drawn, jaundiced face. There was one thing, though, that my parents couldn't lie about or hide. Through his lawyer, my father had been served with a notice that he was being formally investigated for insider trading. I didn't need either of my parents to tell me about this; it was in the paper and on the evening news.

I wondered if some of my father's serenity came from the knowledge that he wouldn't be around for the final stage of this drama. I wondered, too, if in some part of his soul he was speeding up his own death, willing his body to deteriorate, to let him escape. The more I thought about it, the more likely it seemed... and I wasn't sure if this was something for which he should be blamed or admired.

When I got back, it was dark; I turned on lamps in my house, but the walls seemed to move in on me. The wind was rattling the window glass that needed to be caulked. It sounded like an insistent voice. I left and drove down to the bar in Topanga Center, not caring whether or not anyone I knew would be there. But the canyon was small and often incestuous—there was usually someone you knew anywhere you went.

I sat on a stool at the long wooden bar, ordered a glass of wine— cheap, screw-top-bottle wine—but I wasn't there for the wine list. I was there for the dim lights, the hum of voices at the bar and from the tables behind me sunken into the dark, smoky air. I was there for diversion, and for whatever the night would bring.

What it brought was my name called out from one of the tables. I turned around on the bar stool, sent my eyes out like searchlights to probe the shadows, and I saw Al, a canyon regular who had fixed my van and chopped firewood for me in exchange for a bag of grass. I and my glass of screw-top wine left the bar and slid in beside him at the table.

"What are you doing in here all by yourself?" he asked.

"Am I only supposed to be in here with an escort?"

"No, the partner rule only applies to prom nights and deep-sea diving," he said. "And mountain climbing, I guess. I like to see you in here by yourself—I don't have to worry about some guy pulling you away."

"Or challenging you to a duel?"

"Right. That, too."

"Actually," I said, "I came in to try and drown my depression. I'm hoping it's just a viral depression and a couple of glasses of wine will kill it."

He laughed and his chipped front tooth winking from under his mustache made me cross my legs to stop the heat that suddenly bloomed there.

"Honey, that shit'll kill everything," he said. "If you had a tapeworm, it'd kill that."

This unexpected attraction for his chipped tooth and untrimmed mustache made me check out the rest of him in a new way—dark, curly hair falling over his ears, a body made hard and compact from years of doing canyon things like chopping and hauling wood, hiking into the mountains, fixing his own roof.

"So, why are you depressed?" he asked, hazel eyes watching me from under a fringe of lashes that I wished were mine. The other people at the table had given up on us and retreated into their own conversations.

"My father's sick," I answered.

"Oh, I'm sorry. That can be tough. Serious?"

"Yeah," I said abruptly, like a period at the end of a sentence.

"Want another wine?" he asked, happy to follow me down another avenue of conversation—whichever one I chose. I was grateful that he was letting me be the guide.

"Okay. Good thing I don't have a tapeworm. I'd have to feel guilty about his death. I'd have to start making funeral arrangements."

I watched him walk to the bar. I watched his ass, his legs...and recrossed mine as the heat spread its petals again.

"So, I guess I was just trying to take my mind off everything by coming in here," I told him when he sat down beside me again and handed me a full glass.

"Oh yeah?" He smelled like cigarettes and canyon air. "Is it working?"

"It's starting to," I said, thinking about running my tongue across his chipped tooth.

We sat for a few minutes, drinking, talking with our eyes, fucking with our eyes. He slid his hand over mine—a rough hand, calloused from gripping ax handles and chain saws, scratching the city girl's pale skin.

"How's your van running these days?" he asked. "Did I fix everything okay?"

"Uh-huh. It runs great."

He moved my hand beneath the table. At some point, he'd unzipped his jeans; for a second I wondered when. Probably when our eyes were busy saying other things. I let him slide my hand inside, to the night's diversion I'd been hoping for. I leaned over and circled my tongue around in his ear—a small, wet secret hidden under his dark curls.

"Let's go," I whispered, and then glanced away from his ear, from his face, from my hand inside his jeans. My mother materialized in the corner, propped up by shadows, sipping a daiquiri, a look of shock and revulsion on her face.

It was all I needed to propel me into the rest of the night, with no thought of turning back. I was high from the wine and no food, high in the black canyon night, walking a wire with no net beneath me... exactly where I wanted to be. I would never fall as long as my mother was there watching—waiting for me to fall, to fail. I could float on my own defiance.

Back at my house, with logs burning in the stone fireplace, the comforter on the floor, and our bodies moving between the layers of heat, she was still there, ankles crossed, hands folded in her lap, prim and protective—appendages doubling as a chastity belt. I heard her gasps of horror beneath my moaning, felt the steel of her eyes moving in and out of me, following Al's rhythm. Only when my body arched and shuddered and I felt his come wash into me did I release her—let her drift off into the night, back to safer neighborhoods where good girls didn't look for hard-ons under barroom tables. I didn't need her there anymore that night. I had won again.

"Your father's in the hospital," my mother's voice announced over the telephone two days later.

"So how are you going to tell him?" I asked, more gently than I intended.

"I already have."

"And?"

She let out a long breath that seemed ragged and tired; I wondered if she'd been crying and if she would start again.

"He took it quite well," she answered slowly. Her careful voice— measuring out what she wanted to say against what was really there. "He's... quite ill," she added, less carefully.

He was not quite ill, he was dying. And we gathered for the vigil that would be our last family venture—a dinner-table reunion around my father's death bed.

Each day, I drove from Topanga into Santa Monica, to Saint John's Hospital, to watch as my father's life withered.

On a Friday morning, almost a week into it, I woke up in my corner of windows, with thin clouds over the hills and cold air drifting into the house. I usually didn't go to the hospital until afternoon, but I made coffee, got dressed, and got in my car—urged on by a nagging feeling that I should alter my schedule that day.

My father was awake; no one else was in the room.

"Hi, Father."

"Carla, I wanted to talk to you," he said weakly, as though he had known I was coming.

I sat down beside the bed, waiting for him to marshal the strength to talk.

"Your sister—" he began, and then hesitated.

"Lily?"

"No. Your sister who died. Our first child."

"Yes," I said, feeling another secret crawling out of its hiding place, shaking off sleep after hibernating for too many winters.

"She didn't die like we said. She was never born."

"What?"

"Your mother had an abortion. She didn't think we could afford a child right then. It hadn't been planned."

He stopped and let his breath feed his vocal cords for a few seconds.

"You were poor?" I asked, wondering how many secrets were going to crawl out of this confession.

"No—but we weren't as well off. She just didn't think we should yet. So she...didn't have it. I wanted you to know."

I sat silently beside my father, watching his eyes close with the exhaustion of having pulled this secret from its sealed cave. A deathbed confession—I didn't quite know what to do with it. Was it a gift? Should I thank him?

He fell asleep as I sat thinking about the nights I'd gone to sleep with my fantasy sister hovering on the dark air in my bedroom, watching over me like a guardian angel. She had buoyed me, made my life lighter, this ghost-child who was never real, but was to me.

Fool, I thought, you should have known it was a lie.

34

Have you ever wondered how much time we spend in our lives waiting?" I asked Rainbow, three days before my father died. We were in my living room drinking an expensive bottle of wine, which meant one that came with a cork.

"Never thought about it," she said. "I guess a lot."

"Yeah, I mean when we're young, we wait to grow up. When we grow up, we do stupid things like wait by the phone for some guy to call, or wait for his car to drive up. And now, every day, I go down to the hospital and wait for my father to die. It's the morbid side of waiting—it just feels so barbaric to me."

Rainbow nodded, lost somewhere in her own thoughts, that had been washed by wine and dimmed by the amber lights which had replaced every white bulb in the house. I had turned my home into a cave of soft colors—a safe place to crawl back to after the white glare and Lysol smell of the hospital.

"You know what the worst part of this is?" I said.

"What?"

"I don't really know who that is in the hospital bed. My father is dying, but I have no idea who he is."

The tears came then for the first time since he got ill. Rainbow opened her arms and let me fall into them. Warm tears rolled down into the amber air, falling into empty space, as empty as the place they had come from—a tunnel inside me where vague pain rumbled like a freight train with no place to go.

"I don't even know why I'm crying," I said. "I can't even put a name to it."

"It's okay—that doesn't matter," Rainbow told me, hands stroking my hair, her arms tight around me. "It only matters that you need to cry. You don't have to label it."

"My whole life with my family feels like a tour through a foreign country where I don't know the language and don't understand the customs."

Rainbow pulled back enough to meet my eyes, colored lights dancing between our faces. "Are you sure you don't know the language?"

"No, I'm not sure," I admitted. "Maybe I do. Maybe that's the problem. I'm trying to become less fluent in my native tongue."

"We're either learning or unlearning," she said.

"Yeah—or waiting."

It was getting worse every day. I went to the hospital the following afternoon, with the wine Rainbow and I had shared still pounding in my head, and I found my father lying trancelike and vague between my mother, on one side of the bed, and the doctor on the other.

"But what is this odor?" my mother was asking the doctor, in a voice that brought my childhood screeching up behind me. "They're not washing him. We're paying for good care at this hospital and we're not getting it."

"Mrs. Lawton, the odor has nothing to do with lack of cleanliness," the doctor explained patiently. "It's a symptom of the disease. It's what happens in pancreatic cancer as the liver fails."

Lily came up behind our mother. "Mother, you're upset. Maybe we should get you a cup of tea or something."

"Yes...I...tea sounds nice. I haven't been sleeping well, with all this. And I've had no appetite. I just can't eat. I'm starting to get weak from lack of food."

"I'll ring for the nurse to bring you some tea," Lily said. As if the hospital were a hotel with room service.

With my father lying jaundiced and thin on the bed below her, his stomach bloated from cancer that was gnawing its way through his insides, my mother was worrying about her loss of appetite. I looked at Lily to see if the absurdity of this had registered with her, but she was buzzing the nurse, waiting for room service.

I felt like screaming at both of them, but I swallowed it, just as I had everything else that was truthful.

When my father's kidneys failed, the doctor said it would only be a matter of days. No, I thought, it's been a matter of years. This is all this family has been doing for years—watching life seep out, like scientists with clipboards, conducting a study on the effects of accumulated pain.

It finally happened early one morning. I was the sole witness. For two days, I had gone home only to sleep, returning to the hospital in the gray, early hours and staying until dark.

For some reason, on this morning, my mother and Lily had not yet arrived.

I sat in the room alone with my father, staring as he wrestled with death. At moments, his head would snap back and forth, saying no to something. Then his voice would follow.

"No, not yet," he said weakly. "Not yet...no...no..."

He was conducting a dialogue with something only he could see. Selfishly, I wanted him to share it with me. I wanted to be inside his vision for a quick second; I wanted that to be his parting gift to me.

I watched as he struggled with these unseen forces. I glanced around the room, suddenly afraid that I was being spied on, that someone would overhear what I was about to say to this man whose light was sputtering like a tired flame.

"Just go," I whispered, satisfied that no one could hear me, but afraid that I was committing some undefined sacrilege. "It's okay—just let go now. There's no reason to stay."

I had his hand in mine and whatever was traveling between his flesh and mine snapped in two, like an electrical current suddenly gone dead.

I looked at his face for movement; I put my other hand in front of his mouth to feel for a whisper of breath, but there was only the stale, motionless air of the hospital room between my palm and his lips.

Something was changing in the hand I still held in mine. Flesh without life. I shivered and let it slide away from my grasp, and just as I did, my mother and Lily walked into the room.

My voice didn't need to identify what my eyes told them, but it did anyway.

"He's gone," I said.

My mother crumbled as though a heavy object had struck her in the abdomen. Lily helped her into a chair and stared at me, tears shining on her face.

"Were you here?" my sister asked me.

"Yes."

"Did he suffer?"

"No," I said, thinking of his secret dialogue and wondering if that qualified as suffering.

My mother was sobbing silently, bent over like a tree battered by wind.

"Did he say anything?" she asked, her voice falling into her lap.

"No, not really."

"What do you mean—not really?" my mother said, raising her head.

"Nothing coherent. Nothing I could understand."

Her eyes met mine then, hurling a lifetime of history at me—old furies and ancient rivalries that had been melted in flames and cast in the shape of sins. Now, another had been forged from soft metal. It would sit on a shelf with all my other crimes against my mother and stare down at me with the permanence of something lifted from the earth's core.

I had pirated the moment of my father's death, I had held his hand in mine as he crossed an invisible line and fluttered away—a soul finally free from the odorous decay of his body.

And, to make it worse, I wasn't crying. Tears were there, somewhere in my body, somewhere in my spirit behind tall, guarded gates.

The only other one not crying that morning was my father, who was, I was certain, watching from some high, blue vantage point, swinging on ropes of light and wondering why he had been part of a family that always felt the need to be heavily armed.

The rest of the day felt like a long river, and I was a slow boat negotiating the currents that flowed over the cold mud of dying. Lily gave me some phone numbers to call—death announcements. Death protocol. She had another list of calls to make herself.

Looking back on it, I think my mother's silence began then. It just took a while for her vocal cords to fall in line with the order.

The day had the good taste to remain gray, and I sat in my parents' house, listening to Lily on the phone in the next room, listening to my mother's silence. I thought of tides and unsailed oceans, and a child who looked to her father's face, hoping to see answers where the sky and sea met in his eyes. And I thought of tears that I hadn't allowed myself to cry.

I slept in my old room that night, with death rattling like bones in the darkness, the sky outside scraped clean of clouds, and the moon moving across the floor.

When the door opened and Lily came in, I returned for a second to the edge of childhood, to two small hands clutched in a moonbeam. But we were older now, and our father had just died.

"Mother wanted to be there when he went," she said.

"I know that. What should I have done? Asked him to wait?"

"She thinks he said something to you and you're deliberately keeping it from her." Lily's voice barely filled up the room.

"Why are you passing this information on to me, Lily?" I asked my sister. "Jesus, it's like this family has relay races with every unkind comment that's ever uttered. We pass them along like batons."

"Let's not fight, Carla."

"Okay," I said, and reached for her hand.

Our fingers rested together for a moment. But we were outside the moon's thin beam, so it didn't really count.

35

Beck's key turns in my lock just as the coffee is completing its drip passage through the filter and the house is starting to smell like it's supposed to in the morning. I haven't seen him in over a week—since the day his lawyer arranged his bail and I picked him up, saying nothing about the man he beat and left in a pool of blood on a Santa Monica sidewalk.

I come around the corner from the kitchen and hug him quickly, our mouths touching out of habit.

"How are you?" I ask him.

"Okay, I guess."

"Want some coffee?" I go back to the kitchen, feeling his footsteps close behind me.

I take down the mug he always uses; the small habits, I think, string them together and you have a relationship. Or do you?

"Carla, I feel like I've let you down," he says, as we wander into the living room and fold ourselves into the couch, a little farther apart than we usually sit, our coffee cups guarding our faces.

"I could probably feel like that, too, but I think you're hurting yourself much more than me. Although I've probably assisted you in that process. I've been an accomplice—in a way—on this dark journey you've embarked on. I haven't said, 'Enough already—let me off.'"

"And are you saying that now?" he asks, his eyes searching me out through the coffee-cup steam.

I think about his question, turn it over in my mind. I know the answer he wants, I just don't know if I can give it.

"I don't know," I say finally. "You've changed—we've changed. Or maybe we've always been this way and it just took this long to become obvious to us."

"It's not obvious to me, Carla. I don't want to lose you. I know I've been rough to be with lately, but...I was just hoping we could get through it. I mean, I'm trying to get through it."

I look past him to the sky outside the windows—a dull gray like the day we met. Suddenly it's the color of the day, not Beck's words, that stirs up my sadness. Images emerge from the muted light, tumble from the sky, press against my mind's eye. Driving down the Coast Highway with Beck in my rearview mirror, the afternoon sun faint behind a gray gauze sky, his hand touching new scars and old wounds, his mouth following the paths his fingers had drawn.

"If we get through it," I ask him, "what's on the other side? Beck, we have all these barriers that have been set up in this relationship—all these No Crossing signs and traffic signals. I don't know if that's what I want. I'd rather have an open road and I don't know if you and I ever can. It's more than just this Joseph Conrad trek-into-darkness you've been on—that probably only served to bring things into focus. We've been circling each other almost the entire time we've been together. We're always warning each other in small ways not to come too close."

"Maybe that can change."

"Maybe, but I don't really think so," I tell him, trying to make my voice as gentle as possible.

"So that's it?" he asks, his face looking like he should be standing under a streetlamp on a deserted corner, waiting for a stranger to say hello.

I move closer to him, trying to say hello, trying to say something other than what I've already said.

"I don't know" is all that comes out.

My hand finds the back of his neck and rests there, as if it can make his head feel lighter, or make the whole morning feel lighter.

So here we are, I think—somersaulting into a black hole that was always there. We created a universe to cushion ourselves from a fall, but we forgot to include gravity, and now we're spinning out into space.

"I guess I should go," he tells me, and gets up to leave.

We walk to the door and I kiss him—a long kiss, a kiss from deep space, a bonding of unsaid words, and words that never seem to come out right.

When I close the door behind him, Tully walks over and pokes me with his nose, asking me what's wrong in dog language. I kneel down and wrap my arms around his neck.

"You know something's wrong, don't you?" I say into the soft warmth of his neck. "You probably knew for a long time. Could we work out some signal where you could let me know as soon as you figure these things out?"

Tully and I go down to the beach, and I let the morning close in around me, hoping it will whitewash the memories that seem too vivid. I look back over the acreage of Beck's and my relationship, and I have trouble finding both of us. One lonely figure darts through an empty field, looking for something lost, something imagined.

I realize that most of the moments when I felt closest to him, he wasn't there. It was the creation of him in my mind that I would turn to at times when I needed to feel his eyes. I'd put him over my shoulder like a guiding star, or beside me on the road, to keep me from making a wrong turn. I would hold his voice to my ear like a shell and I'd hear whatever I wanted him to say. I'd hear everything but the distance.

When we were together, we mirrored each other. We were both intent on navigating our way through the stormiest waters of our histories, fishing for truths we'd thrown back before. Eventually, one of us had to turn away; I just happened to do it first. Because we couldn't escape ourselves when we were together; each was a reminder of the other. The stories were different, the memories weren't identical, but the priorities were the same. And it all added up to baggage, piled on top of this fragile relationship we swore we'd get around to nurturing—just as soon as...when I finish...right after...

The sun is starting to burn through by the time Tully and I get back to the house. I think of how eagerly I bought this house after my father's death and the execution of his will. It was as though I was afraid the money would be taken away from me if I didn't sink it into a house quickly.

I bought the second house I was shown, knowing my father would want me to be close to the sea.

I moved in the fall, just weeks before my sister called and told me our mother had been rushed to the hospital.

"Carla—" Lily's voice was choked and barely audible over the phone. It was raining that day; drops pelted the windows and weighed down the sky. "Mother's had a stroke."

The hospital corridors, familiar by then, took me on a different journey that time—to my mother's bedside, my mother's retreat from the world, and the transfer of her power to Lily, who willingly took on the role.

"It's one of those things in medicine we can't really explain," the doctor said, after weeks of trying to figure out why my mother had become catatonic.

I can explain it, I thought. She just decided she had nothing more to say to anyone.

"The physical damage is minimal," the doctor continued. "But psychologically—"

"Physical damage has never really been the problem in our family," I said.

Lily shot me a look with deadly accuracy. I turned and tried to see my sister—the child she once was—tried to remember the few moments when I had felt close to her. But I only saw her becoming our mother.

"We all end up leaving each other, don't we, Lily?" I asked softly.

She frowned her confusion at me and the doctor cleared his throat, feeling awkward, as if we had suddenly started speaking in a foreign tongue.

My mother was home before Christmas, or as much home as she would ever be. Lily ordered a tree, organized a tree-trimming party with some of our parents' friends, and hurried around the house all day, snapping orders to the maids.

People came to the house that night bearing gifts and wearing cheerfulness like freshly applied perfume. They drank, nibbled on canapés, and talked to my mother as if she could hear them, as if she would answer. As if she gave a damn.

I drew a circle around all of them and stepped outside of it—the orphan child, nose pressed to the glass of a frost-ring window, looking in at the blinking colors and tinsel cheer of a Christmas that seemed far away from her. I looked carefully at my mother, forced my eyes to stay on her even when they wanted to move away. In her frozen state of silence, she still commanded the room; rigid and vacant, she could still bring people to her side, have them dote on her, try to please her.

As I stared at her, I saw the shape of a child sitting at her feet—head bowed, legs pulled up tight beneath her, trying to make herself small. Her hands reached out hesitantly, not sure she wanted to be noticed at all, but needing that from the woman towering over her. I let the child raise her head and looked into my own eyes. And I knew for the first time in my life that I would never become like my mother, that I would never raise a child in a war zone where all the heavy artillery was mine, that I would never leave her arms hanging timidly, not knowing whether to hug, or hit, or pull back and guard her face.

My hands slid across my stomach and moved down over my womb, as if to protect it, but they were too late. The surgeon's hand had already done its work. I wanted it back—the chance of someday having a child of my own.

It would mean another hospital, another operation, another doctor's hands reaching into my body. It was three years before I had the courage to do anything about it.

T he problem is," the doctor said, pointing to the X ray illuminated on the white screen, "your tubes were cut very close to the uterus and I don't know how much is left on the ends. I have to bring two ends together. I can't tell from the X ray how much I'll have to work with."

His hands were trying to add description to his words; his fingers were aimed at each other, moving in, touching—representing, I supposed, the two ends of one of my tubes.

I stared at my inner body on the screen—my uterus made to show up white from the dye they'd injected into it, and the two fallopian tubes that I'd chosen to have butchered. They were stumps now, not at all what they were supposed to look like under normal conditions.

"So what do you recommend?" I asked, feeling my stomach tighten, not wanting him to tell me to go home and forget it. He was a large man with black-framed glasses; his hands looked like they should be sculpting horses from mountains of clay, not making tiny stitches in fallopian tubes, putting them back together again.

"Well, we can give it a try," he said. "I won't really know for sure until I get in there and see what's going on."

I thought of him being "in there"—my body slit and spread open, hands diving in, assessing the damage, patching things together. A wave of fear rippled through me.

"So there's a chance you can't do anything?" I asked him.

"Yes, there is that chance. But I'll do my best. We should talk about your plans for pregnancy. It's curious that you want to do this now when you tell me you're not married and not involved in a relationship."

"It's a decision that has nothing to do with anyone but me," I said evasively. "It's something I need to do for myself."

His face looked concerned. "I usually recommend that a patient try to get pregnant a few months after the surgery. Do you plan on going to a sperm bank?"

This was an idea that had never occurred to me and, for whatever reason, made me start laughing.

"No... no," I said, trying to stop my laughter, but failing. "I mean, I don't think I could do that. Pregnancy without sex is a difficult concept for me to embrace."

"Well, that is an alternative," the doctor said.

"Sperm from a vial? That comes from a bank? I don't think so."

He watched me calmly as I struggled to bring my laughter under control; this was probably not something they trained him to deal with in medical school.

"There is something else," I said finally, moving back from laughter into more serious areas. "I don't want a general anesthetic. I want an epidural block instead—numb from the waist down but a perfectly alert mind."

He cleared his throat and leaned forward on his elbows. "Carla, this is going to be a long operation—four hours at least, maybe more. You obviously feel strongly about this, but..."

"I want to be awake."

He stared at me, thumbing through this new demand I had slid across his desk.

"But it's an unusual way to do this," he said. "I don't know if you realize how difficult it might be."

"That doesn't matter. What matters is that I'm conscious for the whole thing. Please understand—this is an important thing I'm doing and I don't want to be put out for it. I want to know what's going on." I paused and studied his face to see if I was convincing him. "It's not negotiable," I added softly.

"All right," the doctor said after a few moments that seemed endless. "We'll do it your way."

Rainbow moved into my beach house two days before the surgery. She made me fresh carrot juice and tea from herbs that were so bitter I had to hold my nose to get them down.

"What the fuck are you giving me?" I said the first time I tried this concoction. "Poison? This tastes like you're trying to do me in before I make it to the hospital."

"They're very healing herbs," she answered. "I looked through a lot of books to find the right formula. It's a very old remedy. So stop complaining and drink."

"But there's nothing to heal yet."

"Carla, you have to build up your body."

"Build up the healing mechanism?" I said, deciding that a bitter aftertaste was probably the least of my worries at that point. "Like military reserves, right? Ready to fight if the need arises."

"Yeah—prepare your body. It's very important before surgery. You should be taking extra vitamins, too," Rainbow told me. It was a recent transformation for her. She'd given up Gallo wine and an occasional unfiltered Camel and gone into herbs, acupressure, and holistic healing.

"Rainbow, what if he can't do anything? What if he looks in, shakes his head, and closes me back up?"

"Don't think like that," she said, grabbing my arm as if to stop me from wading out into a swamp. "Think only the most positive thoughts. You deserve this, Carla. You deserve to have it work."

I arrived at the hospital at dawn. The sky was an uncertain shade of gray, the color of lint, the color of dirty snow. The color of sorrow.

An hour later, I had one of medicine's magic potions dripping into my spine, paralyzing me from the waist down. They took me down to the surgery room in the basement—below daylight, below people walking along the sidewalk on their way to work or breakfast. It reminded me of bomb shelters.

"This is reassuring," I thought. "If the big one goes off, it won't interrupt the surgery."

I paid attention to everything—the sounds, the instruments that were asked for and used, the ice-white of the lights, the expression on the doctor's face.

But when my body started shaking so much that my teeth were chattering, they added Valium to the other potions leaking into my bloodstream and I fell asleep.

I dreamed of a wide, empty horizon, the sky brushing the land like a sheet of silk. In the distance, I could see puffs of smoke, white as blizzard snow, spiraling into the sky. Smoke signals. Telling me there is a place where darkness is not something that chases you down; it's just something that happens before dawn.

When I woke up, four hours had passed. The doctor leaned over me and said, "You have one healthy tube. We're working on the other one now." He was so close I could smell morning coffee still on his breath.

"Humpty-Dumpty fixed at last," I said in a sleepy voice. "It was a hell of a fall, too."

It took weeks for the pain in my abdomen to stop nagging me, to let up enough that I could walk somewhat normally, rather than like an arthritis victim. It would be weeks more before it left me completely.

There is an illusion to healing, the illusion being that it only needs to go as deep as the flesh.

A deeper wound surfaced as the surgery pain diminished. At first, it came at night, like something breaking inside me, a crack in my soul. It came in my sleep, slapping me awake with a feeling that I couldn't catch my breath. My body would be shivering cold, my heart racing. I would lie in my dark room imprisoned by a terror that I couldn't identify. A nameless enemy.

Eventually, it followed me into the daylight. It could come over me at any time. Suddenly, my lungs would refuse to allow air into them and I would tremble with a cold only I could feel.

Rainbow was the only person I told.

"Maybe you haven't forgiven yourself," she said simply.

We were walking on the beach and I looked out to the water, to a pelican diving for his catch.

"For what?"

"Look—you just went through major surgery, Carla, because of a decision you made years ago that you came to regret. Sometimes when we go back and correct something, we come up against feelings we've been shoving aside and not dealing with. Maybe when this thing comes over you, you should crawl inside it—examine it—figure out what your body's trying to tell you."

I had no other advice to go on. The next time I woke up breathless and terrified, I didn't try to make it stop. I let it hold me in its grip, and I shivered there, sending questions out into the dark.

Suddenly, my room was crowded. My mother and Lily were in one corner, their faces hard and judgmental, their eyes shiny with victory. My father moved in and out of the shadows, head bowed slightly. I had disappointed him again. Floating above them was a thin ring of light, like a ring around the moon, but there was no moon in the middle. It had fallen out and rolled away to someone else's night—someone else's lie. It was all that was left of the sister I thought had returned from death to watch over me.

With tears, my breath came back, my heart slowed, and my body warmed to its normal temperature. When I looked again, I was alone. I touched my scar, still swollen and tender; I wiped tears from my eyes and spread them across it. It was finally part of me—a wound that had healed a deeper one. I wanted it to feel my tears, to know the salt-sting of pain that would never go away completely, but would learn to feel better about itself.

37

The story should end there, but stories never do. They trail on, like echoes, bouncing off mountains and filling valleys until they find other listeners.

I still visit my mother's silence every week, but I no longer scrape at it, desperate for what may be underneath. The empty places in my memory seem calmer now, like tidewater trapped between rocks. I can wade into them, knowing there is nothing living there; my feet don't have to be careful about where they step. But I don't look for that anymore. There is an ocean beyond if I just climb over the rocks, and it's an easier climb now.

I am gentler with Lily these days. My sister looks more like our mother than our mother ever did. I watch her and smile over the sadness that rises up in me. Because I remember her differently. They are scattered memories, but I catch them when the wind rises and stirs them up.

I remember her when we first moved to California and our parents took us to the beach. We stood in the water, looking down at the white foam swirling gently around our legs. A small fish, silvery and thin, slid past my ankles. There were sand dollars then, some bigger than fifty-cent pieces. And starfish—Lily and I would lift them off the sand and place them softly back in the waves, talking sweetly to them so they wouldn't be frightened.

There are no sand dollars anymore, and I haven't seen a starfish in years.

Sometimes, I feel Lily's scar across my own wrist; I feel the damage in my veins. And when the nights turn silver, I still find myself reaching for her hand, believing that I will feel it again, soft and tiny in mine. I know this phantom touch is only in my imagination, but it makes the nights go by easier.

It is Sunday. High waves crash on the sand. There was a hurricane somewhere and the Pacific has picked up on its anger. The water is almost up under the houses.

My home is a little less cluttered, and only one side of the bed is undone. Beck doesn't stay here on the weekends anymore. I miss the feel of him beside me, but then I don't know if I'm missing the times he was here or the times I imagined him here.

We still have dinner sometimes and, occasionally, we make love. We still need to touch each other, to get tangled in each other's lives for a few hours. To remember. I don't ask anymore about his book, although I know he's still writing it. Its darkness is in his eyes, on his fingers, staining them and making them less willing to reach for me. But I turn my eyes away, and pretend I don't notice this.

I take some of his darkness inside of me; I wrap my legs around it and invite it in, feeling it wash through me—warm and wet and sad. Part of me knows that a child will never come from any of these nights. But I'm not sure it matters anymore.

There is another child with me now. I let her run between shadows and light—wherever she feels more comfortable. I hold her hand when she needs that, and forgive her for her fears. There are other times when she shows up brave and races the wind; she thinks, if she's fast enough, it will lift her over the rooftops, and I don't discourage her.

She still cries inside my eyes sometimes, still runs to the blackest corners of night, still searches through pools of moonlight for magic lost long ago.

But she has words now, and stories that don't need to hide.

Sometimes, when the shore is wide and flat, and sea birds are screeching around me, I hear her laughter coming up from behind, tugging at me like a friend I forgot to notice. I turn to see her writing in the sand, not caring that the next wave will wash over her words. Because she can write them again. She can run along the tide line, shouting her stories, send them winging into the sky. No one will stop her.